WHO IS FAYE?

FRAN O'BRIEN

For Dolores
with many thanks
Fran

McGUINNESS BOOKS

McGUINNESS BOOKS

WHO IS FAYE?

This novel is entirely a work of fiction.
The names, characters and incidents portrayed
in it are the work of the author's imagination.
Any resemblance to actual persons, living, or
dead, events or localities, is entirely coincidental.

Published by
McGuinness Books
19 Terenure Road East
Dublin 6.

Fran O'Brien asserts the moral right to be
identified as the author of this work.

A catalogue record for this book is
available from the British Library.

ISBN 978-0-9549521-3-6

Cover photography by James O'Brien

Typeset by Marlone Press

Printed and bound in Great Britain by
CPI Cox & Wyman, Reading, RG1 8EX

www.franobrien.net

For all our family, friends and clients who support our efforts to raise funds for LauraLynn House at The Children's Sunshine Home Hospice Project.

Jane and Brendan McKenna have been through every parent's worst nightmare – the tragic loss of their only two children. Laura died aged four following surgery to repair a heart defect. Her big sister Lynn died less than two years later aged fifteen, having lost her battle against leukaemia – diagnosed on the day of Laura's surgery.

Having dealt personally with such serious illness, Jane and Brendan have seen a huge need for a "Home from Home" for children with life-limiting and life-threatening conditions, and the Foundation was established to raise funds to build Ireland's first children's hospice.

The main aim of the children's hospice is to provide respite care for children, and support and comfort for parents and siblings for whom life can be extremely difficult.
When the end comes, it provides a peaceful environment where a child can die with dignity if their home is not a possibility.

Now LauraLynn Foundation has merged with Sunshine Children's Home in Leopardstown, Dublin, and the children's hospice LauraLynn House will be opened there in 2011.

ACKNOWLEDGEMENTS

Our very special thanks to Jane and Brendan who always amaze us as they face into each day with such courage. Their friendship means a great deal to both Arthur and myself and we look forward to helping them achieve their dream.

Thanks so much to all my friends in The Wednesday Group, who gave me such valued critique. Many thanks especially to Muriel Bolger, who once again took on the arduous task of editing the book for me. And very special thanks also to Vivien Hughes, who did the final proof readings on this occasion also.

Grateful thanks to my nephew, James, who took the photo for the cover of the book, and special thanks to Fiona who allowed us to use her beautiful image. Also many thanks to my brother Jimmy, a wizard on the computer, for giving so much of his valuable time to keep the project on track.

Many thanks to my sister Mary, my sister-in-law Marie, and all our family, and Arthur's family too, and our many friends and clients, who sell the books for the charity. Also, to all the shops who support us, and especially those who take no margin for themselves. And to people who have made donations to LauraLynn House – their generosity is very much appreciated.

Thanks to all our friends at the Nenagh Farmers Market for their friendship and support for the charity.

Thanks also to everyone at Martone Press –Yvonne, Martin, Deirdre and Phyllis – and most especially Dave who creates the final look of the novel.

Thanks to our printers CPI Cox & Wyman who always do a great job.

Thanks to Craftprint, Superquinn, Tesco, Tipperary National Spring Water, Topaz, and Marquees Nationwide.

A million thanks to everyone at Cyclone Couriers – especially Mags – who continue to support us by delivering the books free of charge to shops all around the country. We really appreciate their generosity.

To my darling husband, Arthur, who works even harder than I do to raise funds for the LauraLynn.

Prologue

It seemed as if she had been here forever.
Had no will of her own.
Her voice played hide and seek behind glistening white tissue.
In a wild rush of blood it was carried to the heart and lungs.
Up down and around.
Plucked sinewy ligaments like the strings of a harp – enjoying itself.
But refused to express a mind growing ever dim.

Chapter One

It was always hot on Helen's birthday. December 6th. High summer in Alice Springs. Ever since she could remember, they had made a day of it. Her earliest memories took her back to when she was about four years old, and they picnicked under the eucalyptus trees on the edge of the desert where saltbush, ghost gums, and mallee shimmered gaunt in the arid heat. Even as a child Helen was both fascinated and repelled by the emptiness, loneliness, and mystery of the vast expanse which stretched away into the distance and took her mind with it to unknown people and places.

Her mother, Carmel, had blossomed over the years since they had emigrated from Ireland in 1980, happy beyond her wildest dreams. They enjoyed their life in Australia. The weather, the people, everything. Tom had set up his own hardware store which had thrived and given them a comfortable standard of living and above all else, status. And the most important person in their lives was their daughter, Helen.

But underneath all the happiness and contentment a destructive fear still lurked deep within Carmel. It turned her into an over-protective woman, terrified to let Helen out of her sight. Weighed down by guilt which sat on her shoulder like a vulture.

'Mum, why have I no gran and grandad? Where are they?
And I'm the only one in class with no uncles and aunts.' Helen stared accusingly at Carmel with wide blue eyes.

'Your grandparents are in heaven, and all of our relations live a long way from here - on the other side of the world.'

'Can we go see them?'

'No I'm sorry, love, it's too far away.'

'Some day?'

'Yes, sweetheart, some day.' The questions were never-ending, and Carmel hedged, backtracked, and lied too. She justified it. Excused it. Telling herself there would be time enough later.

Helen could always get around her Dad. She had helped him in the store at weekends and holidays since she was a small child. Now the bright pretty teenager, dressed in jeans and colourful shirt, bounced around the shop, full of energy. She was popular with the customers, and Tom burst with pride when she tossed her shining hair, and smiled at him. Her father was always the one she went to first. He could refuse her nothing and she knew it.

'Tom, you'll spoil her.'

'Not at all. Anyway, why not? Who else is there to pamper?'

'Too much freedom isn't good.'

'She's a sensible girl.'

'You never know with teenagers. Remember ...'

'No worries. Nothing's going to happen in a place like this.'

Miles and miles of Australian bush. The golden tones of layered dust dominated the landscape which was windblown, and sun blasted. White light dazzled the eyes and caused temporary blindness. But the bird with clipped wings could see way beyond the blue sky and longed to fly away but didn't know where.

Helen overheard her parents talking and arguing more than once. Carmel wanted to hold on. Tom wanted to let go. And Helen was caught in the middle.

'Cut your beautiful hair?'

'But, Mum, it's so old fashioned.'

'No, I forbid it.'

Filled with rebellion, she did it anyway. Cut off the red tresses, and wondered did her mother ever forgive her?

'Helen, who is this boy?'

'No-one particular.'

'We'd like to meet him. Bring him around for tea.'

'Mum, we're only friends.'

'Is he going to be at this party tonight?'

'We're all going. All the gang. Don't be worrying.'

'Your Dad will collect you.'

'No, there's no need, Mum, we're getting a taxi. It's arranged.'

'I'll wait up for you.'

'Don't. I'll be late.'

It was always a tug of war between them.

'A trip to Europe?' Carmel's expression showed disapproval.

'Yes. After the exams.' Helen could not contain her enthusiasm.

'Where will you get the money?'

'I've a bit put by, and I thought you and Dad might lend me some? I could pay you back.'

'I don't know. You'd be away for so long.'

'Just six months or so, Mum. It will be the trip of a lifetime! Before we go to college.'

'But you're only eighteen.'

'Everyone does it nowadays, all the girls, there will be a few of us going.'

Carmel didn't want her to go. The tension increased between them. Her headaches became worse. She couldn't eat. She was hospitalised.

Helen's plan to travel to Europe was put aside and it was ten years later before it became a reality.

Chapter Two

In the stables, Jenny saddled up Swift Eagle – a black with a white diamond on his forehead. She ran her hands over the smooth shining coat, and led the horse out into the yard.

'OK Jenny?' One of the stable boys waved at her.

'Fine, thanks,' she smiled and mounted, wearing black jodhpurs, boots, windcheater, and hat. It was just six o'clock in the morning, and there was a sharp chill in the air but it didn't bother her. She trotted out across the meadows surrounding the house, and then pressed her legs into Swift Eagle's flanks. He responded, breaking into a canter and the horse and woman, a graceful pair, moved as one across some of the hundreds of acres that comprised Ballymoragh Stud. She passed the jockeys training the racehorses on the gallops and waited for a moment to watch them as they thundered along. Then she followed, her head low, until eventually she turned and continued uphill. The rhythm of the hooves echoed and she let the horse take her, the wind whistling past as they chased across the broad green sward. Then into the shelter of the trees, dodging an occasional low branch, and out again climbing up, and galloping on. Reluctantly, she turned back a little later, aware of the time. As she cantered through a grove of pine and out the other side, the large Georgian house came into view. Dating from 1760, it looked magnificent in the distance, surrounded by beech trees, carefully tended lawns, box hedges, the rose garden, and a maze. It was a long way from the home in which she had grown up. The unwelcome thought pushed its way into her head, and a sudden longing swept through her. If things had only been different. If she had been older.

Stronger. Then what?

She had always considered herself lucky to have met her husband, Michael Halloran. Admittedly, he was a widower, twenty-one years her senior with two grown sons, but he had persuaded her to marry him with protestations of love and she had said yes, responding to the romance of candle-lit dinners, weekends in Paris, New York, Monte Carlo, and the novelty of sharing her life with a man for the first time in her life.

She remembered Annabelle's enthusiasm when she had announced her marriage to Michael.

'He's a good catch!' she had encouraged. 'You'll never have a day's worry about money, and you'll be living down at Ballymoragh, what a delicious prospect.'

'We're doing well in our own business, money doesn't interest me, once I've enough to live on,' Jenny had said, wondering whether this was the right decision.

'Go for it, you're not getting any younger, and if you want to have a family then you must find a man soon, otherwise it will be too late.'

'Can you imagine me with children? No, I don't think so.' Jenny pressed her fingernails into her palm. Anxiety swept through her.

'Is Michael interested in having more?'

'No way.'

'Have you discussed it.'

'Of course.'

'But having a baby would be wonderful, surely you'd love to be a mother, isn't it the most natural thing in the world?'

'Not for me,' Jenny was unusually curt. She didn't want to think about babies. Stop talking about it, please, Annabelle, she wanted to scream.

'Such a pity, I was looking forward to being a grandmother by proxy, babysitting, kidsitting, teenagesitting, anything.'

She was disappointed, Jenny could see it. And was sorry.

'So there'll be no patter of little feet around the place – didn't you ever want kids?'

'Never thought much about it,' Jenny said. There was silence. 'When will that consignment arrive from Spain?' she asked after a moment.

Annabelle never mentioned children again. Dear Annabelle. Jenny had felt guilty at the time, wishing she could have granted her wish. She loved her. The woman who had given her that first chance in life all those years ago when she had been adrift in an unfamiliar world unable to find a secure landing place, confused, bewildered, until a job had been offered in her fashion salon – Venus. Part-time at first, she helped behind the scenes unpacking the clothes, pressing and hanging, waiting to be told to find the perfect colour and design for a particular client. She served her time and slowly she became more useful, and made opportunities for herself. She loved the work, happy to have found a niche. She was indispensable to Annabelle and eventually ran the salon singlehanded. Then she took over the buying and when Annabelle retired she offered Jenny an opportunity to purchase forty-nine per cent of the company. Married now, she had some money saved, and the bank provided the balance. Michael had offered to fund her, but she said no, preferring to be completely independent of the family. So they had developed the company. Annabelle's partner Guy had joined them and they opened branches in the U.K. and America – it was a great success.

Twelve years later, increasingly doubts about her decision to marry had invaded Jenny's mind. She had never loved Michael in that wild heady sense, but over the years they had eased into a comfortable relationship. He left her to her own devices most of the time. Occasionally, she had to play at being hostess. Something she didn't particularly enjoy but became accustomed to eventually. He liked to show her off. The clothes she wore. The jewellery he bought. But now she found him more demanding, wanting his own way in everything, her opinion unimportant.

'You don't know yourself,' Annabelle had said recently.

'What does that mean?' Jenny asked.

'It's turned out even better than you hoped – marriage I mean.'

'Yes, it's good.'

'You look happier and more contented than I've ever seen you, Jenny Halloran.'

'And you know what's strange. You'd think by now they'd call me Jenny, none of the family ever do, even Michael, it's always Jennifer. Except all the staff, Maureen and the lads working down at the stables, they're more like my family,' she smiled ruefully.

Jenny had carved out her own place in the Ballymoragh household, and had a good relationship with Michael's mother, Pearl. She had never stepped on her toes and the matriarch was left to run the place as she had always done. Michael's sons, Conor and Eoin had both moved out, but everyone worked in the business. The horses they bred were exported all over the world, they trained for wealthy owners, and owned a stable of winning thoroughbreds.

Just before eight, she came back into the yard, dismounted and unsaddled the horse. She brushed him down for a while and then led him out into the paddock, loathe to leave him. But she had to get back to the house which was quiet at this hour, no-one else around the place except the staff. She went into Michael and found him still sprawled among a tangle of sheets. She kissed him. He didn't move. She kissed him again. This time he groaned.

'Wake up, you've an appointment at ten o'clock and you'll need time to get there.'

He half opened his eyes. 'Who am I meeting?'

'The trainers.'

'Yea.' He pushed himself up. 'Oh, my head.'

'Will I get you something for it?'

'Strong coffee.'

'I'll bring some up.'

'What was I drinking?'

'God knows,' she smiled, anxious to start the day well. These times the smallest thing could erupt into a row. 'Do you want me to run the shower?'

He nodded.

She went into the bathroom and switched it on. In the old days, they would often spend time soaping each other sensually, usually as a prelude to making love and now she was almost tempted to slip out of her clothes and be there waiting for him.

'Where's that coffee?' The bark took her out of the reverie, and she hurried down to the kitchen, where the housekeeper Maureen was already preparing the food for lunch.

'Michael has a hangover, and ordered some strong black coffee,' Jenny grinned.

'It's already made, and I've the aspirin on the tray, do you want me to take it up?'

'No, there's no hurry, he's in the shower.'

'What about you, love, would you like something?' Maureen asked.

'Tea will do, thanks.'

'I'll make some fresh, and something to eat, toast and eggs maybe? You're probably ravenous after your ride.'

'All I want is some of your lovely soda bread, but I'll get it myself.' She cut a couple of slices.

'Just made this morning.'

'Gorgeous.' She spread honey. 'What are you cooking for lunch today?'

'Roast beef. And Karen is coming over with some friend of hers but they'll only want lettuce leaves.'

Karen was Michael's younger sister. A rebellious character, she had done her own thing and turned her back on the family, spending most of her time in India. It was only last Christmas that she had arrived back unexpectedly, and to everyone's surprise, had taken up residence in the lodge. She was an unusual woman, into alternative living, a vegan, and practiced acupuncture and reiki. Jenny liked her.

In the early days at Ballymoragh Jenny had felt like the heroine in the old film "Rebecca". She couldn't think of the name of the actress who played the part, but remembered the rather strange housekeeper, Mrs. Danvers, who was more like her mother-in-law,

Pearl. But she had mellowed over the years and at eighty-seven wasn't quite so irascible as in times past. Still, she demanded a lot of Jenny's time.

She took the tray up and as Michael was dressing she left it on the table in his room. Was he bored with her after all the years? Perhaps she was away from him too much? There were no obvious signs. They still made love, but somehow these days it was more rushed. Something to be over and done with. She remembered last night and her passive acceptance of his advances. In the past she had always been anxious to make their lovemaking as pleasurable as possible. But Michael was a man of the moment to whom satisfaction came quickly and was over before Jenny had even begun. She had never experienced orgasm at all with him but had become expert at faking it.

It was just before dinner when he had put his arms around her. 'Maybe we have time?' He kissed her, his lips hard. He wasn't giving her a choice. He took off his jacket and flung it across a chair.

'I still have to change, darling,' she tried to dissuade.

'Quickly.'

He took her arm and drew her towards the bed. He pushed up her skirt and groped. She lay there and let it happen.

The ceiling was ornate. The cornice picked out in blue and gold. The cascade of crystal in the chandelier threw shadows across, like sunshine through the branches of trees. Suddenly, it took her back to a woodland glade. The scent of grass, wild flowers, birdsong, the softness of another man's lips, to whom she had given herself unconditionally.

Chapter Three

David cast the line out and watched it drop slowly into the rippling water. He loved to take the boat out and spend time fishing the lake which bordered his land in Lackenmore, regretting the amount of time he had to spend away from home, his music career taking him on tour too often.

The boat drifted. Steve hummed softly. He shared David's love of fishing and the two took any opportunity they could get to take off on their own.

'There are a good few people in for the weekend, some nice cruisers there.' Steve looked back to the marina.

'The tourist season has been OK, although we're coming to the end of it now.'

'And this is the finish of our season until February. I'll miss the chance to do some fishing out here on the lake, and escape from the kids. Bit of peace and quiet.'

'And I need to escape from that mad house back there,' David laughed.

'I like the tracks we've recorded so far, slightly different to your usual.' He reeled in an empty line.

'Some of them are OK.'

'All of them are good, you're just too critical,' Steve put a new fly on the hook.

David Taylor and Friends were recording their latest album with all original material written by him. The group's preferred genre was pure blues and experimental, but David had found a niche in the popular jazz market when one of his compositions had achieved number one in the top ten for a famous American singer. And just to add to the pressure, having written some film scores, he was now inundated with requests from producers who liked his style.

'We should manage to launch the album for Christmas.'

'At a push.' Steve cast again.

'We're nearly finished, just another couple of weeks' work.'

'And then on the road again, living out of a suitcase.'

'Maybe we're getting too old for it. Four middle-aged men,' David laughed.

'I wouldn't mind easing back, although we're committed for the next two years.'

'There will always be jobs at the studios, enough going on there to keep us all busy. And we can still record.'

The studios had been David's brainchild when he inherited his father's estate. A large country manor house which was ideal for accommodation, with plenty of space to build on. All the necessary back-up services were provided and they offered the level of expertise required by top recording groups who now came to Lackenmore. With the onset of the digital age of television they had expanded into media post production, which kept them going around the clock. David was glad to be able to give something back to the town in which he had grown up.

There was a tug on his line and a sense of excitement rippled through him as he reeled it in, really pleased to see a wriggling trout on the end of it.

'That's a big one.' Steve caught it in the net.

Grinning, David took it off the hook and weighed it. 'Two and a half pounds - a beauty.' He held it up and Steve took a photo. 'Right, back you go.'

The stocks in the lake were depleted and they always replaced any fish they caught.

The sky in the west was a dull red through the clouds. But as evening drew in, they stayed there, loving the solitude of the place. They didn't talk much, and just sat comfortably, two fishermen, aware that nothing could better this.

They motored back to the marina a little later, Steve to go home, and David over to the holiday development which he had built along the shore of the lake. Several small cottages among the trees could be used by clients if there was not enough space at the house. Here also was the Arts Centre for the community which was really a self-indulgence, and not meant to be commercially viable. Free of charge, it was used by many groups in the town and surrounding area for art, drama, music, and other social events.

He went in to see Breda. She was a jolly no-nonsense sort of person in her mid-thirties, who managed the holiday development and the marina. Utterly reliable and honest, she was invaluable to him, particularly when he wasn't around to deal with the everyday nitty gritty of such a venture. In return, he paid her an excellent salary, gave her a company credit card for expenses, and any of the cars at the house was at her disposal whenever she liked.

'Fix up one of the cottages for me, the best, I've a temperamental soprano flying in on Saturday and she insists on staying in one of my "little houses" he did a good imitation of the American twang and laughed.

'No prob, Dave.'

'I've explained how basic they are, but there's no getting through to her. Put the central heating on full blast. She comes from the deep south and no doubt will think this is the Arctic. Stock up the bar - Dom Perignon, the best wines, use your initiative.'

'Plenty of that,' she laughed.

'New towels, bedlinen, flowers, gold card treatment.'

'Like all your clients.'

'I don't relish the job of looking after them, I'm lucky to have you.' Relaxed, he leaned against the desk, long legs crossed. 'I wish I wasn't away so much,' he smiled and his face brightened as he glanced out the window at the setting sun. 'There's nowhere like Lackenmore, best place in the world.'

He was just back at the house when his phone rang. With a slight sense of misgiving he noted the number. It was Vanessa.

'Where have you been? I'm annoyed with you.'

He could visualise her large blue eyes accusing him, her beautiful face sulky. The same look she would have if he had not noticed the new designer outfit supposedly worn just for him.

'Sorry, I've been really busy.'

'You could have spared time to phone, or text.'

'Sorry.' He felt like a small boy being ticked off by his father.

'You've no idea how upset I am.' Her voice quivered.

'Come on Vanessa, you know what my life is like.'

'Unfortunately.' There was a rush of tears in the whispered word.

'Forgive me then,' he bantered.

Vanessa, late twenties, twice divorced, actress and daughter of a billionaire, had taken a fancy to him.

When in LA, he had enjoyed the hectic social whirl in her company, but lately it had all began to pall. And it was with relief that he had returned to Lackenmore to rejuvenate his soul.

'When will you be over?'

'Don't know, there's so much going on here, I just can't tell you when.'

'So you won't be coming down to Acapulco with us?'

'Sorry, but thanks for the invite.'

'You just don't care, do you?'

'Whether I go with you?' He was being deliberately obtuse.

'No, about me,' she whimpered. She could do it so well if things didn't go exactly as she had planned.

'Of course I care about you, Vanessa,' he had to say it. Had to give the expected response.

'But not enough.'

'You know we talked about that last time, let's not go over it all again,' he said softly.

'I thought if you hadn't seen me for a while you might miss me, maybe even realise how much you love me.'

'Go on the trip and enjoy yourself, I'm far too old for your crowd and well you know it.'

'But you're not too old for me.'

'I'll give you a shout next time I'm over and we'll get together.'

'Promise?'

'Promise.'

He put down the phone and stood for a moment looking at it. Tall, dark haired, his brown eyes seemed dejected. Perhaps he had given the wrong signals, encouraged her to see more in their friendship than was actually there – and it was only a friendship as far as he was concerned.

It was a long time since he had been involved with anyone. Always holding back from total commitment. He had learned his lesson the hard way and gave up looking for someone who would fill that void which existed deep within. For David, it had to be one hundred per cent.

Chapter Four

'I'm going to get my hair done tomorrow,' Chris announced, looking in the mirror over the fireplace.

'Why?' Her mother, Pauline, asked.

'Why not?' She ran her fingers through the frizzy mop.

'You never go anywhere except Mass and the shops.'

'Well, someone might call.'

'Faye is coming later on,' Pauline smiled.

'Who?'

'Faye. Don't you remember your sister?'

'Of course I do.'

'She told me she'd be here at four.'

'We haven't seen her for years, God knows where she is now,' Chris muttered.

'She's beautiful.'

'Don't I know that. She was the one who got all the looks in this family. And then she went off and left me here with you.'

'You should be glad to see her.'

'It's Sean I want to see.' Chris wandered towards the window. 'Any minute now he could drive into the yard.'

'He can't come in here.'

'Who says?' Chris flashed.

'We can't have a strange man in this house, I won't have it.'

'You don't have a say in it. He's my son and this is his home whether you like it or not.'

'Who's home?'

'Mam, will you put a sock in it, I can't take any more.'

'Of what?'

Chris sighed deeply and wandered around the kitchen. Repositioned a plate on the dresser. Settled a curtain. Blew a speck of dust from the top of the range. Then she went back to the mirror and stared at herself.

A widow of ten years with one son, Sean, she lived with her mother Pauline on the family farm just outside the town of Lackenmore, as she had done all her life. Sean had emigrated to the States some years before and he had shown no interest in returning home. So she was forced to allow her neighbour Corcoran work their land. They had an agreement which ran for eleven months each year. She expected him this evening when he would come to make sure that the land was his for the next eleven months. Pay his debt for the previous year, counted out in a mixture of dirty notes and coins which were shaken out of a brown paper bag on to Chris's clean pink-flowered table cloth.

She hated the filth of it. The smell of old pockets. The touch of grubby fingers. But most of all she hated the inequality of the trade. How could God's fine clean earth equate with the thirty pieces of silver spilled on the table. Each year, she vowed that it would be the last.

But this evening she was forced to entertain him. She needed the money he owed her.

'Whiskey?' She poured a small measure into a glass and pushed it across the table towards him.

Corcoran's eyes were small and cunning. She felt as if he was mentally stripping her. Then he pounced. Snared. Impaled. She should have anticipated. Should have known he would do it again. But he was always one move ahead and took the breath out of her with his stomach-churning propositions.

'Why don't you sell? You can't run it yourself,' he urged.

She didn't reply.

'I'd give you a good price, fair, after all we've been working it for nigh on ten years.'

'It has always been a Brophy farm,' she muttered.

'My boys are grown now, and we've looked after it for you.'

She shook her head. Knowing he was going to continue on. And not wanting him to. Yet wanting.

'But there is another way,' he paused, pouring himself another measure from the bottle. 'Maybe this year you might see it different.'

She was silent. Watching him.

'How about it, Chris? Marry me and we could join the farms together. I've no-one at home except the boys and we could do with a woman about the place. You'd be a missus again instead of a widow woman. You'd have your own man. I wouldn't disappoint you, promise you that.' He leaned across the table towards her, leering.

Chris didn't reply. Simply screwed the top of the bottle closed. Tight.

'That bloody development at the lake could destroy us. We might stop his gallop together if we joined the farms. He wouldn't know what hit him with his lines of little white cottages as far as the eye can see. We don't want that, do we? Land is for cattle and crops, not white boxes for them strangers.'

'The price has gone up another one hundred euro.' Her voice formed the words like a snowball with a stone in the middle and threw it at him with pleasure.

His mouth, pink, fleshy, gap-toothed, fell open with surprise. 'What?'

'Everything goes up.'

'But I can't afford any more.'

She said nothing.

'Chris, this could bankrupt me.'

She almost laughed.

He choked on his spittle with a suck suck sucking noise, like that made by a cow trying to drag itself out of mud.

Chapter Five

To make up for her absences from home, Jenny joined Michael and the family at the Prix de l'Arc de Triomphe race meeting at Longchamp. The weather was still pleasant and Ballymoragh Stud had a number of winners.

'You look wonderful, I love the outfit.' One of the other wives there kissed her on both cheeks enthusiastically. 'Where did you get it?'

'It's one of the designers we carry,' she said.

'What's the name?' Another asked.

'Chevalier.'

'I've heard of him.'

'That lilac and white tone is delicious, and the flowing lines are so graceful.'

'Thanks.'

'Maybe you'll win the best dressed prize.'

'I think not,' she laughed, self-conscious.

'Didn't see you at the party after Fairyhouse.'

'I was in New York.'

'You missed a good night,' another woman said, and they giggled together continuing to chat about who was getting together, who'd broken up , who was sleeping with whom, and so on. There was a gust of wind, and they had to grab the brims of the confections on their heads, hanging on to glasses of champagne and designer bags, amid more laughter. The group grew larger as some other people joined them. Introductions were made. Voices raised in gossip.

A man's hand grasped hers, a hardness in his grip. 'Do I know you?' He peered at her curiously.

'I told you, Ralph, this is Jenny Halloran, you know, Michael's wife.' One of the women leaned closer to him.

'I know that, but I seem to remember you from years ago. Way back in my youth.'

Jenny shook her head. 'I don't think so.'

'Where are you from?'

'Kildare,' she said abruptly, suddenly feeling distinctly uncomfortable.

'But before that?' he pressed.

'Don't say you can't remember such a handsome man,' the woman giggled, 'I'd never forget you.' She put her hand on his sleeve possessively.

'I'm from Galway - Lackenmore - the back of beyond,' he said, grinning.

'The race is starting, come on,' someone shouted and en masse they moved and she was left wordless, her heart beating rapidly. Lackenmore. She had become expert at pushing the associations with that place out of her head, and now she drifted without direction across the green sward, dotted with the refreshment tents. Moving through the crowd, excusing herself in her soft voiced way, until eventually she found herself close to the track, forced to stay there, packed in, the people around her cheering on their horses. The noise was loud, deafening. Her ears buzzed. She felt light-headed. Like a dried dandelion floating into the air bit by bit until only the darkness of her mood was left.

When the race was over she wandered back to the *rond de presentation*.

'Jennifer?' Michael called out as soon as he spotted her. 'I want to introduce you.' The name didn't register. She hadn't met the man before, and didn't want to, or his wife either. She was dressed in a dramatic orange and black outfit, with a feathered creation on her head which wobbled as she moved. Jenny felt alone, even though there were so many people around. The group moved over to the bar for champagne. She was left behind until a hand touched her arm drawing her after them.

'Jenny, let's keep up,' her stepson, Eoin, said. He was the gentle one. She liked him better than Conor who was brash and more like Michael. They were both in their thirties now.

'Let's meet for coffee when we get home, I haven't had a decent chat with you in ages,' he suggested.

When they arrived back to the hotel after dinner, Michael ordered more champagne.

'What a day, four winners.' He raised his glass in the air.

Jenny had no choice but to join them, although she was tired by now. She sipped the fizzy drink slowly but Michael knocked his back fast and quickly poured another.

'Mandrake ran well, although even up to the last we weren't too sure whether he'd make it,' he beamed, 'and Barnstorm, Grafter, and Corry Boy wiped them all out.'

'After the race we thought that Barnstorm had a slight limp and the vet had a look at him,' Donal said. Michael's younger brother was semi-retired but still took a keen interest in the stud.

'What?' Michael straightened up sharply.

'It's not serious.'

'Hope he'll be OK for Leopardstown.'

'Should be, we'll keep a close eye on him.' Her step-son Conor was equally concerned.

'Can't afford to have anything wrong with him, he's one of our best horses, so bankable.'

Jenny smiled at his wife Aoife but she was caught up in the conversation too. All of the family was involved in the business and while Jenny loved horses, and particularly her own Swift Eagle, sometimes she felt out of it. But she had to be patient tonight and it was much later when they all drifted off to their own rooms and left them alone at last.

'C'mere to me.' Michael stretched out his arm. 'Jennifer?' He took her hand and stood up unsteadily. 'Come to bed.' He put his arm around her and they walked slowly into the bedroom. Once inside he pulled her close, kissing her sloppily, but his intoxication suddenly hit him and caused him to sway. She helped him to the bed and he sat down, his eyes drooping.

'Let's get some sleep.' She took off his tie, and began to unbutton his shirt.

He wound his arms around her but dozed off on her shoulder.

She lay him on the bed and covered him with the duvet. So glad she didn't have to perform tonight, she relaxed and watched him. He was on his back emitting a low snore every now and then, and tonight he seemed every bit his sixty-seven years. His face was florid and the bald head inclined towards her. Jenny was forty-six now, and she saw that the signs of age had crept up slowly on her as well. But to an outsider Jennifer Halloran was still a beautiful woman. Slim, with that striking red hair, and large blue-green eyes, she hadn't changed very much at all since she was young. Her clothes were superbly-cut designer creations and she always stood out from the crowd, with an allure of which she was quite unaware. She had no interest in going down the route of plastic surgery like some of the other women she knew. The thought of having various parts of her anatomy padded, stretched or reduced was unpalatable so she had decided to put up with the way she was. She couldn't trim off the years. Anyway, if Michael was bored with her then no matter what she did it wouldn't make any difference. Maybe that was to be expected when you reached a certain stage. The brightness of the early years dulled by dark autumn shadows.

'Michael, would you fancy staying on for a couple of days, just the two of us,' Jenny asked the following morning before they went down for breakfast. The bedroom opened out on to a balcony and she stood at the French door holding back the white lace curtain which flipped and flopped in the breeze. She waited for his reply, or perhaps the warmth of his arms to curve around her, the weight of him confirming that he would like that too. But the silence was heavy with unsaid words and she turned to find that the room was empty. He appeared out of the bathroom patting after shave on his face.

'Nice aroma,' she murmured, moving towards him.

'You ready?' he grunted.

'Yes.' She picked up her handbag from the table.

On the corridor they waited for the lift.

'As I was saying, what about spending some extra time here, you and me, we could explore Paris, see some of those places we used to love years ago?' she asked again.

'I'm going to London. Must see a few people. Won't be back in Ballymoragh until Thursday. Stay on yourself if you want.' He pressed the button again a couple of times. 'Bloody lift, takes ages, drives me mad. I'm not staying here again.'

It whirred, and clunked, and eventually arrived at their floor.

They stepped in and when the doors had closed, she turned to him and kissed him full on the lips. 'My love, stay on with me, I feel we're going in opposite directions these days.'

He returned the kiss with a puckering of his lips.

'I miss you,' she smiled, and touched his face softly.

'What are you on about?'

The lift doors slid open. They stepped out and walked the corridor to the first floor dining room. She stared down at the cream carpet, the toes of her maroon courts marching ahead. She was being taken somewhere but wondered had she any control over herself as they swung through the double doors of the bright room. The high drapes of cream silk caught with thick black tassels swung downwards in pools on to the carpet. The furniture was ebony, the upholstery matched the curtains.

Hands waved.

Voices welcomed.

They joined the family at the big table.

'You two are late.' Donal bit into a large croissant and crumbs caught on his dark moustache, in strong contrast to his grey hair.

'Enjoying a lie-in?' Conor grinned and poured milky coffee from a pot.

'Jennifer, sit here beside me.' Karen patted a chair.

But she didn't want to sit there, she would have preferred to be with Michael, but he had already taken a seat beside Eoin.

'Sleep well?' Karen asked.

She nodded.

'You're looking beautiful as usual.'

Jenny smiled, thinking that these words were the very ones which Michael should have said to her already this morning.

'Don't know how you do it, let me in on your secret will you? While I'm vegan and so fussy about everything that passes my lips, my skin never had that translucent look of yours. What is your routine?'

'Nothing unusual.'

'No secret potions?'

'No,' Jenny said, smiling.

'Must be genetic then.'

Jenny poured coffee for herself, a slight quiver in her hand as she lifted the heavy silver pot. Reaching for the milk jug she noticed Conor and Aoife smiling at each other. Suddenly, it seemed there was something intensely intimate about the little scene. Something which was missing in her own life.

Chapter Six

Helen was going to Europe at last. By now her mother Carmel had accepted the fact that her daughter was old enough to make her own decisions. After college, she worked as a journalist on the local newspaper writing a column each week, and now planned to send back articles from the various places she visited hoping that her regular readers would be interested in her adventures.

But there were still moments in the weeks leading up to her departure when she caught Carmel watching her, a strange look in her blue eyes. And there was an air of tension in the house too. She would walk into a room and find herself on the tail end of a conversation that stopped abruptly, a guilty look passing between her parents. She would wake suddenly in the middle of the night and hear whispers floating just out of earshot, and then sit up to listen until the silence of the house reassured that she had probably imagined it. She became conscious of happenings just beyond her which she couldn't quite reach. A light switched on in another room, shadows moving, a low discordant note droning in the distance like there was another entity in the house with them. It made her edgy and while she should have been full of excitement each time she put another item on the pile of things she intended to take there was an added sense of guilt.

For over a year Helen travelled extensively through France, Italy, Greece and Turkey, leaving Ireland – the most important – until last. Finally she flew into Dublin Airport on an October evening, to be met by her father's brother and his wife.

Noreen enveloped Helen in an enthusiastic bear hug. 'You're here at last! I can't believe it.' She stood back and smiled at her.

'Hey, am I getting a look in here at all?' Paddy planted a kiss on her cheek and pulled her close. Her heart contracted. He was so like her Dad she was immediately whisked back to Alice Springs.

'Come on, let's get out of here. I'm sure you're dying to have a rest after the journey.' Noreen put her arm around Helen affectionately as they led the way out of the bustling airport.

She was drawn into the family immediately, surrounded with love from Noreen and Paddy who were delighted to have a young person around the house again, as their own two daughters were working in the States. Years of longing to escape the claustrophobic atmosphere of Alice Springs had now landed her here, a place she could only have imagined. She had been born in this country and now had come back to find her roots, like so many Australians she knew who wished they could go back. Her parents hadn't talked much of Ireland, and although she had asked question after question as she grew up the answers were vague and told her nothing.

'I'm thinking of going to Lackenmore in a few days,' Helen said. She had been staying with her aunt and uncle for a couple of weeks. They had taken her sightseeing around Dublin, and now she felt it was time to move on, she didn't want to overstay her welcome.

'You'll love it there. Maybe we could take you, we haven't been back in years,' Paddy suggested.

'Well, I won't be going direct. I want to visit a few places on the way,' Helen said gently, reluctant to hurt their feelings.

'Paddy, you're embarrassing poor Helen,' interjected Noreen.

'Am I?'

'She doesn't want two old fogies coming with her, she wants to do her own thing.'

'No really, if you'd like to come that would be great,' Helen said.

'Your aunt is right, as usual, Helen. Don't you worry, no need to explain. Maybe it's important for you to go back on your own.'

'I was thinking of taking some photos as I go along, and I'll probably just stop the car and get out on the spur of the moment, so my progress could be quite slow.'

'You'll need a map, never find it otherwise.' Paddy got up and searched in a drawer.

'What are you looking for?' Noreen asked.

'Something to write on and a pen.'

'There's a pad in the top press.' She directed him.

He opened the door.

'There, see it, with the orange cover, and here's a pen.'

'Your mother and father made a good decision to emigrate when you think of how the small farmers have fared since we joined the EU.' Paddy carefully drew a map for Helen. Neatly printed names. Winding roads. Arrows. Left. Right. Straight ahead.

It wasn't quite what she had expected. Which was? She asked herself. Well, something quaint, old fashioned, shabby, the way her dad had described it. But this small town which nestled at the head of a wide lake was certainly not shabby. In pristine condition, it announced the fact that it had won the Tidy Towns Award three times and urged everyone to make sure that Lackenmore won first prize next year as well. Its buildings clustered around a broad main street, two church spires pointed skywards and on an outcrop of rock above the town towered an ancient ruined castle which dominated everything else in sight.

On that first night, she took a room in the only hotel in town and on the following morning drove out around the lake to discover some pretty holiday cottages built at a marina. The place was deserted except for a fisherman working on his boat, and he directed her to the cottage with a red door where she would find the woman who managed the development.

Helen found Breda to be a really friendly individual who was very welcoming. The cottage nearest the water was available and she carried in her bags, warming to the tall dark-haired girl. She unpacked and a little later Breda knocked in again.

'Brought you over some brown bread, eggs and a pot of marmalade for your breakfast.' She put the bag down on the counter, folded her arms, and leaned against the unit obviously in no hurry to leave.

'Thank you so much.' Helen took the brown bread out of the bag and breathed in its aroma. 'It's still warm, how lovely.'

'I make bread every day so if you like I'll drop some in, if you're not in you'll find it in the porch.'

'It looks really good, thanks.'

'If you need anything, just give me a shout.'

They chatted on for a while and gradually, Helen felt more at home, excited that she was at last back in this place where her parents had been born.

The weather was still pleasant and Helen wandered around the town and its environs getting to know Lackenmore. Breda proved to be particularly friendly and they spent the evenings together in the local pub, where she was introduced to many of her friends. Planning to go shopping in Galway one of the days, Helen strolled over to Breda's bungalow but stopped when she saw a black Land Rover parked outside and decided to walk down to the edge of the water until whomever was visiting had left. But after a moment, Breda opened the back door and beckoned her in.

'I saw you outside there, come and meet David.' She led the way into the kitchen where a tall dark man sat on the sofa.

He stood up immediately, hand outstretched. But as Helen grasped it he stared silently at her with piercing brown eyes.

'Helen's from Australia, David, Alice Springs,' Breda said.

'It's good to meet you.'

'Have we covered everything, David?'

'Yes, I think so.' He picked up a file from the table.

'Us girls are heading into Galway for some retail therapy, so we'd better get started.' Breda picked up her large silver handbag.

'Don't let me delay you.' He walked ahead of them out the door. 'See you tomorrow.'

'Sure. Enjoy yourselves.' He climbed into the jeep. The engine roared and he turned with a screech of tyres, drove up the road at a fast pace and disappeared around the bend.

'My God, he seems to be in a bit of a hurry, I was nearly going to suggest he join us in Galway,' Breda sighed.

'To go shopping with us?' Helen laughed.

'Well, for lunch maybe.' She seemed wistful.

'Do you like him?'

'Yea, I suppose I do.'

'He seems a nice enough guy.'

'Not for me though.'

'Why not?'

'He's on a different social scale.'

'He just seemed like a regular joe to me.'

'No way. He's a world famous musician, used to mixing with glamorous people in the entertainment world. I wouldn't fit in there.'

'Why not?'

'Come on, Helen, he's never shown any interest so I'm just dreaming. You're the only person who knows about it, so keep it under your hat, I don't want the whole of Lackenmore knowing I'm mooning after the most eligible bachelor in town.'

'Sure, your secret is safe with me,' she laughed.

They enjoyed the few hours wandering around the shops in Galway, Breda particularly anxious to pick up an outfit for a party to be held on Saturday night at the studios, delighted that Helen was with her to help choose the deep blue chiffon dress which she finally bought.

'You know you're invited to the party as well.'

'Am I?' Helen was surprised.

'Everyone's invited, including all the staff, and guests. I didn't want to say it earlier in case you felt you had to buy something special just because I'm splurging.'

'I've got a little black number with me, the one and only.'

'That'll be fine.

'They had lunch at Cava, a Spanish restaurant, and lingered chatting, enjoying the tapas and the atmosphere of the place.

'I was wondering if you might help me,' Helen asked hesitantly. So far she hadn't told Breda the purpose of her visit to Ireland.

'Shoot.'

'I've been trying to find the house where my mother and father lived.'

'I mightn't be much help. We've only been here about twenty years, blow-ins you might say.' Her laugh was warm and infectious.

'I have a map, my uncle gave it to me.' She took it from her bag and gave it to Breda. 'The house is somewhere along this road. He said you can see the lake from it.'

'Who's living there now?'

'No-one, it's derelict I think. I've driven around but couldn't see it.'

'Have you any family still living here?'

'No. My parents emigrated to Australia just after I was born, we were the last of the McLoughlins around here.'

Breda took the piece of paper from Helen.

'Well, that looks like the Corcorans, and that must be the Brophy place.' She peered at Paddy's squiggly lines and arrows.

'My father sold the land to the Brophys before they left.'

'Then we're not too far away. You continue on our road and take a right turn, then it's the third farm along. Do you know, I think there is an old house a bit back off the road, that could be it.'

Helen followed Breda's instructions and it was easy now to spot the old farmhouse that Carmel and Tom had left so long ago. Up a narrow laneway, and snugly positioned among a grove of tall beeches, it stood abandoned by the family it had sheltered. There was no-one about, and Helen climbed the gate which was thickly rusted and impossible to push open. Most of the roof had collapsed, windows and doors yawned bleak and empty. She stepped inside. Ivy twined and twisted, weeds carpeted the floors, even the branches of a tree protruded through the wall. It seemed as if nature had taken over and would swallow everything before long. She identified the living room, kitchen and bedrooms, and tried to imagine what it must have been like living here. She could even see the remains of an old couch and armchair and imagined her mother and father sitting there of an evening after the work was done. Or waking up each morning to see the land sweep down to the lake and reach up out of the still dark water to the mountains on the other side. And her mother carrying her in her arms – a tiny child only weeks old. But now this house had a terrible air of abandonment and loneliness. A husband, wife and daughter left it one day and never came back. Closed the door on a family born and bred for over two hundred years in this place. Helen wished she had been raised here, and that their family tree had continued to grow where its roots were embedded.

Before she left, she took a photograph to email to her Dad, knowing how much it would mean to him.

Chapter Seven

Jenny drove down to see her sister-in-law, Karen, to get away from the stultifying atmosphere of the house. The lodge was an old-fashioned place, decorated in striking earthy colours, terracotta, yellow, red, the furniture swathed in the bright patterned throws of India. Low lamps and the flames of many candles created a rosy glow.

'Organic wine?' Karen held up a bottle.

'Sure, why not, I can always walk back up,' Jenny grinned. She always enjoyed Karen's company, so different from anyone else in the family.

'You wouldn't want to be seen stumbling along, your reputation could be ruined,' Karen laughed.

'No-one would notice.'

'Don't believe that for one second. If your image is tarnished you'll pay a price. The family wouldn't approve, particularly mother,' Karen quipped, shaking her large silver hoop earrings as she spoke. She wore three different sizes which jingled.

'I almost don't care at this stage.' Jenny sipped her wine, relaxing back into the soft cushioned couch. It was so very different from the house, where there was always an element of formality, a stiffness which caused the bones to ache just a little, and kept everyone slightly on their toes.

'I sense a low mood.' Her sister-in-law sat back on a low armchair, wearing a loose red cotton dress, her greying hair caught up in a mother of pearl comb. 'Not like the perfect Jennifer we all know and love.' Karen leaned forward towards her as she spoke. 'Do tell, do tell.'

Jenny hadn't intended to say anything, but the words slipped out at her encouragement.

'Things aren't going well between Michael and myself.' Jenny stared into the leaping flames.

'I'm sorry,' Karen murmured, 'but I could have told you. He doesn't understand women. Never did. Horses are the only creatures who mean anything to him.'

The blunt words cut through Jenny.

'When you go into a relationship it's like walking into a fog, God only knows what awaits you.'

'I don't know what to do.'

'There are only two choices where Michael is concerned. Stay or go.'

Jenny stared at her, shocked.

'You won't change my brother.'

'I don't want to change him radically, it's just how we are together. There's so little talk. We never go anywhere alone, it's always connected with horses, racing, that whole scene.'

'You married a man with equine blood in his veins. How well did you two know each other before you got hitched?'

'It was a whirl. We had a great time. You name it, we did it. Although I didn't realise what motivated Michael above everything else.' Jenny reached her hands out towards the heat of the fire. The warmth was comforting.

'You were a bit of a mystery too I think,' Karen laughed, 'the whole family was up in arms when Michael told us he was getting married again. Who is this woman who came out of nowhere? Is she just a gold digger, an opportunist? And she's so much younger than him, it won't last a year, and then she'll go off with half the estate. Mother was worst of all. But it was the first time I admired Michael. He made up his own mind for once in his life.'

'I didn't know how you felt.'

'It was hard to get close to you at first. I still sometimes think I'm only skimming the surface.' She poured two more glasses of wine, and lay back languidly in the chair waving the glass in the air, numerous coloured bangles clinking.

A little uneasy now, Jenny wondered where this was going.

'Who are you really, Jenny? What goes on in your head? The secrets behind those eyes?' She leaned forward with a mischievous smile.

'Nothing worth talking about, Karen,' Jenny murmured softly.

'You were a successful businesswoman, worth a lot of money in your own right. But the deep personal side to you was missing. You must have been very lonely.'

'Karen, the wine has gone to your head.'

'Maybe I've blanked things out too.' She took another gulp.

Jenny looked at her, surprised. 'I think we all have stuff we can't face.'

'And some have more than others.'

They sat in silence for a while each occupied with her own thoughts.

'I'd better go.' Jenny stood up. 'Thanks for a lovely evening.'

'Are you capable of driving?' Karen's voice was slightly slurred.

'I'll walk back.'

'You can stay here if you want.' She leaned her head back and closed her eyes.

'Why don't you go to bed, I'll see you tomorrow.' Jenny took the glass out of her hand.

She was already asleep.

Jenny covered her with a velvet throw, blew out the candles, and put the guard in front of the fire.

'Jennifer!' The tap of Pearl's walking stick was heard more and more throughout the house. Always accompanied by a shrill demand for someone or something. It got on Jenny's nerves.

'I want to clear out some of my things.' She was querulous.

'They're gathering dust.'

Jenny felt she was gathering dust herself. That soft stuff which clogged up the mechanism. Cloaking her heart. Drying up the juices until she crumpled like paper tissue.

'Open that drawer, I want to see what's in there.' Pearl pointed towards it with her stick.

Jenny opened it to find a large number of photographs crushed into the space, barely enough room for them all. She took some out and spread them on the small table which stood beside Pearl's chair. All were old, some colour, some black and white.

'Give me that one.'

Jenny handed it to her.

'Get me the magnifying glass. It's somewhere around, I had it earlier.'

Jenny searched through the pile of newspapers and found it underneath.

'Do you recognise him?'

Jenny examined the photo but hadn't a clue as to the identity of the man who sat astride a white horse. 'No, I'm sorry.'

'You should know. He's my brother. He was killed taking a fence. A great horseman.'

Pearl was quite annoyed when Jenny took a guess at the identity of this or that person, but never got it quite right. Thankfully, after an hour she grew tired and instructed Jenny to put the photos back. As she did that, she had a fleeting impression of faded albums. Photos lovingly inserted into thick cardboard pages, a delicate tracery of flowers in beautiful colours framing the edges of each one. The heavy leather-bound covers closed with a tiny brass lock. The image of a man with bent head sitting at a table forced itself into her mind. Someone took her hand and drew her closer. She was young then. It was a time of innocence and she knew with certainly that nothing could come between them. He turned to look at her. She wanted to hold on to him. But he drifted away. So close one moment so far the next, the distance between them only counted in seconds.

'Let me see some of your family photographs.'

The curt demand sent a quiver through Jenny.

'I don't have any.' Her hands twisted nervously.

'What?' Pearl stared fixedly at her.

'No.' She couldn't look at the old woman.

'Nonsense, everyone has photos. Surely your mother and father took some of the family?'

Jenny shook her head.

'What about when you were young, days at the beach, at school with your friends, I can't believe you haven't even one.'

'They were lost along the way.' The vision of the man came into her mind again, and her heart twisted.

'Well, you should go about finding them and getting copies. Maybe your brothers and sisters have some?'

Jenny didn't reply and tried to change the subject. 'Would you like to go outside, Pearl, it's a lovely day for this time of the year?' she asked. 'I could push you in the wheelchair and wrap you up well, the fresh air will do you good.'

'I'm not going out in that thing. I hate it.' She shook her head vehemently and the pinned up white hair drifted down into her eyes. She pushed it back. 'No, there's something else I want you to do for me.'

Jenny sighed inwardly, and stood there waiting, although she longed to get out of the room, feeling unnerved after Pearl's remarks about family photographs. What is it with the Hallorans? Karen last night, and now Pearl. Trying to force me to talk of stuff I can't even bear to think about.

'I want to go through my clothes, I might give some to Maureen, she always knows someone who will need them.'

Jenny opened the heavy mahogany door of the large antique wardrobe. This was something Pearl did regularly and now Jenny could see herself being stuck here for hours. The rows of dresses hung limply. She took one out and held it up. It was turquoise with a cream collar.

'I like that, keep it.'

Jenny put it back. She showed her another, a pale pink floral.

'No, fed up with that, dump it.'

Another was produced, navy with brass buttons.

'Show me the back.'

Jenny obeyed.

'The front again.'

'Back again,' she considered, 'maybe I might ...'

It was replaced.

The walking stick pointed towards a wine creation with a fine pleated skirt. It too was taken out, Jenny's arms beginning to ache by now.

'Will I, won't I?' An out of tune hum escaped the puckered lips.

Then a loud knock on the door, and it was opened abruptly to admit Karen who burst into the room, dressed in a blue fringed poncho and floaty green trousers. The mood in the room changed and prepared for an explosion.

'Mother, did you send one of the gardeners to cut my trees?' She stood in front of the old woman who still held her stick pointing outwards.

'Your trees?' She stretched it as if to ward off her daughter.

'Yes, behind the lodge.'

'They're not yours.'

'Just because they don't have my name printed on them doesn't mean they're not mine.'

'They have to be cut, they've grown too high.'

'But I like them that height, they protect me.'

There was a sudden weakness apparent in Karen's attitude. Something Jenny was surprised to see. She lowered the dress she was holding but said nothing. Normally, she didn't get involved in any arguments which went on between the family. She felt in the way, and longed to fade into the wallpaper until she became invisible.

'They're cut down regularly,' Pearl snapped.

'This is like someone took a sword and cut a huge gash in nature. All the branches broken off, dying, the trees crying out to me, I can't bear it.' She flopped into a chair, in tears.

'They'll grow again.'

'I mightn't be here then.' She wiped her eyes with the edge of the poncho.

'Are you thinking of taking off around the world again.'

'I'm not sure.'

'Well, maybe you should stay here and look after your mother, did that ever occur to you?'

'You don't need me. You don't even like me.'

Jenny stiffened, wondering could she reach the door without attracting their attention. She took a step.

'Stay where you are, Jennifer,' Pearl ordered.

'Yes, Jennifer, do what you're told,' Karen muttered.

'I really should go,' Jenny murmured.

The hostility was now directed towards her.

'Continue with the dresses.'

Her fingers tightened on a soft velvet covered hanger. The dress was old. A party dress. A coming out creation for a young woman. White lace toned to cream. The pink satin sash still bright as the day it had been tied. Jenny let the fabric fall free. It had its own volition and was like another entity in the room asking for approval.

The door banged.

Karen had already made up her mind that her mother didn't like her. She used the word "like" but it had to mean more than that. Like was too nebulous. It wasn't the half of it, not when you went beyond. Jenny thought of her own emotion within this family. She only went as far as "like" too. The other word that was bandied around so freely meant nothing to her. Love you. Love me. So perhaps it meant nothing to Karen either.

'This is beautiful.' Jenny fingered the delicate collar.

'Put that back,' Pearl snapped. There was a deep flush on her cheeks.

Jenny did so.

'I'm tired.' The old woman leaned her forehead on to her hand.

'You've done too much. Would you like to rest for a while?'

There was a sound at the door and Michael appeared. 'Where is everyone? I bring my buyers back for a coffee and the place is deserted.'

'We've been busy, Michael,' his mother snapped.

'Where is Maureen?'

'She's on a half-day.'

'Jennifer?' He raised his hands in a pleading gesture.

'I told you we were busy, can't you make a cup of coffee yourself?'

'For God's sake, I can't leave the buyers sitting in the study on their own while I potter in the kitchen, Mother, you're putting me in a very embarrassing position.'

Pearl tut-tutted. 'Jennifer, go make this helpless man some tea or whatever he wants.'

'I won't be long.'

'Don't be.'

Michael held the door for her and together they went downstairs.

'Thanks so much, love, don't know what I'd do without you.'

Jenny smiled. But inwardly she wondered at the veracity of the remark. Old. Hackneyed. Used so much it had lost any real meaning.

She quickly rustled up brown bread, smoked salmon, a cheeseboard, and some of Maureen's best fruit cake. That should do them, she thought, as she set the trolley, brewed tea and coffee, and went in.

'Steel Rock is a well-bred three year old, and he has won his last two races.' Michael was showing the group of buyers from Dubai a DVD of the horses on the wall sized screen. 'There you see Brownlow Boy coming up to the winning post – he was ten lengths ahead of the rest of the field.'

'Would you be interested in training some of our stable?' one asked.

'Certainly.'

They reeked of extreme wealth, thought Jenny, as she handed out cups and poured, only vaguely aware of the conversation The words tossed about. Bloodlines. Sires. Mares. Stallions. Foals. Form. Training. Unbelievable billions to spend on horseflesh. It was a sin with so much poverty in the world. But then her own position flashed across her mind. She hadn't been born into this world of money and the place in which she had grown up had long since been pushed into the deeper recesses of her mind. Just like today, occasionally something would remind, but she was a different person now and any feelings which drew her back were kept under wraps.

If she was honest about herself, she had to admit she was a rather unemotional being. Never plunged into a morass of sensation about anything. She didn't like this side of herself. The fact that she was always the one who held everyone together. Who didn't allow a tear to escape. In contrast this was a woman who could suddenly find herself overcome with sadness at an old black and white movie of long ago. But no-one else saw this side of Jenny. It was her secret self.

Chapter Eight

David's fingers slid over the ivory keys of the piano. The sound tinkled in the higher register like distant church bells. In the lower it was dark and threatening – the two combined in the middle somewhere and made music.

These were the times he hugged to himself. The house quiet. Cut off from the activity in the studios which often continued unabated all night. Through a combination of notes, he searched for a melody, slow, fast, a ripple of sound which darted in and out of his head. Tonight he needed to be distracted. His mind dwelling on the moment when he had met Helen McLoughlin.

He often worked through to the small hours trying to pin down that elusive note. That perfect sharp or flat which would complete the piece and send him rushing to record, listen, fine-tune, until at last he was satisfied. He played the piece over again. There was something distinctly familiar about the melody, and concerned that he may have plagiarised it inadvertently, he went over it again with slight variations, but always came back to the same theme.

Later, he sipped a Jameson and listened to the DVD. His mobile rang. Reluctantly he answered the call, not overly pleased to hear Vanessa's rather husky tones. He went through the usual ritual of enquiring after her health, glad to hear that her recent fractious mood had disappeared.

'What are you doing tomorrow night?' she asked, her voice teasing.

'We're recording at the moment so it's busy.'

'Do you think you could take some time off?'

'Not at the moment, Vanessa.'

'Not even if I gave you a really delicious surprise?'

'What are you planning?'

'Surprise surprise,' she giggled.

'What are you at?'

'I'm not going to tell you.'

'Come on.'

'You don't deserve it.'

'I probably don't, I'm a cranky old guy.'

'That's true, but I can't help loving you even if you are cranky.'

He hesitated. Suddenly not knowing how to respond to her. Vanessa told everyone she met that she loved them and so far he hadn't taken too much notice of it. 'How's the filming going in Nice?' He changed the subject, and continued the conversation about the part she was playing. Vanessa was only ever truly happy when talking about herself.

In the middle of the session the following evening, they were interrupted by one of the guys on the sound desk.

'Sorry, David, there's someone outside looking for you.'

'Can't it wait?' he asked.

'According to Susan it's urgent.'

He wasn't pleased to be called away and couldn't think who it might be. Hope nothing's wrong, he thought. But stepping out of the lift, he was unable to believe his eyes when he saw Vanessa sprawled on one of the sofas in the foyer, surrounded by a collection of bright pink luggage.

'Vanessa, what are you doing here?' He stared at her.

She sprang up, dressed in matching pink leather trousers and jacket. Her blonde hair caught up in a diamante comb. 'I told you I had a surprise for you.' She threw her arms around him, and hugged tightly.

'I thought you were filming?'

'They don't need me for a few days.' She broke away and wandered around. 'So this is your place. It looks fantastic. And the old house is so cute.' She peered into one of the glass display cabinets which held various awards, gold and platinum discs, and other memorabilia. 'Are these all yours?'

'Some.' He followed her around, not knowing what to do with her.

Chapter Nine

Una had been a close friend of Jenny's when she was young. At a particular time of her life when she couldn't see beyond the narrow environment in which she lived Una extended her hand and she took it. That trust in this woman gave her the opportunity to develop herself as a person and take those first tentative steps which led to where she was today. But somehow, they had drifted apart when she married Michael and her old life was left behind, until recently memories had forced their way to the surface of her mind and took her back to those days when Una had been the only person who mattered. So she wrote to the address she had. Not really expecting a reply but hoping, excitedly hoping.

When Jenny arrived, Una was already sitting at a table in Bewleys, and stood up as soon as she saw her. They embraced tightly.

'It's so good to see you.'

'You haven't changed at all, I can't believe.' Jenny stared at her.

'Except for putting on a few extra pounds which I can't shed,' Una laughed. Her pretty face was transformed and she was again that girl who had reached out to mend a broken mind. 'I arrived earlier and I've already had a cup. What would you like?' she gabbled.

'Black, thanks.' Jenny pulled a tissue from her bag and dabbed her eyes.

Una waved at a waitress and gave the order. Then she reached for her hand and squeezed it. 'Don't be upset, it's only me,' she said softly.

Jenny tried to overcome the wave of emotion. She had promised herself she wouldn't cry.

The waitress brought coffee, and fruity buns. Una played mother, cut the buns in half and spread the butter and jam thickly. 'Have one.' She pushed the plate towards her.

It was very sweet and crumbly. But Jenny couldn't finish it and she wiped her mouth with the paper napkin. Her fingers were sticky. She took time to clean them conscious of a palpitating silence between them. A waiting for something to happen silence. To her relief, it was broken by Una.

'You look well, but a little on the thin side.'

Jenny managed a smile.

'It's been too long, we shouldn't have let so much time pass without a phone call.'

'I know, it's my fault, I'm so involved in my own business and the family.'

'And I'm still at St. Joseph's.'

At her remark, Jenny had a vague image of the large high-ceiling rooms, the sound of doors being locked with heavy bunches of keys, and noise, always noise. And most of all the smell. A mixture of boiled cabbage and urine – she put her hand over her mouth to halt its invasion.

'Are you OK?'

'I'm sorry, it's just the thought of that place.'

'It's different now, there have been big changes.'

'I was surprised when you called, I didn't really expect a reply to my letter.'

'I've often wondered how you were getting on, so it was lovely to hear from you.'

'For me too.'

'I kept the house in Galway as an investment, not that it's worth as much as it used to, but there are always nurses anxious to find a place near the hospital so there has been a stream of girls staying over the years. They sent your letter on to me.' Una chatted on.

'I'm glad.'

'What made you write now, I wondered about that,' she asked.

'I don't know.' Jenny looked deep into her grey eyes.

'Have you been back home?' she asked.

'No.'

'Perhaps you should. Sometimes it does you good to face the fears.'

'I wanted to see you again.' Jenny drew shapes on the table with her forefinger. 'You sent me off into the world and told me I could do anything I wanted, and when I did exactly that it took me away from you.'

'Maybe it was time you grew up.'

'I was a late starter,' Jenny admitted.

'It was better to make your own way. You wouldn't have thanked me for hanging in there like an overanxious parent.'

'You gave me strength.'

'And look how you turned out. A successful businesswoman married to a multi-millionaire.'

'Sounds very materialistic.'

'Isn't that what it's all about.'

'Let me know if you ever need anything, it's the least I could do.' Jenny felt guilty. There was so much comfort in her life. No shortages of any kind.

'Don't worry about me. I'm fine.'

'I'm sorry for not thinking of you but my life changed radically when I married Michael. I've often felt as if I were one of his trophies. Pampered. A priceless asset. I could only see straight ahead.'

'But you're happy surely?'

'Yes, I am' she said, vehemence thrust its way into her voice.

'And you're still in love with Michael, and he with you?'

She nodded. There had been men in her life before Michael. She had thought she was in love with different men more than once. That excitement of a first date. Getting ready. Choosing what to wear. Nervously wondering how he must be feeling. Was he imagining her too. Did he feel a little in love? Or was it just sex with dinner a preamble to the final conquest. With Michael it had been different. She had truly believed he loved her. But the glow in his eyes had faded quickly like a photo image on paper left in the sun for too long. 'Yes,' she said, wanting to believe.

Chapter Ten

Chris sat at the table and flicked through the pages of "Hello" magazine.

'Give it to me,' Pauline demanded, 'it's mine.'

'I'll give it to you when I've finished reading it.'

'When will that be.'

'When I'm done.'

There was a silence.

The pages rustled.

'Are you finished yet?'

'No.'

'You're so cruel to me.' Pauline's lips trembled.

'You're spoiled rotten.'

'I'm going to tell the Gardai you're keeping me here against my will. You won't let me go home.'

'You are home, Mam.'

'I'm not your Mam.'

Chris looked at her sadly.

'I'm going to get the bus.'

'Off you go if you want, don't let me stop you.'

The old woman pushed herself out of the armchair and shuffled to the door. A pathetic figure dressed in a blue floral housecoat, wearing shapeless slippers which flopped off with each step she took. She turned the handle, pulled open the door, and stepped out into the darkness.

'Mother,' Chris yelled, and with an angry grimace she got up and hurried after her. But the bent figure had already disappeared. 'Mam,' she called out, 'come back in here immediately, you'll catch your death.' She ran inside again, found a torch and flashed it into the shadows, but could see nothing. She walked across the yard, worried now. It was a very cold night and there was already a fine misty rain falling. The concrete surface of the yard was slippy and she had to step carefully. She flashed the torch ahead of her and was finally rewarded by a glimpse of a figure in the doorway of the barn.

'Get back inside, it's freezing cold.' She grabbed Pauline's arm.

'Let go of me, I'm going home, Mammy will be waiting for me.'

'Will you stop that mad talk about your mother, she's long dead, and we're getting soaked.' She tried to pull her back in the direction of the house, but the old woman dragged against her, surprisingly strong.

'She'll have my tea ready.'

'I'll make it for you and we can open that packet of biscuits I bought today. They're Custard Creams.'

The old woman abruptly stopped her efforts to get away, and looked up at her. 'Custard Creams?'

'Yes.'

'I'd like some of them.' She turned, and meekly walked back across the yard and into the kitchen with Chris. 'Where are they?'

'In the biscuit tin.'

'Is my tea ready?'

'I'll boil the kettle.' She filled it with water.

'Don't forget my Mam.'

Chris stared at her with exasperation. Then she plugged in the kettle, and took down cups and saucers.

'Where's she gone?'

'The shops.' She decided to go along with the fiction instead of constantly arguing. It was sometimes easier.

'What for?'

'Something for the dinner.'

'She didn't tell me.'

The kettle clicked off, and the tea was made. To satisfy her mother, she included an extra cup for her grandmother who had died many years before.

'I don't take sugar.' Pauline suddenly waved and knocked the cup over. The tea spread over the white tablecloth.

'Mam, will you look at what you've done.' Chris reached for a towel and soaked it up. Then she poured a little milk on the stain and rubbed it in. 'My clean cloth, it's a right mess.'

'My tea's gone, I want another cup.'

'All right, just give me a minute.' She moved the cups and saucers to the counter, took off the cloth, plunged it into a bowl and turned on the tap letting the water flow over it.

'I want my tea.' Pauline crumbled the biscuits.

'OK, OK.'

'Want tea.' She thumped the table.

Chris poured another cup, added milk, and banged it down in front of her.

Her mother sipped it.

'There's no sugar in it.'

'I thought you said you didn't want any.'

'I always have sugar. I have a sweet tooth.'

'Put it in yourself.' Chris pushed the sugar bowl towards her.

'Mam always does it for me.'

'Then wait until she comes back.'

Pauline began to cry. Short childish whimpers.

Chris went back to rinsing out the tablecloth.

The old woman rocked.

Her daughter turned up the volume of the television, a large modern flat screen which looked incongruous in the old-fashioned surroundings of the farmhouse. The signature tune of Coronation Street blared.

'Shut-up now, Corry's on.'

The cries diminished suddenly and Pauline's eyes were riveted on the screen. The two sat in silence until the programme finished.

'I knew that was going to happen. She had her claws in him. The bitch,' Chris pronounced.

'I like her.'

'No-one likes her.'

'Dot does.'

'Dot?' Chris laughed, 'who's Dot?'

'The one with dark hair.'

'In Corry?'

'Yea.'

'She's not in that programme, she's in one of the other ones I think.'

'What's the difference?'

'They're not the same people. Can't you see that?'

'They're all on the tele.'

'You're so stupid. Don't you understand that they're real, and we see what happens to them in their lives, every little thing, it's like we were living in the same house.'

'I don't want to live with them.'

'I wouldn't mind, I could invite them over.'

'There's no room.'

'People like that talk about Ireland, they love the scenery and the green and all that. They come and stay in those white cottages, you see them sometimes, weird looking they are.'

'I won't let any of them in here.'

'We could do the same thing,' Chris mused, her eyes suddenly wide with excitement.

'What?'

'Have them to stay, we could tidy up your bedroom and then you and I could bunk up together.'

'In the one bed?'

'We could charge them the earth.' She stood up and looked around the kitchen.

'I'm not sleeping with you.'

'You'll do what I say.'

Pauline grimaced.

'We'll put an ad in the paper, get some of them Americans. They'd love it here.'

'I hate Americans.'

'They have money, that's all we're interested in.'

'There'll be no room for Faye.'

'She won't come back here.' Chris shook her head.

'She will.'

'I'm not going to share this place with her. It belongs to Sean. And when he comes back I'll send you to a nursing home.'

'No, Chris, no, please don't.' She buried her face in her hands.

'If I hear any more guff out of you that's where you'll go.'

'Faye wouldn't put me there,' she muttered staring out through her fingers.

Chris stood over her for a few seconds.

The old woman fell silent.

Jealousy swept through Chris. She had always been envious of her younger sister. Always so popular. So many friends. Once Chris was finished school it was expected that she would help her mother on the farm. She had wanted to get a job, but Pauline insisted she needed her at home. Faye was going to do a business course, and that was what Chris had wanted to do too. Maybe to go to Dublin or London or even New York. Like her friends, all of whom had moved away. She had fantasised about that. How marvellous it would be. But that's all it was. A dream. Four years older than her sister, she often longed to be the same age as Faye. To go out with her friends. To discos. To the cinema. To join in. Be one of the gang. But then Faye had stolen a march on her and left Chris always catching up.

Chapter Eleven

'I'm getting married,' Eoin said with a grin. He left that gem of information until they were having their coffee after lunch at the Shelbourne.

Jenny smiled, 'I'm delighted. It's about time. Who is she?'

'Her name is Maria.' He took a sip of coffee, but his eyes were looking beyond her across the restaurant and he seemed suddenly uncomfortable.

'Tell me about her?'

'Well, she is Croatian.'

'So what? You sound as if that's some sort of disease,' she said, laughing.

'The family could see it like that.'

'Don't be ridiculous.'

'They're not all like you,' he grinned.

'Tell me about her.'

'Well, she's beautiful,' he said shyly.

'Naturally.'

'We met just after she arrived. It was about two years ago.'

'And you've waited this length of time to mention her?'

'I prefer to keep my private life private. Working here sort of keeps you entangled with the family, even though I've my own house in Naas, I never feel I've achieved my independence, Dad keeps the tentacles of his empire fairly taut.' He looked away from her and focussed on cutting a slice of brie, and spreading it on a cracker.

'Bring her around to meet us some evening. Just let me find my diary.' She rooted in her bag and produced it. 'Right, next week I'm in London. How about this Thursday?'

The dark-haired girl was nervous. Jenny could see it in the way she clung on to Eoin's hand when they came in.

'It's lovely to meet you, Maria.' She hugged her. 'Michael is still down at the stables but he should be back soon. I didn't tell him you were coming.'

'Thanks for that, I want to surprise him,' Eoin said.

Jenny tried to put Maria at her ease, and served drinks and finger food.

'Where do you come from in Croatia?'

'I live in Split, it is a beautiful place,' she smiled, and her large dark eyes filled with moisture.

'I've been there, and also to Dubrovnik.'

'Oh, many times I visited too.'

'We went over for a few days and really enjoyed it.'

'I met Maria's parents last summer,' Eoin said, smiling.

'I'd love to go back, maybe I might persuade Michael to take a break next year,' Jenny said.

'We could all get together then.' He squeezed her hand and their eyes met in a loving glance.

'So tell me, when's the big day?' Jenny asked.

'Sixth of December.'

She stared at him as the date resonated with her.

'What's wrong?'

She shook her head.

'Are you all right, you look a bit shook.'

'It's just ... that date.'

'Something special happened?'

'You could say that.'

'I know, Dad and you met for the first time?' he turned to smile at Maria. 'They're a pair of lovebirds you know. If we're as happy we'll be doing well.'

Jenny nodded, going along with his suggestion although it wasn't that at all. 'So where are you getting married?'

'The Registry Office.'

'I'm really happy for you.' Jenny was unexpectedly envious. There was so little love in her own life she would have given anything to be as happy as Eoin and Maria seemed to be. 'Are you going to tell everyone or surprise the family with the news after the event?'

'Whichever, it doesn't matter, we're just having a quiet ceremony with two of our friends.'

Michael never appeared, and by the end of the evening, Maria was quite relaxed and Jenny could see exactly why Eoin was attracted to her.

'I'm sorry Michael didn't make it.'

'Don't worry, it was really nice, just the three of us,' her step-son assured, a wide smile on his face.

'Eoin called and brought his fiancée, it was a pity you couldn't get back. He wanted to surprise you.'

'What?' Michael's eyes swivelled around.

'She's very nice.'

'Who is she?'

'Her name is Maria, and she's from Croatia – Split actually. Do you remember we had a great holiday there a few years ago?'

He stared at her, his mouth open, the paper crumpling in his lap.

'They're getting married in December.'

He lurched upwards and marched across the room.

She didn't know what else to say.

He took his phone from his pocket and stood waiting while it rang, his hand on his hip, tension filling every bone in his body.

'Eoin, Jennifer's been telling me you're getting married. How come I'm the last to know?'

Jenny listened uneasily.

'You're living together?'

There was silence.

Jenny twisted her hands tightly.

'I'll see you tomorrow to discuss this.'

He pushed the phone back in his pocket and whirled on Jenny.

'Why didn't he tell me himself?'

'He wanted to surprise you this evening, but you weren't here.'

He fumed.

'He's very much in love.'

'In love?' he snorted.

'She means a lot to him, they're great together.'

'Yea, I can imagine.'

'I'm surprised at you. Eoin is thirty-three years old - a grown man.'

'The family is everything to me. My sons are everything to me. I hate to be left out of things. He seems to have more faith in you and you're not even one of us.'

She felt excluded, but wasn't going to be browbeaten. 'Michael, he doesn't need your say-so to do anything.'

'What do you mean, my say-so?' he became enraged.

'Surely it's obvious.'

'My sons have me to thank for all they have.'

'But you can't expect them to bow down and kiss your feet.' She wasn't going to let it go.

He turned on her, his face flushed red.

'Don't get involved Jennifer, it's not your place.'

'What do you mean by that?'

'You're not their mother.'

'I'm your wife and their stepmother. I've taken their mother's place and have always been there for them.'

'That's as may be but what goes on between me and them is private.'

'So I've to put my head down and keep my mouth shut?'

'Yes.' His voice lowered, but the venom in it was clear.

'Well, I'm not going to do it.'

'You'll do what I say.'

'I have to obey your orders?'

'If you want to put it like that.'

'Let me tell you, Michael Halloran, I'll never take orders from you.' She turned abruptly and left the room.

Michael stared gloomily at the television, a glass of whiskey in his hand. She leaned down, kissed him, and they made some light conversation. Things had settled between them since that evening when the row had erupted about Eoin and Maria. He had apologised later. He hadn't meant it. She forgave him. She was never one to hold a grudge. But he hadn't been in good form since and she hated the tension between them. All spontaneity seemed dead. She went downstairs and talked to Maureen about dinner, and then checked the dining-room table. It was the family gathering which took place once a month and she checked the table setting, repositioned a silver fork, and folded a napkin. She hoped that Michael's mood would improve. He could be such a bear.

She heard the front door open and hurried down into the hall.

'Eoin, you're early.' She put her arms around him and hugged. 'Did you bring Maria?'

'No, she's working late. How's Dad?'

'He's all right, grand.'

'I've been keeping out of his way during the day, but I want to have a decent chat with him this evening.'

'Try to hold yourself back, there's no point in getting into a row over it because he'll come around in the end, you know he always does. He's all bluster really.'

'Well, I'm not going to change my mind. Maria's my partner and that's it. If he's not prepared to accept her, then we'll just do our own thing without his approval.'

'I'll say a prayer.'

'Thanks.' He kissed her.

She had a shower, changed, and was ready to go downstairs when Eoin knocked on her door.

'How did it go?' she asked him.

'Not good.'

'It's like something that might have happened years ago, not in the twenty-first century.'

He flopped into an armchair. 'He's put out because I didn't tell him first. It's ridiculous. I won't stay for dinner, hope you don't mind?'

'I do mind.'

'I'm sorry, but it would spoil the evening for everyone else.'

'Don't worry about this, he'll be fine,' she tried to persuade.

'He'll have to. If work gets too difficult, I'll go and work at another stud. I won't be browbeaten.'

'There's a car.' She glanced out the window. 'It's Conor and Aoife, won't you please stay?'

'I'll go out the back way, just give my apologies, make up some excuse.'

Later, Eoin's words echoed and reminded of another young man standing up to authority. A long time ago he had told her they would be together no matter what, and that their parents would have to accept it. Emotion swept through her and she buried her head in her hands.

Chapter Twelve

On the night of the party, Helen wore the black dress. It was quite plain with narrow shoestring shoulder straps and she always felt good wearing it. Following Breda through the crowd, she was bowled over by the beauty of David's home. The high ceilings with wonderful plaster work, the glittering crystal chandeliers, and the sweep of the stairway which led up to the gallery above where people were grouped, sipping champagne.

'Let's see where David is, I'd like to offer my services although he told me to take the night off.' Breda flounced ahead.

The house was packed, and they went from room to room, hardly able to hear each other above the level of conversation and shrieks of laughter. A waiter passed and Breda helped herself to the some prawns, and Helen chose a pakora. 'Delicious, come on, dig in!' she laughed, 'the food's always great here, I deliberately didn't eat.'

They made their way to the library where some people were gathered. David smiled and stepped out of the group when he saw them.

'Dave, this is a fantastic night, do you need me to do anything?' Breda asked.

'The caterers are handling everything so just enjoy yourself.'

'Thanks for inviting me,' Helen said, 'your home is wonderful.'

'Delighted you're here.' His brown eyes met Helen's and she felt very strange. It was like he could see deep down inside her. Could identify every little sinew, muscle, vein, organ, like he even knew what she was thinking.

'Meet Vanessa.' David introduced them and they both shook hands. Helen glanced at Breda and could immediately see disappointment in her eyes. Vanessa was a stunning blonde, wearing a skin-tight silk dress in ivory with deep décolletage. Her golden skin gleamed, and expensive jewellery sparkled. Although Breda was a very attractive brunette, tall and slim, unfortunately no-one could compete with Vanessa tonight.

'Helen is one of our guests, and Breda works for me. She is invaluable, I couldn't do without her,' he smiled.

'What do you do?' Vanessa looked slightly put out.

'I couldn't tell you how much she does. The list gets longer all the time.'

'I deal with the properties, bookings, guests, etc. It keeps me going.'

'It sounds like fun.' Vanessa now clung tightly to David.

'Helen, let me introduce you to everybody.'

She was glad to chat with them. Innocent light-hearted conversation which held no threat of anything. What brought that word into her head, she wondered. Was she threatened here? She swallowed the last of the champagne in the glass and unexpectedly wanted more, feeling self-conscious holding an empty glass. A waiter appeared and refilled it. She was relieved and sipped the cool fizzy liquid. But now she felt heady and couldn't really follow the conversation which whirled around her. Someone told a joke. Everyone laughed, but she didn't get it. She smiled vaguely.

'You probably don't understand our wit,' David said.

'Honey, will you explain, I didn't know what it was about either,' Vanessa simpered.

'Come on, if you didn't get it first time around, forget it,' the man chortled.

'Here's a better one,' someone else said.

After a moment or two Helen didn't have any difficulty understanding the rather vulgar anecdotes and even giggled a little, never one to find those sort of jokes funny, although Breda was enjoying herself hugely. They continued on then, the guys trying to outdo each other, although she noticed that David didn't contribute anything.

'Let's have a tune, come on lads.'

'Haven't got our instruments, but David will plonk on the piano.'

He demurred at first, but was persuaded after a few minutes, and sat down, Vanessa standing close by. 'OK, I'll play something from the album.' His fingers were long and slender and they caressed the keys. The music was soft, a piece of modern jazz which reminded Helen of evenings spent on the porch at home, the bush stretching out and beyond into the darkness, a sky peppered with bright twinkling stars. Suddenly, she felt lonely and had an immediate urge to phone home and talk with her Mum and Dad. But it wasn't possible to do that, she hadn't brought her phone.

'He's great, isn't he.' Breda dug Helen with her elbow.

'Yea.'

'You should hear the group together, they're something else.'

The party was wild. Disco in one area. Jazz in another. Irish folk in the third. Food was served in an enormous marquee, a fantastic selection of Thai, Japanese, Indian, Mexican, and other dishes she couldn't even name. They had drifted away from the group and Breda introduced her to so many people she felt that she must have met everyone in the town.

'What a night, Breda, I can't decide where to go next, what to eat or drink.'

'Try everything, that's my motto.'

'Breda, are you going to introduce me to this gorgeous girl?' A young man appeared beside them. He was fair, with tight-cut hair, and friendly hazel eyes.

'Peter, meet Helen.'

They shook hands.

'How come I haven't come across you before?' he grinned widely.

'We don't frequent the same fleshpots as your crowd,' Breda laughed.

'The pubs of Lackenmore are legendary. How about a dance, Helen?'

Peter was good fun and Helen enjoyed herself hugely. He was the first man she had met since coming to Ireland who appealed to her and he monopolised her for the night. It was a lot later when they caught up with Breda again.

'Hey you two, do you know what time it is?' she asked.

'Haven't a clue.'

'It's four o'clock, and I'm going to have to get home.'

'I think we'd better get a taxi, I've had far too much to drink,' Helen admitted. 'I'd be a danger on those little narrow dark roads. Probably end up in the ditch. I'll pick up my car tomorrow.'

'I've already booked it, I didn't think you'd feel like leaving yet.'

'No, it's late, we'll go together.'

David was seeing some people off at the front door.

'We're going too, and just want to say thanks for a great night,' Breda said when they got a chance to speak with him.

'It's not over yet,' he grinned.

'Only Breda told us the time we'd probably be still here in the morning,' Peter put his arm around Helen and pulled her closer to him.

They left Peter at his apartment in town, and grinned at each other as the taxi drove on to the marina.

'I think he fancies you,' Breda said.

'We just had a bit of fun.'

'The trouble with him is that he's usually after anything in a skirt.'

'Thanks.'

'Just keep an eye on him, he hasn't got the greatest of reputations.'

'I've been around, Breda, I'm not all that green.'

'Just telling you.'

'Well, I enjoyed his company, and it was a great night.'

'Yea, but my David seems well and truly tied up.' Although they were driving in a large seven-seater and had kept their voices low, she still put her forefinger on her lips.

'Vanessa seemed like a bit of a bimbo to me, hardly his type.'

'I'm probably letting myself get carried away, but he's such a peach,' Breda sighed dramatically.

'Are you really serious?'

'Of course I am.'

'Maybe you should bat your eyelashes at him a bit more, femme fatale!' Helen giggled.

'Wouldn't I look good with my wellies on. Can't compare with our bimbo.'

'She's over the top.'

'Some men like that, particularly the older ones, makes them feel young again.'

'He's not that old.'

'He's about forty-eight now I think.'

'He doesn't look that.'

'No, there is something quite youthful about him.'

'You'll have to get someone to do some matchmaking.'

'Do I look like I need that sort of intervention?'

They dissolved in peals of laughter, and then Breda yawned. 'I'm exhausted.'

'Stay in bed a bit later tomorrow, today I mean.'

'No rest for the wicked. There's a crowd of fishermen arriving in the morning. I have to be up and about - one woman welcoming party, that's me.'

'I think I'll catch the dawn, grab a few hours sleep later.'

'Rather you than me.'

'There's nothing like it around here.'

'How long do you plan to stay?' Breda asked curiously.

'It's open, haven't decided yet.'

'Until the money runs out?'

'I've enough work for the moment. My column is attracting a lot more readers.'

'Maybe you'll never go back.'

'I miss home,' Helen said wistfully. The taxi drew up outside her cottage, and she reached over and kissed Breda on the cheek.

'Thanks so much.'

'What for?'

'For everything.'

Helen climbed out of the car. 'Goodnight or should I say good morning?'

'G'day, g'day.' Breda mimicked her accent.

She went inside. Made a cup of coffee, and ate a slice of Breda's fresh brown bread and marmalade. Then her phone rang and in a matter of seconds her life changed irrevocably.

Chapter Thirteen

'You're heading to LA and I'm stuck in Nice. You're so mean. Why couldn't you change your plans and come to Nice for a few days first. We could have a lovely weekend. Please honey, please?' Vanessa begged, tears welling up in her large blue eyes.

'We've got gigs lined up, and some business to do as well,' David laughed at the very idea. 'Have some coffee, it's fresh.'

'No, I've been drinking too much, you know it affects my skin tone, I told you that.' She opened the large Sylvini leopard-skin bag, pulled out a mirror and inspected her face.

'Forgot.' He poured coffee for himself. There were so many things he had to remember about Vanessa, and most of it went completely out of his head until he was sharply reminded.

'Tea?'

'Yes, if you have camomile.'

'I'll check.' He went into the kitchen. When he was home he lived here at the back of the house in his own apartment. It was small and intimate and gave him that sense of seclusion when he wanted to get away from it all. He brought her in the tea and they sat on the couch, the tiny mini skirt riding up to reveal almost everything.

'You know I love Ireland.' She curled her legs and pushed nearer to him like a languid cat.

She was very beautiful, he had to admit, but was far too young for him, and although he had held back from becoming more involved, Vanessa was the type who would entangle any man no matter what his head told him. It would be nice to have a woman in his life, he mused, but couldn't imagine Vanessa fitting into that role.

'I think I could even live here.'

'You would be very very bored.'

'No, I wouldn't, I can just imagine the two of us here in the evening all alone. Tell me how much you love me?' She ran her fingers through his short dark hair.

'Vanessa, I like you a lot, but love is ...'

'Love is wanting to be with a person every second of every day.' She reached to kiss him, lips pouting.

'I suppose it's something like that.'

'Love is ...' she chanted. 'Doing all those personal little things you let no-one else do.' She ran a long finger slowly down the side of his face, her blue painted finger nail sharp. 'Love is - buying you everything you ever wanted. Bringing you breakfast in bed, lunch in bed, dinner in bed and staying there all day and all night with you.' She flung her arms around him. 'And I want to get a dog, and we could take him for walks together. I love animals but I can't have any in my apartment but you could have lots of them here. Oh, it will be so cool. I'm so looking forward to it.'

'You'd think we were both working nine to five, Vanessa,' he laughed lazily, almost enjoying her craziness. 'We could never be together, our lives are just too different. I'd drive you mad.'

'We're both in the entertainment business, that's something we have in common.'

'I know but I don't think that counts.'

'Pussy cat!' She kissed him wetly. 'Don't be so negative.'

'I'm serious.' He shifted on the couch in an effort to escape her grip. 'And I don't want you to be disappointed. You'd be far better off with a guy your own age, he'd be much more fun. Any of the fellows in the crowd you hang around with would be better than me.' He put his arms around her and hugged her. 'Next year you'll be doing something much more exciting and will have forgotten all about this. Who's your leading man on this film?'

'Josh. He's OK, but I don't like him, it's you that I want.'

Her phone rang.

'Ya?' she listened, and made a face. 'Honey, can't you just delay it for a little longer? It's Pierre,' she whispered, 'I really need some more time. I'm very busy.' She leaned down and kissed him. 'Yes, I am, it's family,' she grinned, 'that's really cool, Wednesday will be fine, thanks so much darling, *merci, au revoir*.' She put away the phone. 'Isn't that great, I've got a reprieve, one day, I don't have to be back on set until Wednesday. That gives us tonight, all day tomorrow and tomorrow night.'

'Vanessa, I've got to get into the studio in an hour, and we're booked for the next few days, sorry.'

'I'll play along, there's a lot we can do in an hour,' she giggled.

There was a knock on the door.

'Ignore it,' she leaned closer to him and covered his mouth with hers.

The knock was repeated.

'Have to see who it is.' He tried to get up.

'No, you're staying here with me.'

'Vanessa, please?' He disentangled himself and reached the door, but she followed still hanging out of him as he opened it.

'Dave?'

It was Joe. 'We're running through some of the recordings, thought you might like to hear them before we start the next session.'

'No can do, he's all tied up with me,' Vanessa giggled and peered around the edge of the door.

Chapter Fourteen

In Alice Springs, the sun beamed through the windows of the waiting room at the hospital. It was hot, but the air conditioning kept the temperature cool inside. Helen stared at the serious expression of the doctor and the knot in her stomach tightened. She wanted to stand but couldn't, her legs suddenly weak.

'How is my wife?' her father asked.

'She's comfortable.'

Comfortable? They always said that. So pat. So nothing. Helen thought. 'How will my Mum be affected by the stroke?' She asked the doctor. Her fear for Carmel waited on the edge of control like an animal stalking its prey. She had managed to keep it at bay on the journey, but now it was going to destroy her.

'They're not too sure yet, Helen, I told you,' her father murmured.

'Will she make a full recovery?' she addressed the doctor.

'With luck and plenty of rest and care,' he assured, 'she has some loss of movement on her left side, but luckily her speech is not too badly impaired. You can go in and see her now.'

Tom took her arm and she managed to stand up. They followed the doctor into the ward. The curtains were drawn around the bed. Pink roses on a white background. So pretty. She hated herself for even noticing such unimportant details. She pushed through. Inside Carmel lay in bed attached to various monitors, an ill-fitting blue hospital gown draped around the thin frame. It looked so ugly, Helen thought, angry. Her Mum loved soft silky lacy things. Everything was wrong. The drip inserted into the distended purple vein. The display panel lights which flickered eerily. The measured bleeps indicating her life force.

For one crazy second, Helen wanted to scream that this woman in the bed was not her mother, deny that anything had happened to Carmel and run home to find her in the kitchen preparing dinner. But instead she drew closer to the bed and tried to control the tears. 'Mum?' She touched her shoulder and bent to kiss the pale cheek.

Carmel opened her eyes. There was a look of confusion in the blue depths. 'Helen?'

'How are you feeling?'

'Don't know,' she whispered, her voice slightly slurred.

'I'm sorry, I should have been here sooner.'

'So happy to see you.'

'Carmel, love, I've brought in some fresh things for you, I'll leave them here,' Tom murmured. The paper bag crackled loud in the quiet, and drew Helen's attention away for a couple of seconds.

'Don't let me die here,' Carmel said, as a tear sprang and dribbled slowly down her thin face.

'You won't die, you'll be better in no time.' Helen tried to convince her mother, and herself.

'Will I?'

Helen stayed in the hospital that night and her father went home. He had stayed up the previous night and needed his rest, and she was persuaded by the nurses to stretch out on the couch in the waiting room rather than sit in the uncomfortable chair beside her mother who was sleeping. But it took a long time before she could slow her racing heart and even relax a little. At last, in the small hours she fell into a light sleep, but jerked awake immediately when a nurse touched her shoulder and said something. She followed her and swung unsteadily through the door of ICU. Two doctors stood in conversation by the bedside. The nurse caught her arm.

'She's had a bit of a turn, your father is on his way.'

Helen could see a huge change in Carmel. She lay limp on the white pillows, her complexion ashen. A film of moisture clung to her skin and there were blue shadows around her nose and mouth.

'Mum?'

'Helen?'

She bent closer.

'I'm sorry.' Carmel whispered.

'What for?'

'There's something ...' She tried to raise her head.

'Don't move, Mum, you must be quiet.'

'Mrs. McLoughlin, please lie still,' the nurse said.

Carmel's breathing became more laboured.

'You'll be all right, Dad's on his way.'

'I want to tell you ...'

'Mum, it will take too much out of you, try and rest.' Helen sat by the chair at the bed and took her mother's hand. Their fingers entwined.

'I was afraid.' Carmel tightened her grip around Helen's hand.

'Come closer.'

She leaned down to her.

'I'm not ... your real mother.'

★

Carmel's mind drifted into dream state. Images came and went. She remembered how she held a tiny child, rocked her gently and kissed the soft fair downy cap on the little head. She breathed in that special baby aroma. Happiness spiralled through her.

'Shush baby, shush, don't cry. My God. I can't believe, Tom? Tom?'

'What's up?' He came into the kitchen.

Carmel held out the baby.

His jaw dropped.

'What is it?'

Carmel smiled. 'It's a baby. Are you blind or what?'

'What's it doing here?'

'It's Faye's.'

'You're not serious, sure she's only a child.' He stared.

'I know. But it happened. Obviously.'

'Who's the father?'

'Don't know, she never mentioned him. Just said her mother was going to get rid of the baby. She was very upset and wants us to take her to Australia.'

'What?'

'Tom, it's a miracle. The baby we lost a few months ago has been given back to us. She would have been the same age as this little one. God sent her. We can't give her back.'

'No Carmel, it's not our baby.'

'You know I've longed for a child. And you too. Now Faye has given us what we've prayed for.' She hugged the baby to her and began to cry again. 'Don't take her away from me, Tom, please don't. I couldn't bear it, please, I beg you.'

'You can't just walk off with someone else's offspring.'

'But Faye asked me to look after her.'

'What if she changes her mind.'

'Then I'll give her back.'

'But we'll be in Australia.'

'I'll write and tell her where we are.'

'God, I can't believe this is happening.' He sat down slowly.

'We'll have to pass her off as our own baby. Baptize her. She's called Helen – Helen McLoughlin.'

'But we won't be telling the truth. It's illegal.'

'It will be worth it. What's a few white lies?'

'Carmel, are you mad or what? This has gone to your head altogether.'

'Tom, I'm not giving up this baby. I don't care what happens. I'm not.' She stared up at him with fierce determination, the thin frail face radiant now, blue eyes blazing with love. 'I was never so sure of anything in my life.'

'Jesus, give me strength.' Tom pulled a large white handkerchief from his pocket and mopped the globules of perspiration which stood on his forehead. 'What will we say to Larry when he arrives?'

'Nothing. I'll sit in the back of the taxi and pray she doesn't cry.'

'Some hope with a new baby,' he retorted as he walked out of the kitchen.

Carmel smiled. Thrilled. She had won him around.

In the sitting room, she laid the baby in an armchair and put another against it at right angles to prevent her rolling off. Then with feverish haste she emptied the contents of one of the smaller bags out on to the couch in an untidy heap, and chose a white towel which she folded into the travel bag, and another to put on top of her.

'Carmel, what are you doing?' Tom reappeared.

'We'll put Helen in the small bag. No-one will guess. Now I'll use that towel as a nappy, it'll have to do, I hope it won't be too scratchy, the poor little thing.' She was already changing her. 'Will you put the things on the couch in one of the other bags? If it doesn't fit, leave it there. Where's that bottle of whiskey you bought for Paddy?'

'That's just what I need, a stiff drink.'

'I want a little for Helen.'

He stared at her, speechless.

'We'll just give her a tiny drop, it'll make her sleep.'

'How will we feed her?'

'I was just about to throw out the rest of that milk, thank God I didn't.' Carmel took the bottle out of the fridge. 'I'll heat it, and put it in the flask.' She searched in the pantry and found it, so glad that she hadn't given it to Pauline. She had already told her that she could take anything left in the house when they had gone.

'She can't drink it out of that.'

'I'll buy a proper bottle in Galway.'

'God help the poor child.'

The taxi arrived just after seven and the luggage was loaded into the boot. Carmel placed the small bag carefully on her lap and hugged it. Tom sat in the front with Larry and they took no notice of Carmel who leaned her head back and closed her eyes, feigning sleep. All the time she prayed, losing count of the decades of the Rosary she said. Helen slept peacefully.

It was the longest journey in Carmel's life, but eventually to her

73

great relief they arrived at the railway station in Galway with plenty of time to spare. Now it was Tom's turn to sit with the bag on his knees, hiding behind a newspaper terrified someone would recognise him. Carmel shopped. She bought baby formula, nappies, clothes, feeding bottles, and a soft pink rabbit. There wasn't much time to spare when she rushed back, and quickly they gathered their things and boarded the train looking like any ordinary family, but feeling anything like it.

They must have been half way to Dublin when Helen began to cry. Carmel rocked her gently but it didn't soothe her. She stared at her husband for help.

'Tom?' she whispered.'

'What?' His voice was irritable.

'She's crying.'

'I can hear that.'

'What'll we do?' She glanced around conscious of the sympathetic smile from the woman sitting across from them.

'You'd better shut her up quick, we can't be drawing attention to ourselves.'

'What is it Helen, what's wrong?' Carmel rocked her but she cried all the louder.

'Carmel, will you pull yourself together, she must be hungry or something,' Tom growled.

'Of course, that must be it. Why didn't I think of that before. Will you hold her, Tom, while I get the flask.' She handed the bundle to him, and he took it awkwardly, staring down at her. Unexpectedly, she stopped crying and he smiled.

She rooted in the bag in search of the flask, and poured the warm milk into the bottle. 'You give it to her.'

He pushed the teat into the wide open mouth and to their surprise, she gripped it tightly and sucked until the bottle was empty.

'What an appetite, Tom, can you believe it.'

'Next time she cries, don't lose your head.'

'I'm sorry, Tom, I'm so nervous I just froze,' she laughed, 'I'll never do it again.' She leaned across and put her hand on his.

In Dublin, they were met by Tom's brother, Paddy, invited to stay with him until they would fly out to Australia.

'A baby? How wonderful. Why didn't you tell us?' He hugged her.

'We were afraid to tell anyone until everything was OK, you know, after all the other disappointments,' Carmel blurted out. It sounded plausible. Could be true, well, almost.

'Is it a boy or a girl? My God, Noreen is going to hit the roof, congratulations Tom.' He shook his hand. 'Now, is this all your stuff? Let's go, I've the car outside.'

Suddenly, Carmel felt everything was going to be all right. And it was. Within a short time, she believed Helen was hers. There was no need to invent the tiredness, her night's sleep broken as she fed, changed and walked the bedroom floor in an effort to keep Helen quiet. She made up stories about the pregnancy. Described all those months praying that she would carry this child to full term. Their joy when she was born. Their hopes for the future. Tom said nothing. But he was the one who went to the office of the Registrar of Births, Marriages and Deaths to fill in the appropriate forms. All the time terrified they would be found out. But it didn't happen and now it was official, Helen was Carmel and Tom McLoughlin's daughter.

★

In the rush of staff, Helen was pushed out of the way. They tried everything but it was too late.

'I'm sorry, but there was nothing we could do.' The doctor seemed more sympathetic now.

'Mum?' She leaned over her mother. She wanted to see Carmel smile. Wanted to prove him wrong. But there was no movement from the person who lay on the bed. Now she seemed relaxed, as if she had just fallen asleep. Helen touched her arm. 'She's still warm, look, feel. She couldn't be dead, she's going to wake up in a minute,'

75

she kissed her mother's cheek and stroked her soft silky hair, the possibility that she was actually gone too horrendous to contemplate.

'Helen, let me get you a cup of tea, your Dad will be here soon.' The nurse took her arm.

She wouldn't let go of Carmel.

'You can come back in a little while.'

The gentle voice of the nurse eventually made an impression on her and she allowed herself to be taken out of the room and into another. All the time the nurse emphasised how much better she would feel after – and Helen wanted to shout that she wouldn't. It would be worse, much worse. Grief exploded within her, gathered momentum and overwhelmed like a tidal wave. They should have been able to save Carmel. Helen was bitter. Why had her mother been taken? She was only sixty three. She was young. She didn't deserve to die.

Her father arrived a short time later and when he put his arms around her she leaned against him and cried for the first time. Long despairing sobs which went on and on. He didn't try to stop her. Just held her close.

She wasn't really present at the funeral. While she may have been there in person, in spirit she was somewhere else. Wandering through the past with her mother. Remembering. And most of all questioning the meaning of her last words. She wanted to tell her father. But couldn't. Not even sure if she had heard correctly.

'Are you going to stay home for a while?' Tom asked her a few days later, as he sat watching her mix a salad for lunch at the counter in the kitchen.

'Of course I am.' Helen tossed mixed leaves, and poured dressing.

He smiled and seemed to relax. His thin frame softened. Shoulders eased their tense posture in the beige sweater which he wore. He leaned back in the armchair, his spine sinking into its usual position, and some of the strain which had marked his features since

Carmel had died disappeared.

'It's lovely to have you back, I've missed you.' He pulled a handkerchief from his pocket and blew his nose loudly.

She smiled.

'Every time I look around I think I see her. Hear her voice telling us the tea's ready, hurry up you'll be late or some such.' He snuffled.

She said nothing, unable to trust herself. She wasn't able to help him. Didn't know what to say to a man who had lost the most important person in his life. How to fill the void which existed now inside him? A daughter could only know a part of the man. Couldn't understand the depth of his pain. What went on behind the bedroom door in those secret moments between two lovers. What they said to each other when they turned off the light, or awoke in the morning. She had wondered if they talked of those early days when they first met. Were they boy and girl at school? Was theirs a long courtship, in love, over many years? It wasn't something they ever talked about in her presence. Almost reticent about their lives in Ireland before they emigrated.

She went back to her cooking and added red and yellow peppers to the salad, onions, corn, radishes.

'There was something,' she whispered suddenly into the stillness.

He looked up.

'Mum said ...' she hesitated and then regretted mentioning it.

'Helen?'

'I'll just put the steaks on.'

'What did your Mum say?'

'I'm not even sure I heard it correctly. I may have misunderstood, her voice wasn't very clear.' She took the steaks from the fridge, went out on to the deck and placed them on the hot coals of the barbecue.

He followed and stood at the door watching her. She poured cool beer into long glasses. They sat in the shade and sipped staring out over the arc of cloudless blue sky that was afternoon in Alice Springs.

After a while she looked into his eyes and for a long moment they stared at each other until finally she managed to whisper. 'She said something about not being my mother.' A butcherbird trilled into the still air. It was a strange haunting sound. She dragged her gaze from his and looked out across the scrubland, her eyes dazzled by the brightness.

He reached forward and covered her hand with his.

'Is it true?' she asked softly.

'Yes.'

'Are you my Dad?'

'No.'

Acrid smoke drafted across, but they didn't notice the charred steaks at first until Tom stood up and took them off. 'I'll put on some more.'

'Not for me, thanks.'

'You have to eat.'

'Couldn't.'

'A sandwich then?'

She shook her head He said nothing and proceeded to make them anyway.

'It's tough to hear something like that at this hour of your life, I tried to persuade your Mam to tell you over the years but she found it very difficult. I think she was afraid that she might lose you. But just remember that we loved you, I love you.' He came closer and put his arms around her. 'When you were given to us, it was like a miracle. God had granted our wish and our lives were never the same again.'

'Do you know anything about my real mother?'

'She was our next door neighbour and just arrived very early one morning with you and asked us to look after you.'

'What was her name?' she asked slowly.

'Faye Brophy.'

Helen's mind tossed the name around.

'She was only seventeen.'

'And my father?'

'We never knew who he was.'

That evening they sat in the sitting room. Tom dozed off, the newspaper crumpled on his lap, and Helen sat staring into space. She couldn't get her head around it. Suddenly, she had another life, another family, and was so disappointed that the man sleeping in the chair was not her father. The past swam around her and took her back down the years to when he was the most important person in her life. She picked up a family photo which stood on a side table and stared at it. She shifted in the armchair, the silky covering causing her to slide forward just a little. Her back ached. She had always hated these chairs. The occasional chairs her mother had called them, proud of the gleaming gold satin upholstery and rich mahogany. Helen felt guilty then. Remembering how it used to be between them. Arguing. Flaring up over the slightest thing. Demanding her way. Hating almost. And then regretting. That most of all.

Chapter Fifteen

One evening David walked the land. Crossed fields. Jumped ditches. Until he came to the river which flowed slowly along unerring as the cattle wandered down to slake their thirst each evening. He stepped from stone to stone across the flow, noting that the level had not changed that much since he had been here last.

Suddenly in his head a question came out of nowhere. Carried on the whisper of breeze which rustled the leaves. In the chuckle of the river as it curled and eddied. In the full-throated trill of a lark high above.

Do I want to open up wounds never fully healed?

Or lay the ghost to rest finally.

But he didn't seem to have a choice and his mind swept him back in time to youthful uncertainties.

To follow a dimly remembered path.

Through thick groves of leafy trees.

Long grasses.

Deep banks of palest green fern.

Until suddenly he was there.

Recognised.

And remembered.

Chapter Sixteen

'What do you know about Eoin's girl?' Pearl asked.

'I've met her, she's very nice,' Jenny said, anxious to give the right impression to Pearl. Her opinion really mattered in the family.

'Take me nearer to the fire,' she ordered.

Jenny stood up and moved the position of the wheelchair, and then topped up the embers with more coal. She sat down again, glancing out the window to see dark clouds massing.

'The weather is terrible, so much rain, the place is saturated.' Pearl rubbed her hands together. 'When you're my age you really feel it in the bones, I never seem to be warm.'

'Will I get you a rug?'

'No thanks, if I get too cold I'll go to bed.'

Jenny leaned back and stared into the flames which hissed and crackled loudly, against a background of the sound of heavy rain which lashed against the old windows.

'You know I was in the same position once.' Pearl fiddled with the silver fob watch she wore on a long chain around her neck, her thin misshapen fingers rubbing it over and over again.

Jenny looked up, curious.

'I met Tony in nineteen forty when I was staying with my aunt in London. He was a naval captain.' She opened the front cover of the watch and stared at it pensively. She motioned Jenny closer. 'Don't you think he was very good-looking?'

Fitted snugly into the cover was a black and white photograph of a young man in uniform.

'He certainly was,' Jenny agreed.

'We were in love.' Pearl's voice was soft.

Jenny was astonished to see this side of her mother-in-law, who was generally a rather strident domineering woman.

'But my father didn't approve. He wasn't good enough.'

'I'm so sorry.'

'We used to meet secretly – it was wonderful.' She glanced up at Jenny with an impish gaiety in her eyes. 'We were going to get married before he had to rejoin his ship but my mother came up to London and forced me to return home with her. I never saw him again.'

'What happened?'

'His ship went down – a German torpedo.'

'That was so sad.' Emotion surged through Jenny.

'I still love him you know.' She closed the watch carefully.

Jenny didn't know what to say.

'So I understand what it's like for Eoin,' she sighed.

'Michael seemed to think that you would agree with him.'

'In most things I do, but this is different.'

'Do you think you could talk to him?' The situation upset Jenny. She couldn't quite understand why she felt so strongly about it, and why she was standing up to Michael.

'He's stubborn. When he gets something into his head there's no stopping him. I suppose I'm the same usually.'

'But you might be able to persuade him to see it from Eoin's point of view. He will lose him you know if he refuses to accept her. They're going ahead with the marriage regardless.'

'My family would have lost me too if my captain had come back and I wouldn't have cared. He was the man I wanted and I'd have gone to the ends of the earth for him.' She took a hankie from her pocket and dabbed her eyes.

'I can imagine,' Jenny murmured.

She nodded.

They were silent for a few moments.

'I married Michael's father a year later. He was a suitable match. We had a good life but I never loved him as much as I loved Tony.

You probably think I'm a silly old woman dreaming of a man I knew when I was a girl?' she smiled, her blue eyes moist.

'No, to love someone and to lose them is heartbreaking.'

'You speak as if you know what that's like too,' Pearl murmured.

Jenny hesitated for a few seconds before speaking. 'My father died.'

'Ah, the love of a father.'

'It was a long time ago.'

'Time means nothing when you love,' the old woman sighed, 'I don't think I've heard you talk much about your family. Your home is in Connemara, isn't that right?'

'Yes.'

'Are your people still living there?'

'There may be some, but I've lost contact,' Jenny felt suddenly uncomfortable.

'You should go back, it's never a good thing to lose touch with the past.'

They talked on through the evening. Jenny closed the heavy burgundy damask curtains on the night. Replenished the coal in the scuttle. Brought up supper. A hot pot of tea with tiny bite-sized salad sandwiches, and some cream sponge. It was after ten when Pearl yawned, and asked Jenny to help her into the bedroom. A short time later, she was tucked up under the eiderdown.

'Sleep well, see you in the morning.' Jenny kissed her.

'It was nice to talk, I enjoyed it.' Pearl patted her cheek with a hand still slightly moist from the cream she had rubbed in earlier. 'And ask Eoin to bring his girl around to see me.'

Back in her own room, Jenny sat pensively. She couldn't believe how Pearl had opened up to her. Their relationship down the years was definitely mother and daughter in law, and her place in the household was strictly defined. To hear the story of a tragic love which ended in death was so poignant it reminded of her own life. Those days which she had pushed into the back of her mind and never wanted to think about again.

Chapter Seventeen

Helen pushed open the door of her parents' bedroom. Waited a few seconds. And closed it again. She went down the landing and stared out the window into the garden. Carmel loved gardening. Every plant had her touch. The combination of colours in the beds. The balance of shapes. All her darling mother. Since she had murmured those words to her in the moments before she died, Helen had swung in crazy arcs not knowing what to think. Her father had confirmed that he and Carmel were not her real parents, but questions had built up in Helen's head which demanded answers. Mostly why they hadn't told her before now about her real mother and father. Her background. Who were her people. Tears sprang into her eyes. A sudden surge of anger swept through her. They should have told her. How was it that they didn't understand what a shock it would be to hear such a thing at this late stage in her life. If they had simply mentioned it when she was two or three years old she would have grown up with the knowledge. It would have been natural. She was adopted. So what. She had a friend who was adopted. Had always known it. And she had looked for her natural mother and found her. It had been wonderful hearing the story of their reconciliation. Helen felt envious now. Resenting that her mother had waited until the end of her life before telling her. She would have given anything to talk with her now.

She opened the door again. The anger vanished as a delicate aroma of scent drifted around her and she was drawn in. Everything seemed normal. The bed was made, although the cream duvet was rumpled, the cushions which Carmel would have placed carefully along the pillows were thrown on the chair. A pile of books on the glass-topped bedside unit on her father's side. He always had a dozen books on the go at any one time. There was just one on her mother's side. She liked to work her way through a book, Helen remembered, savouring it to the last word before beginning another. She glanced at the title – "The Mystery of the Windmills" – and smiled. Mum always enjoyed a good whodunit. She opened it and the leaves sprang to the page Carmel had been reading marked with a small card. Helen picked it up. There was a picture of a bunch of lilac on the front and inside a curl of red hair. Tears filled her eyes and she put the card back into the book, and left the room.

She threw herself into a frenzy of work until it was dark. Vacuuming. Dusting. Washing. Ironing. The telephone rang several times. She ignored it and let the answering machine record the messages. Her father was meeting with some friends this evening, the first time he had been out since her mother died, and she was glad to be alone. The night was hot and still and she sat in the garden remembering so many other evenings spent out here with Carmel and Tom. The bark of a dingo echoed out of the bush which stretched as far as the MacDonnells range of mountains silhouetted black against the wide arc of deep blue sky dotted with a million stars. The high peak of Mt. Ziel pierced upwards.

She listened to the messages.

'I'll be home about eleven, you go on to bed if you want, don't wait up.'

'Helen, Jim here, hope you're feeling a bit better. Sorry we haven't had a chance to talk properly over the last few days, you seem to be all at a distance. Give me a call.'

'Let's get together as soon as we can, phone soon.' It was Kath.

She didn't feel like talking now, so decided to wait until tomorrow. On her way to bed she stopped at her parents' room again. A sense of unease drifted through her as she went inside. The room was in shadow now, and suddenly she could see a form lying in the bed. 'Mum!' she cried out loud and flicked on the light, but it was just her imagination.

Then a sudden impulse. She pulled the pink nightdress which was still tucked under the pillow and buried her face in its softness, so glad that her father hadn't removed it. It was like putting her arms around her mother, holding her close, having her back again. Then with quick jerky movements, she threw off her clothes and pulled on the nightdress over her head, turned off the light and climbed into the bed. To snuggle down and breathe in Carmel's fragrance, feeling her love encircle. Within seconds, her eyes had closed and she slept soundly all night for the first time since her mother had died.

'Did you have a good rest?' her father asked the following morning.

She smiled, 'I'm sorry, where did you sleep?'

'The spare room. You didn't even move when I turned on the light.'

'It was a spur of the moment thing.' She felt awkward about it.

'Why don't you take that room, I'll stay in the spare, I'd prefer it – so difficult without your mother.' He concentrated on spreading butter and marmalade on toast.

'If you're sure?' She shook flakes into a bowl, and poured milk.

He nodded.

They ate breakfast in silence. There was a tension between them. Unusually for her she didn't know what to say. Again overwhelmed by the questions which crowded through her mind. But somehow she couldn't voice them. It seemed like an attack on him. She was a coward. She could be angry with Carmel who was no longer here to defend herself, but quailed in the presence of this man she had loved her whole life.

Slowly they filtered back into normal life. She helped her father at the store. Took over the work on the accounts her mother used to do. She went through the motions. A person who now felt she didn't belong here. Who didn't know who she was. Who couldn't get back to her old life.

The first time she ventured out socially was to have dinner with Jim.

'It's so good to have you back, all that time you were away seemed like a life sentence,' he smiled. A stocky cuddly sort of guy, grey eyed, tanned from the outdoor. A couple of years older than herself, he had worked at the store since he was a schoolboy and Helen felt he was like a brother.

They ordered and ate their meals, chatting generally

'Your Dad's going to find it difficult without Carmel.' He sipped a beer.

'Yea.'

'We were all very fond of her. She'll be missed,' he said softly.

Tears sprang into her eyes and reduced her to a shaking child, unable to say anything more. She sniffled into her napkin.

'Sorry, I've upset you.'

'Happens all the time

'Another beer?'

'Why not, steady my nerves.' She managed a crooked smile.

'I wish I could help in some way.'

'You are, taking me out, just being there.'

'I'd like to mean more to you, all those months you were away changed things. I was surprised at how deeply I felt.' He swallowed a long draught.

'I really missed everyone at home too.' She was suddenly conscious of the import of his words.

'No-one in particular?' he asked, with a grin.

'You're teasing.'

'Actually I'm not.'

'Jim, you're one of my dearest friends.'

'And that's all?' there was a crushing disappointment in his eyes.

'I've never thought of anything more.' She had to admit it.

'I love you. I've always loved you,' he burst out in a rush. His fingers tightened around the glass.

She was silent.

'I'm probably putting you on the spot now, but I wanted you to know. Maybe you've never thought of me in that way but you could change your mind. I'd give anything to have you in my life, you're the only one that matters to me.'

'What about all those other girls along the way?' She tried to lighten the tone of their conversation.

'I'll admit there have been a few but I didn't realise how much you meant to me until you went on your trip to Europe.'

'You've taken my breath away.'

'Don't say anything now, just think about it.'

'You're looking great.' Helen admired the silk wrap-around skirt worn by Kath. The wonderful vibrant reds and yellows suited her dark colouring so well.

'Thanks, do you like it?' She twirled around in the centre of the room. The fabric billowed, bright and gay. The matching red sandals were glamorous.

'It's lovely. Where did you buy it?'

'That new boutique at the Todd Centre.'

'Are the clothes nice?'

'Gorgeous, but a bit pricey.'

'Wine or beer?'

'Wine thanks, for a change.' Kath flopped down on the soft cushions of the couch and put her feet on the footstool.

Helen poured sparkling white wine. She was looking forward to this evening with Kath.

'Cheers.' She held up her glass.

'Your mother's precious crystal?' Kath exclaimed.

'I know, she'd have a fit if she saw us.'

'Aren't you worried she might be looking down?'

'If she is, we'll raise our glasses to her. Slainte, Mum.'

'Have you thought any more about Faye?' she asked. Always to the point, that was Kath.

'No.' Helen was immediately on the defensive, and was unable to meet her friend's concerned eyes. She didn't want to talk about it. Could feel the disquiet which dogged her lately begin to surge up into something much bigger.

'You'll have to, some time.'

She nodded.

'I know you're grieving for your Mum, but that other matter has burrowed deep and changed you.'

She stared at her friend. Shocked.

'You don't seem to know where you are any more. You go through the motions but you're not here any longer. You know what I mean?'

She nodded.

'Where is Helen McLoughlin? That's what I keep asking myself.'

'I feel so guilty, I can't get it out of my head. One day I want to go back to Ireland to search for her, the next I'm terrified at the very thought of it.' A nerve throbbed at the corner of Helen's eye and she pressed a finger against her skin, self-conscious.

'You'll have to go some day, otherwise you'll be haunted by it.'

'But there are so many questions, Kath. Is she still alive? Married with a husband and family?'

'Do you know if she ever looked for you?'

Helen shook her head.

'She was only seventeen, that means she was probably still at school.' Kath put down her glass on the coffee table with a clink.

'Don't know.'

'How much has your Dad told you?'

'Not much, and I don't want to quiz him, it has to be upsetting for him.'

'Can you imagine what it must have been like in those days, such a disgrace to have a baby without being married. Not much different to here.'

'But who was my father?'

'Probably just an ordinary guy.'

'But what if he was a priest and it was sexual abuse or something?'

'You're crazy.'

Helen twisted her hands together, her palms damp and sticky. 'Or maybe it was incest, her father or brother? It might mean that I'll never be able to have children, or if I do they'll have something wrong with them.'

'Don't be ridiculous, that's the exception rather than the rule, she probably had a boyfriend and got caught out, and had no way of getting the pill.'

'I hope so.'

'And all the more reason for finding out. Here drink up, it'll help you relax.' She topped up her glass.

'Thanks Kath.' She sipped the wine.

'Something like that will never go way unless you deal with it.'

'But I feel so bad about Mum – even though she isn't here any more – it seems like a terrible betrayal.'

'Look, why did she tell you?' Kath waited a few seconds. 'Because she wanted you to know.'

'I suppose.'

'Maybe you should go back to Ireland.'

'But I can't just turn up on my mother's doorstep. She might not want to know me.'

'You could get a social worker or a solicitor to represent you.'

'No, I'm not going about it that way, it's too impersonal.'

'So you are going to do something about it?' she grinned.

'I haven't decided yet.'

'But you might.'

'Yes.'

Kath threw her arms around Helen and hugged. 'But that means you'll be gone off again, and God knows when I'll see you.'

'It will take me a long time to decide what to do so you needn't worry.'

'I've been thinking,' Tom said as they drove home from the shop one evening. 'Why don't you go back to Ireland again and try to make contact with Faye?'

Helen was surprised at his suggestion.

'It will only play on your mind if you don't.'

'I've been thinking I should put it out of my head altogether,' she whispered.

'If you don't deal with it now, you may always regret it.'

'But it seems too soon – after Mum.'

'No, I think the time is right.' He stopped the jeep in the driveway, and cut the engine.

'You're my father, I don't want to know about anyone else.'

'It's often difficult to find a father, so maybe I won't be replaced,' he grinned.

'No-one could replace you.' She gripped his hand.

'Thanks love.' He leaned across and kissed her

Chapter Eighteen

Helen drove along the street slowly. She felt self-conscious, wondering would anyone recognise her, or did she just look like another tourist. In the summer, a fairly common breed dressed in shorts, standing out against the locals particularly when it rained which it did a lot of the time in Lackenmore. But now in the autumn she might be just a person of no consequence passing through town. There was a spatter on the windscreen and she switched on the wipers. People scurried for shelter. Umbrellas of various hues appeared and bobbed along, but that protection wasn't even strong enough for the downpour and the pavements were suddenly empty. Inclement weather does that to people, she thought, it pushes them out of sight.

She went out to the lake and stopped the car to look at its reflective beauty. It had stopped raining but grey threatening clouds massed above and pressed down upon her. The surface of the water was like a mirror, broken only by cracks created by slight ripples. She felt like someone who was suffering from a partial amnesia. Aware that her genes were from a different strain. She's a Brophy now. The family who lived in the farmhouse beside her parents. Mixed with some unknown group of people. A school bus passed filled with children and she stared fascinated at it. Imagining her own mother coming home from school and getting off with a group of giggling friends. She wondered would she suddenly walk past now out for a walk with her dog, or drive, or cycle. Does she still live at the farm or has she long left Lackenmore? Do her relatives pass by in the street, brush shoulders, talk, smile? Helen's imaginings were suddenly interrupted by the beep of a car horn. She glanced in her rear-view mirror to see a red jeep behind hers, climbed out of the car and went back.

'Hey you.' Breda hurried towards Helen, arms outstretched to hug her. 'What a surprise, you never said you were coming. Why didn't you let me know. Only I recognised the head of hair.'

They talked long into the night and Helen told her about Faye. Breda wanted to call on the Brophys first thing in the morning, but Helen wasn't quite ready for that yet, as so many what if's went through her head. But she was glad to see Breda again, and particularly grateful when she was persuaded to stay in her cottage. She didn't want to be alone now.

'David's invited us up for dinner tomorrow night,' Breda announced.

Helen stopped working on her laptop. 'Is there a special reason?'

'Not particularly, when I mentioned you were back he just asked.'

'Have you seen much of him lately?'

'No, he's been away.'

'Are you still keen on him?' Helen asked with a smile.

'I've tried to get it into perspective. It's very unlikely he'll take any notice of me - ever - and maybe it was just physical attraction, a madly in love thing which lasted a short time. It's all about being unattainable I suppose.'

Helen said nothing, reluctant to make some trite remark which would hurt her feelings.

'When I saw him with Vanessa I realised that it was going nowhere. So I'm trying to be sensible about it, although I can't help looking forward to dinner,' she sighed dramatically.

To Helen's surprise there were only the three of them there. She felt shy in David's company, but Breda made up for it and slowly she began to relax listening to the chat. The meal was Italian - a simple pasta and a cool bottle of sparkling white wine.

'What brought you back to Lackenmore?' he asked.

Helen put down her glass, feeling embarrassed. She had wanted to ask everyone she met in the town whether they had known her mother but so far the courage to speak up had failed her. The only person she had told was Breda.

'I'm hoping to find out about my mother.'

'But you're a McLoughlin?' He sipped his coffee.

'My Mum and Dad weren't my real parents. I only discovered it when my Mum died.'

He stared at her and she found herself unable to look away from his dark eyes which held such intensity. There was an awkward silence.

'What was your mother's name?' His fingers gripped the handle of the cup tightly.

'Faye Brophy.'

There was a tense silence.

'I knew a Faye Brophy.' His voice was husky.

Helen gasped.

'Wow,' Breda whooped. 'There can't have been very many Faye's about.'

'No,' David laughed softly, 'it was an unusual name, but her mother was into the movies and called her children after actresses she liked. Faye would have preferred to be called Mary or Pat or anything else.'

'You knew her well?' Helen was quite unable to believe how unexpectedly she had found out exactly what she wanted.

'We were friends. More coffee?'

'Let me play mother.' Breda poured and in the fuss of those few moments Helen had a chance to breathe again.

'Some more cheese?'

Helen thanked him but refused. She couldn't have eaten any more.

'I'll have some.' Breda helped herself.

'Do you know if she's still living here?' Helen asked softly.

'No, as far as I know she isn't. There's just Pauline and Chris – her mother and sister – living at the farm now.'

Helen was disappointed.

'I haven't talked to anyone in that family for many years,' he said.

'What did she do after school, did she go to college?' Helen asked. She had a million questions which needed to be answered.

'I think she may have done when she went to England.'

'Tell us what you know, David, we want to hear everything,' Breda encouraged.

'I never met her again after we did the Leaving Cert – I went to Trinity in the October.'

'But, Helen, you said your mother was only seventeen when she had you, did you know that she had a baby, David?'

'I don't mean to be inquisitive, but when were you born?' David asked slowly.

'Never ask a woman her age,' Breda quipped.

'In 1979.'

'And the date?'

'David!' Breda squealed.

'My birthday is on the sixth of December.' She just whispered it not really aware of Breda's remarks. It was as if she and David were in another world.

His face paled. He ran his fingers across his forehead, eyes hidden from her.

'How did she look, do I resemble her?'

He nodded silently.

'Did you know her boyfriend, David, he might have been your father, Helen.'

'I didn't go around with the same crowd.' His voice was low.

'Am I really like her?'

'Your hair is a bit darker, but you are so alike it's uncanny.'

Helen sat back in the chair, a ridiculous smile of joy on her face.

Chapter Nineteen

David selected the combination of the safe with trepidation and the door slowly opened. Inside lay various personal items, some of which he had not touched in years. His mother's jewellery, and his father's papers. A shiver went through him. What if he couldn't deal with it? Back in the eighties he had forced himself to cut free from anything which reminded him of her. She wasn't his. Would never be. She had made a new life for herself without him.

He had hardened himself in those early years, and buried deep any emotion. But she had always hovered on the edge of his subconscious. A fluttering candle never entirely quenched. Memories triggered off by the unexpected sight of red hair, the sound of laughter so familiar that many times he was almost convinced it had to be her.

He wondered if he was crazy opening up this Pandora's box? He had a good life. Successful. And he had made a lot of money. But all his interests centred around music. It was his one all-consuming passion and replaced all those things other people took for granted. He had met many women over the years and still had friends in various places across the world, including Vanessa. But no-one had ever been able to cut deep enough into his psyche to find the real David.

Now he was on a wild rollercoaster, all logic and sense forgotten. He reached into the safe and touched the old wallet. A thrill spun through him. He sat down at the desk and stared at it. His mind was bombarded with memories so strong everything else was blotted out and he was swept back to those days spent with Faye in the woods above the river. He opened the wallet and immediately she was there with him. Blue green eyes blazed at him, warm and loving, and she smiled at him as real as that day when he had taken the photo, the first with his new camera. Then something rolled on to the desk, finally wobbling to a halt in front of him. It was his gold signet ring.

He remembered the warm summer sunshine that year. It was 1979. The excitement in his heart as he rushed to get there first. He had concealed his bicycle behind some bushes and making sure there was no-one in sight he hurried through the trees and down the steep slope to the bank of the river. He followed it for a few minutes, then took a narrow track uphill again which led to a heavily wooded area.

Faye was already there sitting underneath a wide-branched oak reading a book. Shafts of sunlight broke through the foliage casting a trellis of light and shade on the grass around her. Caught in a web, there was a magical quality about her. David waved and ran towards her. She stood up. Tall, long-legged, wearing a denim skirt, and pale blue top, hair spread over her shoulders shining in the sunlight. He had been away on a family holiday for the last couple of weeks. Such longing, wanting, dreaming. It had seemed never-ending.

'David!' She threw her arms around his neck. He swung her around and they collapsed on to the grass overcome with laughter.

'I missed you.' He kissed her.

'It felt like years.'

They clung together.

'You are wonderful, Faye Brophy,' he whispered.

She raised her face to meet his and their lips met. Soft. Warm. His hands caressed her slim body. There was a rush of warmth from deep within as that craving swept through him. They stretched out on the ground. His lips grasped hers, and their tongues entangled, until he almost shouted with desire. She was underneath him now. His body burned hard and he struggled to move closer, her legs winding around his, holding tight, their movements becoming more and more urgent as their passion grew.

'I love you Faye,' he whispered.

'And I love you, David, come on, do it quickly, I can't wait.'

He fumbled with his trousers, and her regulation school knickers. She helped him. He lay upon her again. Exquisite pleasure spiralled as their naked bodies touched. Awkwardly, half afraid, he entered her.

'My love.'

'Hurry, David, hurry.' She dug her nails into his back.

He groaned, long slow guttural sounds which mingled with her cries, and came all in a rush. He held her tight, and kissed her. Pushed her hair back and cupped her face in his hands. 'Faye, what's wrong?' he asked when he felt the dampness on her skin.

'I couldn't help myself, sorry,' she smiled through the tears.

'I love you so much.' He dried the moisture softly.

'I love you.'

They wound their arms around each other and with eyes closed lay quietly for a while in the warmth of the day.

'I've something for you,' he grinned and stood up, zipped up his trousers, and took a parcel from under his black jacket which lay on the ground. He handed it to her.

'And I've something for you too,' she murmured, feeling the parcel with her fingers. 'But I'd better get dressed.' She waved her leg in the air with a pair of navy knickers hanging from her ankle. They both laughed as she stepped into them and pulled them on.

'Open it,' he urged, looking forward to her reaction.

'Just give me a second to think what it might be. I love keeping myself in suspense,' she had a broad smile on her face waiting a few seconds before she tore the wrapping paper and the pieces curled and drifted downwards. She stared at the red leather-bound book in her hand. A brass lock held each side together and a tiny key swung from a chain.

'I know how you like to keep your diary, so instead of those little things you normally use now you have the real thing.'

'It's lovely, David, thank you so much.' She raised it to her cheek and held it there.

'I'm glad you like it.' He felt sheepish now. Embarrassed.

She hugged him.

'Today David gave me a present – that will be the first entry.'

'What about mine?' He stood grinning at her.

'Well, it's not exactly a thing.' She looked away.

'Come on, don't keep me waiting.'

She sat down under the tree, plucked a blade of fresh grass and sucked it.

He sat beside her. 'Don't tease.'

She looked at him and her blue green eyes blazed into his. He reached for her, immediately wanting her again.

'Do you remember when you asked me to marry you?' She leaned back against the old gnarled trunk of the tree and stared into the green distance. Her white teeth gripped her lower lip which was pink and glistening, and so desirable.

'You don't think I've forgotten that, do you?'

'I've been thinking about it.'

He nodded. Eyes puzzled.

'And I was wondering when we might get married, would it be soon?'

'It might be a bit difficult at the moment. I probably let me heart rule my head when I asked you. I'm sorry, but I'll be going to Trinity in October, and I'll have no money to support us until I qualify. But we could get engaged and that would make the waiting easier.'

'I was going to get a job in Dublin – and you have to get a flat anyway.' There was disappointment in her voice.

'It's not the way to start our life, I want to be able to support you in style, buy our own house, not live in some dingy flat.'

'But you said?'

'We must be sensible.'

She stared at him.

'Is something wrong, Faye?' He cupped her face in his hand, puzzled at her serious expression.

'No, not really,' she hesitated.

'Out with it,' he laughed. Wound his arms around her shoulders and pulled her to him, heads close together.

'David,' she paused, 'I ... we ... we're going to have a baby.'

How do you tell someone that you think you might be their father? The thought of coming out with such a statement shook David. Helen didn't look like him. She was all Faye. The thought that the girl he had loved might have been with another boy at the time slithered across his mind. He shook the unpalatable thought away, unable to contemplate that she hadn't been everything he had imagined her to be. Faye was so loving. So full of life. So honest with her feelings. No, it simply wasn't possible. But denying that left him with the knowledge that Helen had to be his. That the same blood ran through their veins. Their DNA matched.

He remembered his utter shock when Faye told him she was pregnant. But after a few minutes the very idea had become exciting. He adored Faye. He would adore their child.

'When will the baby come?'

'At the end of December I think. I'm not really sure. I'm about three months now.'

'We'll have to get married before anyone notices. Have you told your mother and father yet?'

'No, but they'll have a blue fit.'

'I'll tell my father straight away. He'll have to accept it. So will you marry me, Faye Brophy?' he smiled.

'Yes, yes, yes!' She threw her arms around him.

'Now we're engaged.' He twisted the gold signet ring off his finger and put it on to the third finger of her left hand. 'My mother gave this to me before she died. I'm sorry it doesn't fit but I'll buy you a proper engagement ring as soon as I can.'

David had never forgiven himself for leaving Faye. It was something which had affected him deeply in his youth, and now to be taken back to those days again ignited his sense of helplessness and frustration at his inability to keep his promise to her. Although in his forties, many times he had questioned the reasons why he made certain decisions. Never quite satisfied with his achievements. Never sure of where he was heading. Over the years he had not consciously thought about that time of his life but now those days thundered back with a vengeance his emotions stirred as if it was only yesterday.

Chapter Twenty

The following evening, Breda took Helen to the Brophy farm.

'I'm terrified.' She shivered.

'Don't be ridiculous, they're not going to bite you. They're only two women. God help them, left alone on a place this size without a man to give a hand's turn. The son Sean is in the States and hasn't been back in years.' Breda rang the doorbell.

It took some time before the door was opened by a woman. She had a heavy bulky presence, and Helen felt immediately cowed by her.

'Chris, how are you?' Breda stepped closer.

'What do you want?' She stared at them suspiciously.

'This is Helen McLoughlin, her mother and father were your neighbours years ago – Carmel and Tom?'

Chris began to close the door.

'My Mum died and she left some money in her will for a Faye Brophy who lived here. She was very fond of her.' There was a tremor in Helen's voice. She had remembered that there was a thousand dollars left to Faye in her mother's will and it had given her the excuse she needed.

'Who was Faye, I've never heard of her,' Breda asked.

Chris was silent.

'Is she related to you? Why don't you ask us in, Chris, might be better not to discuss something like this on the doorstep,' she suggested.

Chris opened the door fully and led the way into the parlour. The atmosphere of the unused room had a dampish musty smell not quite eliminated by the strong odour of furniture polish.

'How much money is there?' she demanded.

'It's not very much, just a few dollars,' Helen explained.

'Then it should come to her relations, her next of kin.'

'So she is related to you?'

'She's dead.'

Helen was stunned.

'When did she die?' Breda asked.

'Years ago.'

'How old was she?'

'She was just a girl.'

'How sad, was she your sister?'

'She was younger, look, that money should come to me.' Chris raised her voice.

'The solicitors are handling my mother's will. They'll be in touch with you.'

'Where is Faye buried?' Breda asked.

'Don't know.' Chris fidgeted. One hand rubbing the other nervously.

'Is she buried in Lackenmore?' Breda pressed her for an answer.

'No.'

'Could you tell us exactly? We'd like to visit.'

'In England I think.'

'Would it be London?' It was Breda who made most of the conversation.

'How would I know, it's years ago.'

'But surely you were there?'

'Stop asking me questions.'

'Sorry, Chris, it's just that it's very important to us.'

'I told you I don't know.' She moved to the door and held it open.

Breda and Helen followed.

'Make sure the solicitor knows my name. He can send the money here. It's Christine Aherne, do you want me to write it down for you?'

'No, it's OK,' Breda murmured as they walked down the hall.

Chris caught Helen's arm. 'Don't let them forget about me. That money's mine.'

They walked towards the car. She ran after them. 'It's mine, tell them it's mine.'

'I never expected that.' Helen stared out through the car window. Tears in her eyes.

'Me neither.' Breda drove back to the cottage.

'Now I'll never meet her.' Helen was very upset. She had built herself up since coming back to Ireland and had never even considered that Faye might have died. It simply hadn't entered her mind.

'It's very sad, particularly when she was so young. Wonder what happened?'

'I'd give anything to know where she's buried. Just to put a few flowers on her grave.'

'We'll find out, don't you worry. Oh look, we have a visitor.'

Helen brushed the tears from her eyes, definitely not in the mood for company.

'I'll disappear. I don't think he's looking for me.'

'Who?'

'Peter.'

They drew up in front of the cottage. He was sitting in a black sports car and got out as soon as he saw them.

'How are you, girls?'

'We're fine,' Breda said.

'I heard you were back,' he addressed Helen.

'The local grapevine got it already,' Breda grinned, 'come on in, we'll make you a coffee.'

'I came to ask you to have dinner with me,' he smiled.

She was suddenly glad to see him, excited, but was thrown into confusion, such was her emotional state.

'Go on, it'll do you good,' encouraged Breda, brewing up.

'I've booked a table at The French Connection.' He sat down on the couch, long legs in blue jeans seeming to stretch half way across the room.

'Confident then?' Breda quipped, raising her eyebrows.

'Why not?' he smiled at Helen.

'OK. Just give me a minute to freshen up.'

'Do me a favour, don't take half the night like some women I know.'

'Cheeky. It'll take as long as it takes,' Helen retorted.

'That's right, give it to him.' Breda poured. 'But sit down and have your coffee first, you're not in that much of a hurry, are you?'

Within a short time they were speeding along the narrow roads around Lackenmore.

'It's great to have you back,' he smiled. So handsome her heart flipped.

'We should be in Alice Springs with a car like this. Hood down, hair flying.'

'Give me half a chance and I'd be over.' He put his hand on hers. She shook him off with a screech.

'Peter, both hands on the steering wheel.'

'What?'

'Don't pretend you didn't hear.'

'I didn't.'

'Yea,' they laughed together. To be so much at ease with someone she had known for such a short time was unbelievable.

They ate in a tiny restaurant which overlooked the lake. The candle-lit table was in a corner, hidden from the gaze of the other diners.

'Fancy another glass of wine, or something else.'

'No thanks.'

He stretched out his hand across the table and took hers. His touch was warm and intimate. Excitement erupted again inside her and this time she didn't make any attempt to remove her hand from his grasp.

'You're something else, Helen McLoughlin.' His hazel eyes gazed at her with intensity.

'You're crazy.'

'Yea, about you.'

'Peter!'

'Come on, let's get out of here.'

He drove back to the marina and pulled in before turning for the cottages, and cut the engine. Then he leaned across and put his arm around her pulling her close. It all happened so quickly she wasn't prepared for the touch of his lips on hers, melting almost as they moved slowly, warm and moist. A wave of desire spiralled through her and she responded to him as if it was the most natural thing in the world. But then a tiny voice deep down warned and she forced herself to pull away.

'Peter, it's late.'

He didn't seem to hear her.

'Peter, please?'

He raised his head, smiled, and immediately kissed her again. Long lingering kisses which made her feel almost weak.

At the door of the cottage, he leaned close again.

'Meet me tomorrow?'

She wasn't sure what to say.

'We'll have a few drinks and catch some music afterwards, please don't say no,' he smiled, that broad smile which she couldn't resist.

'OK, you're on.'

'Call for you about seven.' He bent and kissed her softly on the forehead. 'Sweet dreams.'

She waited until the car had disappeared, and then slowly closed the door and went inside. She flopped on to the couch feeling dazed and shaken, unable to believe what had happened. How is it possible to be attracted to someone so quickly, someone she hardly knew? She couldn't find an answer, but was certain that all she wanted was to see him again. Hear his voice, his laughter. Touch him. Kiss him. Just be with him.

It was a wonderful morning, the land shrouded in mist, magical, with an ethereal light which changed constantly. Helen followed the narrow road which wound uphill and parked the car to take some photos of the town which was just a tiny huddle of buildings with two church spires, overshadowed by the castle. She still felt sad about Faye. And terribly disappointed that suddenly her plan to find her mother had been cut short so abruptly.

Later she drove to Athenry. She had received a request from someone in Brisbane who had read her articles and wanted some information about the place his great-grandfather hailed from. She was delighted to help and was looking forward to the trip, to see what she could find out for the man. It meant a lot to him obviously.

She wandered around the town which hadn't changed greatly by the look of it. A lot of the old shops and houses had been restored, and the fronts were the same as they probably were a hundred years ago. She called to the presbytery of the catholic church, and found Fr. McMahon there. He was only too delighted to let her have a look at the old registers which went back to the eighteen hundreds. The man's name was Samuel Bourke and he had been born in 1875. There was more than one Bourke, but eventually they found him mentioned in a list of names written in copperplate script. She was delighted, and had a marvellous sense of satisfaction now that she could tell the man what he wanted to hear - she had found the record of his grandfather's birth. They continued the search and eventually found the record of the birth of his wife Margaret, and their marriage record. It was wonderful. The priest allowed her to take photographs of the register, and the church itself. She offered payment but he wouldn't hear of it. But she did give him some money to say a Mass for everyone but most especially for Faye.

She enjoyed the trip, but didn't realise that this first enquiry would lead to a landslide of requests from people in Australia with Irish roots which would keep her here in Ireland for much longer than she had anticipated.

Chapter Twenty-one

'What are you doing?' Pauline stared at Chris as she climbed up on the chair and reached to take down a large box from the top of the dresser. She put it on the table, undid the string which kept it closed, and took the top off. It was stuffed tight with papers, and she searched through it until she found the old photograph album, opened it and slowly turned the thick pages which were decorated with beautiful floral designs. Pauline stood beside her staring at the likenesses of relatives.

'Look, Uncle Joe.' She pointed. 'And Mam and Dad.'

Chris stopped at a particular page and tore a photo from its place and handed it to her mother. 'There, that one that called looked just like our Faye.'

Pauline moved her gnarled fingers over the shiny surface of the photo. Then she picked it up and kissed it. 'This is Faye.' She remembered her youngest daughter.

'I know that.'

'Faye ...' The old woman's voice was tremulous.

'It's the other one I'm wondering about.'

'Who?'

'The one who was here. She said she was Helen.'

'No, couldn't be, she was drowned.' Pauline was unusually adamant, her tone of voice firm. There was no confusion there today.

'What do you mean?'

'In deep water. Dead and gone.'

'Who?

'Helen – that was her name.'

'You don't mean Faye's baby?'

'Dan searched, but we couldn't find her.' Pauline pulled her rosary beads from her pocket and began to pray. 'Hail Mary full of grace, the Lord is with thee.'

'So it could be her.' Chris sank down on a chair. 'I'd forgotten all about it. You had me brainwashed. Don't tell a soul, you said, this has to be kept in the family, and she was such a gorgeous little thing, Faye didn't deserve her, I always thought she should have been mine. I know I had Sean later, but after him I still wanted a girl, it wasn't fair.'

'I was glad when I thought the baby had drowned, God forgive me,' Pauline whispered.

'I told them Faye was dead.' Chris fingered the photo. 'Maybe I shouldn't have done that.'

'That baby is long gone.'

'What if she finds out I lied?' Chris looked worried.

'She won't say anything, Faye was always such a good girl.'

Today Pauline's mind was very clear, and she remembered how difficult it had been to run the farm after her husband's death. But the love of the land ran deep and strong, and she battled through from morning to night working harder than any man. Often in the late evening as she herded the contented cattle in for milking, some deep down urge for fulfilment was satisfied as she surveyed her achievement. She held out as long as she could but knew that sooner or later she would have to step aside when a husband was found for Chris. The farm was the only attraction that her plain daughter possessed.

So Seamus Aherne married Chris and Pauline was dispossessed. Having two elder brothers he was forced to look elsewhere for land and he grabbed the opportunity to take over the Brophy farm. Pauline had been able to manipulate her husband, but it was different with this man. He had his own ideas and put them into practice without consulting her. Once she had full control over this farm, like her father before her, and his before him, back along the generations, but now she was relegated to a position of no importance. It was the end for Pauline.

Chapter Twenty-two

The matriarch sat on her throne in splendour and everyone bowed, scraped and listened – at least on the surface. Pearl controlled the Ballymoragh household like a puppeteer. Each of them at the end of imaginary strings which she crossed and re-crossed like a large spider weaving its web.

The evening Eoin brought Maria over to meet her was a momentous one, particularly chosen because Michael was away in England on business. Pearl had come downstairs especially but when Jenny walked into the dining room she stared in shock. The old woman was wearing the white lace dress with the pink satin ribbon at the waist. The one which Jenny had taken out of the wardrobe that day and which obviously meant a lot to her. She could smell the scent of old roses from the delicate lace as she bent to kiss the paper thin skin, knowing instantly why Pearl had chosen to wear that dress tonight. It was reminiscent of another era when a girl had danced with a young man and fallen in love. Jenny's heart increased its rhythm and raced away to take her to another time too. But she dragged it back screaming into this evening of expectation.

'This is Maria, grandmother.' Eoin brought the dark haired girl close to the chair in which Pearl sat, and hands brushed together in brief acknowledgement. Pearl nodded, her smile polite, her lips painted a rose pink to match the satin bow, make-up carefully done by Maureen.

'Well, this is very nice.' He rubbed his hands and smiled when they were finally seated.

'Yea, it's really lovely to ...' Jenny spoke at just the same moment.

'Sorry.' He waved at her to continue.

'I was going to say how lovely it is to have Maria here in Ballymoragh,' Jenny smiled at the girl. 'You're very welcome.' As she picked up her napkin she was aware of a sudden tension at the table. She looked at Pearl and could immediately sense the disapproval which emanated from her. For a second she was puzzled as to the reason but then realised why. They were like actors in a play and she and Eoin had missed their cues and spoken out of turn. Pearl always wanted to be first.

Maureen appeared with a large soup tureen on a tray.

'Gran, thanks so much for inviting us.' Eoin placed his large brown hand on the thin wrist.

'It's my pleasure,' the old woman smiled.

Jenny sighed and relaxed a little.

Maureen served consommé and handed around the dish of soft white bread rolls.

Eoin continued talking to Pearl. She asked a few questions of Maria and seemed to like her answers. Jenny ate her soup. Listening to pieces of information being passed from one to the other which would bring Maria into the family fold. If Pearl had asked her the same questions when Michael had introduced her to the family, would she have found answers to them? She shrank into herself. That day Pearl had enquired about photographs of her family had sent her into shock.

'Maria, come sit closer to me,' Pearl said.

'You have beautiful hair,' Pearl admired Maria's dark shining tresses. 'Once I had hair like that too.'

Jenny had a sudden recollection of a heavy scissors cutting through her own hair and she shivered. Chop, chop, and the soft shining red mass had landed on the floor. Drifted. Settled. Like autumn leaves to eventually wither and die. Like she had almost died in that place.

'Jenny, have you finished your soup?' Maureen enquired.

'Yes thanks.' She was aware of a slight air of concern from the housekeeper. 'I'm not very hungry this evening.' They were close,

Maureen and Jenny.

'A proper wedding will have to be arranged, not some hole in the corner affair,' Pearl announced. 'I'm sure you'd love to wear a beautiful white dress and veil,' she addressed Maria.

'Yes, that would be wonderful.' The dark eyes were excited.

'It will be in our local church. I'll talk to the parish priest.'

'We've arranged a quiet ceremony in the Registry Office. Just ourselves and two friends,' Eoin explained.

'That's your own business, the wedding proper will be here.'

Maureen reappeared and served rack of lamb. Busy with the food there was no more talk of weddings and the conversation was light – about the weather, which horses were running, who was doing this and that.

'Do you ride, Maria?'

She shook her head

'You'll have to learn. Everyone in this family rides. It's a tradition. Why even Jennifer loves her horses, although I seem to remember she didn't know how to ride when she first came here.'

'I often ride my horse Swift Eagle in the morning before I go to work. I could give you some lessons if you like. Start you off on a very quiet animal,' Jenny offered.

She smiled her acceptance.

'We can all go out together, you'll enjoy it.' Eoin reached for her hand under the table, his love quite obvious to Jenny.

Jealousy swept through her. Hot. Burning. An emotion which left her head spinning.

Chapter Twenty-three

Helen was happy. Happier than she had been in a long time. She was in love with Peter. He was in love with her. She couldn't believe life could be like this. Endless days of excitement filled with longing for him. To catch that first sight of his smile. Feel his hand touch hers softly. His lips cling with passion. She shivered. He would be here in half an hour and she couldn't wait.

'Peter coming around again tonight?' Breda asked.

'Yes, we're going out for a meal.'

'I hope you don't mind if I sound a bit like an elder sister, but the two of you have become very close.'

'I know, isn't it wonderful?' Helen smiled widely, happiness obvious in her blue eyes.

'Maybe you should hold back a bit.'

'What do you mean?' Helen was puzzled.

'He has a reputation.'

'I know, you told me that already,' she became slightly irritated.

'He's been engaged a couple of times, did he tell you?'

'Of course, we have no secrets from each other.'

'And he was the one who couldn't commit.'

'How do you know that?'

'I knew both of the girls, they were good friends of mine.'

'Maybe they weren't right for him. I've known a few guys in my time and now I've met Mr. Right, and surely it will be the same for you too, Breda, he's just waiting around the corner.'

'I suppose that could happen and pigs might fly.'

'Don't be so cynical,' Helen laughed. She really didn't want to have a confrontation with her friend.

'So you might be settling permanently in Lackenmore?'

'Maybe, but perhaps that's taking things too fast, I just want to enjoy what I have now, I'm not thinking ahead.'

'There's something else I've been wondering about,' Breda murmured.

'What's with you tonight?'

'Let's have a gin and tonic?' She stood up and poured the drinks, not waiting for a reply.

'Were you wondering about having a drink or was it something else?' Helen grinned.

'I shouldn't mention it, it's really none of my business, and you are a big girl,' Breda laughed.

'Go on will you, say it now, don't keep me in suspense.'

'You mightn't like it.'

Helen sighed and drummed her fingers on the arm of the chair.

'Have you ever thought,' Breda hesitated, 'who your father might be?'

'I have a father and he's the only one I want.' It was a snap. A regretted lapse.

'I know, but your natural father probably came from around here and Peter could be connected with the same family.' She took a sip of her drink.

'What are you saying?' Helen stared at Breda, her blue eyes wide open with shock.

'It's just something you should keep in the back of your mind.'

'That Peter might be related to me?'

'It's possible.'

'It's highly unlikely, one in a million chance, not at all,' Helen dismissed it immediately.

'It's been on my mind lately and I felt I had to say something, so now I've done that, so you can forget about it.'

'Forget?' There was accusation in Helen's voice.

Guilt flashed across Breda's face.

'Have you any idea of what you've done?'

'I'm sorry.'

'To have put such a thought into my head was terrible.' Tears filled Helen's eyes.

'Perhaps I shouldn't have mentioned it,' Breda murmured quietly.

'It was irresponsible. How can I look at Peter now thinking that he might be my brother or my cousin?'

'It won't matter unless you're going to have a child with the guy, so it's better to be prepared. What if you discovered such a thing way down the line, it would be tragic.'

'It is tragic,' Helen retorted. She didn't often lose her head over things but this was something else. On account of a few words her whole life was going down the tubes and all the joy she had known recently had suddenly disintegrated.

'My love, you were very quiet this evening.' Peter kissed her as they left the pub after a rowdy evening with his friends.

'Sorry.'

'There's something wrong?' he was concerned.

'No, I'm just a bit tired.'

His eyes held hers. 'Come back with me and we can have an early night, and a late morning.'

'You know I can't, I don't want the whole town talking about us.'

'No-one will take the slightest notice, come on?' he kissed her.

So far, their lovemaking had been confined to heavy sessions in the car, parked up a secluded laneway or on the shores of the lake somewhere around Lackenmore. Peter was becoming frustrated. She knew that. But she couldn't have brought him back to the cottage, and certainly felt it wouldn't be the thing to be seen going in and out of his apartment. There was too much gossip. But the secrecy had added to the excitement, and she felt very disappointed now that Breda's suspicion about Peter's family had suddenly stolen the brightness from their relationship, like a dark storm cloud obscured the sun.

He held her very close in the car. The aroma of his skin was so sensual she reached for him. Her fingers fumbled with the buttons of his shirt, and as the first one opened she slid her hand through to feel his warm skin, slowly inching up across his ribs, the rest of the buttons popping until there was room to lean forward to press her face on to him, sensing the soft hairs on his chest, her lips gently massaging.

'I love you,' Peter murmured, bent his head and kissed her, drawing closer, their bodies moulding. Even in the tight confines of the small car their passion swept them into a crazy whirl of longing.

'I need you, Helen.' He swept her skirt aside and his hand moved further along her thigh and further, searching.

'No, Peter.' She sat up abruptly.

'Helen, please,' his hand moved.

'I want to, I love you, but I'm not sure.'

'Come on. There's no reason. I've been patient, you can't say I haven't been that, so bloody patient I'm going around the bend.' He kissed her again.

'I know.'

She stared out through the window of the car into the night. The sky was dotted with stars. She was reminded of home. In the southern hemisphere it would be so much more extreme than Ireland. Darker sky. Brighter stars. His fingers curled around her neck. Drew her back. She loved him. She wanted him. She turned into him.

'My love.' His breath was warm on her lips, his mouth repossessed hers, and cut off any hesitation. Her legs wound around his. The gear level caught. She laughed.

'Not the most comfortable,' he murmured, his voice warm. 'Are you all right?'

She moved closer. They fumbled with their clothes. She touched him. Her fingers teased. Swirled. Formed designs. The feel of him did something to her. And all sensibility disappeared. She had worked it out before – the pros and cons, and had decided she couldn't really. Couldn't commit herself to something which held such doubt. Questions of who, what, why, where, darted. But no answers meant no decisions, meant no reasons to withhold, meant go for it. Follow your heart.

'I love you,' he breathed, his voice husky.

'I love you.' It was the first time she had said those words.

He moved. She moved. He was there. She held him tight. She didn't want to let go. He swept on, taking her with him, his momentum increasing. She was part of him. The other half of a pair. Her breathing was fast. Her pulse rate soared. She was in a magic place. Somewhere she had dreamed of. Imagined so many times. Now that she was there it was even more wonderful. She held herself tight. Holding back just a little until he reached a climax and then she let go. Her body releasing, and together, just at the exact same moment, it happened.

She didn't remember very much after that, coming to out of a drifting sleep much later. His head was on her shoulder, eyes closed, and she ran her fingers through his short hair. Silky smooth. She kissed his forehead.

He moved a little, and was still again.

She closed her eyes. Reluctant to disturb him, and wanting to savour these moments. That first time so special. She didn't want to think any further than tonight. These moments were to be kept like a special keepsake in a box to be visited when she wanted to be reminded of this time, and Peter.

Chapter Twenty-four

David had a plan in his head now, loosely drawn. He would try to find Faye. It gave him that sense of direction which he needed, and his first call was to see the doctor who had practised in Lackenmore in the sixties and seventies. He had been retired for a long time but was still living in the same house with his wife.

'He's fairly good today, although sometimes he's so depressed he doesn't want to get out of bed,' the doctor's wife explained as she led the way through to the back room where her husband sat in a chair, dozing. She touched him gently and he jerked awake with a surprised look on his face.

'Dear, this is David Taylor, you remember he was a patient of yours, and his father as well. Now he's anxious to find out if you know anything about another patient, a young girl, Faye Brophy?'

'I don't discuss my patients with anyone,' he grumbled, his thin lined face growing a deep shade of red.

'It's very important, Dr. O'Sullivan,' David spoke gently.

He grunted.

'I was a close friend of hers and I don't know where she is now, so I wondered if you have anything on your files which might help me locate her. She may have attended you in the late seventies.'

'That Dan Brophy's girl? The younger one?' For the first time he looked straight at David, his beady eyes suddenly sharp behind dark-framed glasses.

'Yes.'

'Dan died around that time.'

'Perhaps you could check your files dear? He has them all in

117

perfect order, you know, even after all these years.'

He grunted and made to move out of the chair. His wife handed him a walking stick and took his other arm. Together they walked slowly into the other room and after a few minutes reappeared, Mrs. O'Sullivan was holding a white filing card and as soon as he had managed to sit down again she handed it to him.

'I really shouldn't give you any information,' he paused, 'but it's so long ago, perhaps it doesn't matter any longer.' He peered short-sightedly at the card.

'I'm sorry for putting you to so much trouble.'

'Nothing much happens anymore,' the old man muttered, 'I only saw Faye for childhood illnesses, but then she wasn't well. It was a strange case.' His voice sank to a whisper. 'I was sure it was the shock of her father's death, she was withdrawn and didn't recognise anyone.'

Mrs. O'Sullivan stood closer and patted his shoulder.

'There was a good man at St. Josephs so I referred her to him, I wasn't equipped to deal with it.'

'When was that?' David asked.

'January, 1980.' The card began to shake, and his wife took it out of his hand.

'So you must have attended her when she had the baby?' David chanced the question although at the time he had understood that she had gone to England.

'What baby?' he asked sharply.

'She had a child around that time.'

'She was only a child herself. Give me back that card.'

'Seventeen.'

Mrs. O'Sullivan handed it to him.

'There's no mention of a baby here. I'd have known if there was, I was her doctor.'

'Do you know what happened when she was referred to St. Josephs?'

'You're overstepping the mark. I can't tell you anything else. It's all confidential. I'd be breaking my Hippocratic Oath,' he glared at him.

'I'm sorry.'

Mrs. O'Sullivan tipped David's arm.

'Thank you very much for all your help Dr. O'Sullivan, I really appreciate it.' He shook his hand.

The old man grunted.

'We're lucky the doctor kept such good records. Always a stickler,' Mrs. O'Sullivan smiled.

'You've no idea how much it means to me.'

'We're always glad to help. Would you like a cup of coffee or tea?'

'No thank you,' He was anxious to be away now, and pressed some notes into her hand.

'No, I wouldn't dream of accepting money.' She shook her head.

'Tell the doctor that it's the price nowadays for a consultation.'

'Thank you,' she smiled.

David drove straight to St. Josephs which was a few miles on the far side of Galway city. With a high grey wall which bordered the edge of the narrow road, it was a brooding keep in keep out sort of place. But as he turned in he was surprised to see the gates standing open, in pristine black and gold wrought iron. A large painted sign confirmed that it was St. Josephs Hospital.

A security man appeared and enquired as to his business. After David had given a satisfactory explanation he drove through and swung up the wide driveway. It was a pleasant place. With tall trees. Wide beds planted with mature shrubs. A swathe of sculptured grass swept up to the large Georgian building which had been extended on both sides. Following the signs he drove around the back and parked. In Reception, he asked for someone who might have information about hospital records. While waiting, he wandered around the large foyer and stopped to look out through a high window at a group of people sitting outside. A nurse pushed an old man in a wheelchair. Some elderly women chatted together. While it was a very pleasant hospital now he wondered what it was like thirty years ago. They were terrible places then, and he hated to think of how Faye must have felt to be referred here. His stomach coiled in a tight knot of self-recrimination.

He was brought into the office, and a very efficient woman took the details about Faye. She wasn't particularly sympathetic, and it was so long ago she didn't know where the information might be now.

'Are there any staff still working at the hospital who would have been here at that time?' he asked.

'Well, I started in the seventies but I'm one of the few. Anyhow, it would be practically impossible to remember one patient from all of those who passed through.'

Very disappointed, he had to remind himself that the chance of finding out anything about Faye at this point was optimistic to say the least. It was a chance in a million.

'Are the records on computer?' He tried again.

She hesitated a moment, on the desk her fingers were splayed out, tense, nails polished white. A low tch of annoyance escaped her lips, and the fingers moved one by one from little pinkie to thumb as if repeating a five finger exercise.

'Even if you go down that route, there is the problem of relationship, you are not family.'

Chapter Twenty-five

With the big bread knife Pauline sawed rough slices of bread. They fell, thick and thin. Then she spread butter and placed pieces of ham before joining them together.

Chris came in from the back and stared at her. 'What's this?'

'Faye will be home soon.'

'For God's sake Mam this is crazy, making food for her. You know she's been gone for years, she's hardly going to turn up now and eat this stuff.' Chris took the plate and emptied the sandwiches into the bin.

'Why did you do that?'

'Don't ask silly questions,' Chris snapped.

'I've just made them.' Her mother peered into the bin.

'Why are you on about her now anyway? It's all I hear about these days. Faye this, Faye that, I'm going to lose my mind if you don't stop talking about her.'

'I was a good mother. I looked after my children.'

'You looked after her too well. It was always her.'

'Who are you anyway?' Watery blue eyes peered at her.

'Oh Mam.' Chris lowered her bulk heavily into a kitchen chair. 'I can't take any more of this, it's just too much.'

'You can go home now.'

'I feel like running away somewhere, anywhere.'

'Go back to where you came from. My Faye will be coming home soon, so you'll have to be gone from here.' She went to the door, opened it, and stood waiting. In her mind, today her eldest daughter was a stranger to her.

Chris rushed over and banged it closed. 'Don't be ridiculous, I live here.'

'I was paid off once.' Pauline picked up the knife and began to cut more bread. Remembering the white envelope with the money in it. All that money.

'What do you mean?'

'I have to make it up to her.'

Chris swept the slices of bread off the counter. The knife clattered to the floor. They stared as it moved across the lino and finally came to a halt against the leg of the table. Chris bent to pick it up and held it tightly in her hand. The blade trembled. The fine steel caught the light. It had a dangerous lethal quality.

Pauline gazed at her, silenced.

'I want to hear no more about her.'

'I shouldn't have taken the money. I shouldn't have done that.' The old woman said, the events of that night crystal clear in her mind.

It was almost eleven o'clock when the car drove up the lane which led to the farmhouse. Pauline was still up, kneeling by the fire saying her night prayers. It was always the same. Her own private ritual. But the moment the car entered the laneway, her head jerked up and she was interrupted in the middle of the Litany. Who was coming here at this hour of the night? She went into the hall and peered through the heavy white lace curtains. Large circular lights illuminated the yard, and quickly she took off her apron, patted her hair, concerned now. But at the last moment she went back to the kitchen and took a packet of peppermints from the dresser drawer, popped one in her mouth and hurried to open the door.

'Mrs. Brophy?' The man was tall, and dressed in a worn grey tweed jacket.

She opened it slowly. 'Yes?'

'Professor Taylor.'

He didn't offer his hand, but she knew well who he was. Dan had done business with him, although she had never spoken to him before. Very worried now she led the way into the parlour and switched on the light. The brass lamp hung down from the high ceiling, shadows thrown by the heavy mahogany furniture which crowded the cramped space, a legacy of her grandparents.

'Please sit down.' She indicated a chair.

'No thank you. This won't take long. Is your husband here?' He drew himself up to his full height of six foot four inches and peered at her from under dark bushy brows drawn together now in a deep scowl.

'He's already in bed, I'm afraid, but can I help you?'

'Perhaps you might be the better person to handle this situation.' He cleared his throat.

'It has come to my attention that your daughter and my son ...'

'Chris?'

'No, it's Faye I believe.'

'Faye?' The name was hissed.

'It appears they have been seeing each other.'

'Faye doesn't have a boyfriend.'

'They want to get married.'

'What?' Pauline's mouth fell open.

'I know. It's ridiculous. They're only children,' he laughed, 'needless to say I forbid it. I'm sure you'll be of the same mind. He is going to Trinity in October and has his whole life ahead of him. Marriage at this stage is out of the question. So I want you to talk to your daughter and made sure she realises that there will be no marriage with my son. Now, or in the future. I trust I can leave it in your hands?'

She heard his words, but was unable to respond.

'I'll take my leave of you now. My apologies for the lateness of the hour.'

At the front door, he turned back and took a white envelope out of his pocket. He stared at it for a few seconds before handing it to her. 'I trust this will go some way towards the expenses,' he muttered. Then he strode out the door and marched across the yard to his car.

Shaken she stood watching until the rear lights of the car disappeared, then slowly returned to the parlour. She caught her thumb under the envelope flap and ripped it open. The jagged edges revealed neatly folded twenty punt notes. She counted them slowly. One hundred. Two hundred. Three, four, five hundred punts. She couldn't believe her eyes and counted it again. It was correct. She took a few notes, stuffed them into her pocket, and concealed the rest in the sideboard.

She started up the stairs. She could hear the loud snores of her husband coming from the back bedroom and knew there was no fear of him waking. She stood outside her daughters' door for a moment then threw it open and switched on the light. Chris sat up in bed immediately.

'What's wrong?' She stared at her mother in astonishment. Her round eyes blinked in the brightness.

Pauline ignored her and strode over to Faye's bed, who slept on undisturbed, one hand curled underneath her cheek. Pauline caught hold of the pink candlewick spread and yanked it off the bed. Then the blankets and sheet all in one go. Faye awoke with a scream as she was dragged out of the bed by her mother and fell on to the cold lino with a heavy thump.

'Mam?' she cried out, 'what are you doing?'

'It's not what I've been doing, it's what you've been doing.'

Faye's blue eyes stared stark, her face white.

'Tell me what you've been up to with that boy. Tell me?' Pauline leaned forward and slapped her hard across the face.

The blow stung, and tears sprang into Faye's eyes. The imprint of her mother's hand showed dull red.

'Tell me, or I'll beat it out of you.'

Faye crouched up against the wall as her mother rained blows upon her with increasing ferocity.

Chris watched, incredulous.

'Have you got yourself into trouble? Is that it?' She dragged at Faye's blue cotton nightdress.

Faye crossed her arms in front of her body. It seemed to reinforce Pauline's anger.

'You're expecting, you little bitch. How far gone are you?' She caught the nightdress at the neck and wrenched it in two, the buttons popping open. Then she grabbed Faye's long hair and dragged her upwards. The nightdress fell away, a very slight swelling visible to her probing eyes.

'My God, what have I done to deserve this? We've given you everything and look how you repay us.'

She swung around to Chris. 'Why did you not notice this? You sleep together in the same room. You must be blind.'

She was shamefaced and silent.

Pauline turned back to Faye and stood glaring down at her. The only sound in the room was Faye's quiet sobs. When she spoke again, her voice was low. The words full of venom.

'And I thought you were putting on a bit of weight at last. Always so skinny. What a fool I was.' Her voice trembled. 'You know you've committed a terrible sin? More than one I'll be bound. How could you even know about such things. Where did you go? When did it happen?'

Faye didn't answer, her face hidden by her long hair.

'Did he force you, was that it?'

'No he didn't,' Faye screamed, defiant.

'So you went along with it, you cheap bitch. Do you think that boy is going to stand by you? His father was just here and he told me everything. He'll never marry you. He's already dumped you. I don't know what you were thinking. Trying to catch a well-off husband. Did you think you'd be allowed to marry a Protestant? You stupid girl. You went the wrong way about that, let me tell you. Now you're stuck with his baby. He'll probably deny it anyway.'

'No he won't. David wants to marry me. We're going to live in Dublin.' Faye pulled the torn nightdress around her body.

'Don't be such a little fool,' her mother hissed, 'he was just using you.'

'No, he wasn't, no.' Tears drifted down Faye's cheeks.

'Well, what do you think this means?' Pauline took the notes out of her pocket and waved them in front of her daughter's eyes. 'You've been paid off. Money for services rendered. Professor Taylor doesn't want his son to have anything to do with you or this family.'

'I don't believe you.'

'Believe it or not, I don't care.' She paced up and down for a few minutes, deep in thought. 'You can't walk around the town carrying his baby. We'll be disgraced. A laughing stock. What will your father say?' she paused, 'when is it due?'

'December, I think.'

'My God.' She made the sign of the cross. 'And what is this?' She caught hold of the ring which hung around Faye's neck on a chain.

'David gave it to me, it's my engagement ring.'

'Not any longer, my girl.' Pauline caught hold of it, and the chain snapped. Then she put it into the pocket of her apron. 'And what other things has he given you?' She pulled open the drawer of the locker beside the bed. 'Oh, this is something new.' She took the journal up. 'A secret diary. Have you put all your guilty thoughts in here?'

'That's mine, don't touch it,' Faye shouted.

'Speak to me like that again and you'll regret it.' She stood staring down at her for a moment, then turned on her heel and left the room.

In the kitchen Pauline poured herself a drink and sat down. She pondered on the situation, and finally came to a conclusion. She knew what she had to do. She raked the turf in the range and tidied up as was her usual habit. Then she picked up the ring. She examined it thinking that perhaps it would be better to return it. Taylor might even come looking for it.

She opened the range and tossed the journal into the glowing embers.

It was the following day when she talked with her husband, having finally managed to get her head around it.

'Dan, there's something up.'

He raised his head.

'Faye has got herself into trouble.'

126

'What do you mean?'

'What do you think I mean?' Her voice was filled with derision. She didn't really care what he thought. Still he must be told. She had to get him to agree with her plan.

'But she's only a child herself,' he blurted.

'I know.'

'Who?'

'Some boy.'

'Jesus, who is he?' He rose from the chair, his face in a fury as he opened the press where he kept the shotgun.

'No Dan, that's not the way of it.' She grabbed his arm tight.

'He'll have to marry her.' He shook her off with a growl.

'Put the gun away.'

'No. I won't allow some young fellow to destroy my daughter's life, he'll have to pay.' They struggled with the gun.

'No Dan, it isn't possible.'

'He's already married? Is that it? The bastard.' He gazed at her in horror.

'He isn't, but he's not for Faye either. Put away the gun.'

'I must talk to her.' He hurried towards the door.

'The gun.'

He stared at it.

'She won't want to talk now. She's not feeling well. Anyway, I've dealt with it.'

'No, maybe not.' He put the weapon away and sank down into the chair. 'I can't believe it, she's only seventeen.'

'She's not as innocent as we thought. Every Sunday at Mass you'd think butter wouldn't melt in her mouth. And as for confession, I'm sure she didn't tell that to the priest. Little hypocrite.'

'Was she forced?' he whispered.

'No. It appears she didn't object at all. Can you imagine? Probably enjoyed it. Although for the life of me I don't see how any woman could enjoy that.'

'We must have gone wrong somewhere,' Dan sighed.

'She's the one who went wrong. We can't take the blame.'

'We must.'

There was silence for a few seconds as Pauline thought about what she was going to say. 'This must be kept a secret. If it gets out we'll be the talk of the place, and Chris's chances will be ruined.'

'Sure it'll be bound to get out.'

'We'll make sure it doesn't. She'll stay here in the house until the baby is due. Keep her inside. We'll put the story out that she's gone to England.'

'We can't keep her inside like a prisoner,' Dan objected.

'She deserves all she's going to get. Anyway, she's far better off here than in one of those homes. I remember there was a girl in town who was expecting and it turned out that one of the maids at the house she was sent to lived in the next street. I'm not taking that chance and nearer the time we can arrange something.'

'She'll never agree. Faye's so headstrong.'

'She'll have no choice.'

'I don't like it.'

'Well, what would you suggest? Have you a better plan?' she yelled.

'I want her to rear her child in this family – our grandchild. There should be no secrets. People will accept it.

'That's not going to happen Dan, I've made up my mind.'

Chapter Twenty-six

'It's all arranged, Michael,' Pearl announced.

'What?' He cut a thick slice of Brie and ate it slowly.

'The wedding.'

'Who's wedding.'

'Eoin and Maria.'

He gasped. What was left of the cheese fell from his fingers among the chaos of broken crackers on the white plate.

Jenny put down her cup of tea. She hadn't expected Pearl to burst out with it just like that. She had thought of gently bringing Michael around. A slight nudge this way and that with a few carefully chosen words. Inching him closer to an understanding of where Pearl was coming from. But he had no idea where that was, Jenny surmised. Possibly only herself and Maureen might be the only ones in the family who know the origin of the white lace dress. She noticed too that Pearl constantly fingered the surface of the locket as if to remind herself of what it meant.

'We're having a proper ceremony in our church.'

'But you don't know who she is?' Does she know anyone we know?' he stuttered, taking a gulp of what was left of the wine in his glass. 'Who are the family? What sort of people are they?'

'I'm sure they're fine people,' she snapped, putting her eldest son back into his nursery.

'How would you know?' he gasped, his face flushed.

'Eoin brought her over to visit me and I see nothing wrong with her, she's a beautiful girl.'

Michael's focus changed. His eyes swivelled around to Jenny and his anger gathered force. But he said nothing more to his mother. It was later that night when his venom exploded.

'You know how I felt and yet you encouraged it.' His rage had reached boiling point.

'They were getting married anyway. You'd have had to face it sooner than later.' She maintained calm.

'That would never have happened.'

'Then you'd have been the loser.'

'Me?' He poked his finger into his chest. 'I never lose,' he leered into her face.

She stood there, refusing to back off. They stared at each other, protagonists. He moved closer. She turned away.

'I'm going to bed.' She left the room, closing the door quietly behind her.

'Come back here,' he roared, following quickly behind.

She walked steadily along the landing. 'Jennifer?' His footsteps echoed on the carpet.

She reached her bedroom door and went inside, closing the door in his face. Inside she stood waiting, wondering if he would come in, but nothing happened, and she sank into an armchair as all the fight waned out of her.

She took a long soak in the bath, and went to bed, wondering how to deal with this situation. She slept fitfully, but awoke again after a short time to stare into the dark, her thoughts immediately on Michael. She toyed with the idea of going into his room. But didn't. She drifted off to sleep again, but it was disturbed. Caught in weird inexplicable dreams, she was in a strange dark place. A voice called to her. Gave orders. Blue willow pattern plates waited to be placed. Bowls for soup. Cups for tea. She nuzzled a rough chin. Clung to a thin frame. Panic swirled. Ice cold water swept around her. She couldn't breathe. She went under. Choking. Up to gasp oxygen. Down again lungs bursting. She awoke with a start. Sat up to stare around, so relieved that she was in her room and not in that terrible place of fear. It was only a nightmare she reminded herself, that's all.

'Michael, let's not fight over this,' she said gently as she poured his coffee the following morning.

'I don't want to fight.' His expression was grim as he gazed at some article in the newspaper, shutting her out.

Why was it always like this? Annoyance sparkled. She was always wrong-footed.

He stood up from the table. 'I'll just say one thing. I don't want you involved in this wedding. I have no intention of attending and you won't either. I've made my mind up.' He went out through the door, closing it quietly enough, but leaving a dark storm cloud hovering over her. She wondered what form the thunder would take, and didn't have to wait long. Maureen appeared and told her that Pearl wanted to see her before she left.

But to her surprise, her mother-in-law sat up in bed surrounded with pieces of paper. She smiled at her, with eyes full of excitement and Jenny had not seen such enthusiasm in the woman for a long time. 'You're awake early.' She kissed her and patted the white head. 'And I see you've been busy.'

'I'm enjoying myself so much organising the wedding. These are the guest lists and I've been talking with Maria about the menu, the music and so many other things,' she laughed like a girl. Jenny could see how much it meant. It was a new lease of life for her. 'I've carte blanche to arrange everything. Now I want you to help Maria choose her wedding dress and trousseau. Take her to Paris. I hope it can be done in time? ' A shadow passed across her face.

'We'll manage,' Jenny smiled.

'Michael's being very obstinate,' Pearl said, picking up a sheet of paper. She peered at it short-sightedly and ticked off items.

'He's not happy.'

'He came in here last night like a bull. Said he didn't want you involved. And he won't come. And you're not allowed to either apparently,' she said crisply.

'I've got my instructions,' Jenny's laugh was wry.

'I hope you're not going to follow them.' Even though it was a question there was a certainty there. Pearl was strong. Since Jenny had come to Ballymoragh, she had never known her mother-in-law to be any different. But she wondered if she could be equally strong in the face of Michael's dominance.

'Which one do you like?' Jenny asked.

'They're all so beautiful.' Maria seemed confused as they passed each wedding dress.

'I think perhaps something very simple for you.' Jenny stopped at a white silk strapless dress. 'Like this perhaps?'

Maria nodded enthusiastically.

'Or maybe this one.'

It was cream satin with a lace overlay.

'There is too much choice.'

'Why don't you try on a couple, you can't judge just by looking.'

The sales assistant helped Maria into the first dress and it did look wonderful on her. Then she tried two or three others and suddenly it was quite obvious which suited her best. This was an ivory silk with a tucked bodice embroidered with tiny iridescent beads. The waist was tiny and the skirt flowed softly with the beads glimmering in a design at the hemline. It was beautiful and came with a studded headdress which wound through her long dark hair with sparkling beads drifting through its shining length. It was quite stunning.

'You're going to wow them at Ballymoragh.'

'I hope so.'

It was a hectic few days but Jenny really enjoyed taking Maria around Paris. With the dress ordered and veil chosen, over the next few days they went on to a succession of different salons for shoes, lingerie, and clothes for her trousseau. Pearl's instructions had to be followed to the letter and they had to phone each evening to keep her up to date with progress.

Jenny did some work while she was there and found Maria to be really interested in the business. It crossed her mind that she could fit very nicely into Venus should an opportunity occur. Jenny had no-one interested in carrying on after she had retired so Maria's arrival into the family could be timely. It would be nice to have a daughter. The unexpected thought occurred to her as she brushed her hair after taking a shower. The brush held up as she looked at herself in the mirror. She lowered her hand slowly. In the soft shadows, a child's face glowed. Perfect pale pink skin. Tiny pursed lips. Long eyelashes brushed crescent shadows. Dainty fingers curled around hers. She breathed fast. Uncomfortably fast. Her hand clenched. An unusual scent wafted into her nostrils. She was unable to determine its origin, but after a few minutes she realised it was the scent of orange. Drifting. Warm. Dozy. She went into the bedroom and sat on the bed. Her shoulders drooped as a crushing weight reminded of the loss. She gasped for air but what swept around her masqueraded as oxygen, the atmosphere dry and empty. Her throat constricted. She almost choked as she reached towards the window. Her fingers twisted catches. Turned. Left. Right. Pushed forward. Forced up. At last a tiny gap allowed some air. Just a little. But it was enough and she rested her head on her forearms able to breathe at last.

They flew down to the south to see Annabelle. Jenny was keen to introduce Maria to her business partner. She hired a car and they drove into the rolling valleys of Provence to where Annabelle lived in an eighteenth century chateau.

'This place reminds me of home,' Maria laughed.

'You must miss everyone,' Jenny said, turning a tight corner in the narrow road.

'Ah yes, I do, so much.'

She concentrated on her driving.

'Where is your own home?' Maria asked.

'Ballymoragh.'

'But before you married?'

'I was born in the west of Ireland,' Jenny said, being deliberately vague as she turned in through the gate of the chateau, and drove up the long avenue bordered with tall trees. She said no more. The old house came into view and she stopped in front, tooting the horn. They climbed out of the car.

'It's a beautiful house and the gardens are wonderful.' Maria gazed around her.

'Hello there?' Jenny called out but there was no response. They waited a few minutes. 'She was here yesterday, I phoned. Perhaps I should have mentioned we were coming down. I'll just see if her car's in the garage.' She went around the side.

'Jenny!' There was a screech from the garden.

'Anna?' Jenny rushed along one of the gravelled pathways to where Annabelle was running towards her. They embraced, swinging each other around. Laughing. Crying.

Anna kissed her on both cheeks.

'I've brought Maria, I knew you'd love to meet her.'

'Introduce me then.' They walked up through the garden, arms encircling each other, to where Maria stood watching.

Jenny made the introductions.

'Let's have a glass of wine, I'm dying to catch up with all the news.'

Anna led the way up to the patio which overlooked the magnificent gardens, the place almost overgrown with masses of plants and flowers everywhere. Even at this late stage in the year there was still some colour there. Anna loved gardening and had fallen in love with the house just before she retired. Now she couldn't be dragged out of it.

At first it was all wedding talk, then business, and then dinner. And when Maria had gone to bed, Anna and Jenny stayed up late demolishing another bottle of the delicious wine produced at her vineyard.

'Have you lost weight?' Anna enquired.

'Eh no,' Jenny hesitated, 'well, maybe a few pounds.'

'You're like a stick, and you're not in the best, I can sense it.'

'There's a lot happening at home, and Michael doesn't approve of Maria so I suppose that's enough.'

'It's odd.'

'I think so too.'

There was the sound of a car driving in, and Anna turned to listen. 'It's Guy, another surprise.' She stood up, all flowing chiffon, and rushed to meet him. Jenny's heart dropped. Guy was supposed to be in London. What a pity.

'Jenny, fancy seeing you here.' He kissed her. Looking handsome as ever in white suit and black T-shirt. His dark features were permanently suntanned and Jenny could always understand what Anna saw in him.

So another bottle of wine was opened and the night proved to be a very late one.

The following day all four of them went into Cannes for lunch and Jenny was glad to see that Maria was enjoying herself. Maybe it was the late autumn sunshine, the sea, or the atmosphere of the town, but, whatever, it did something to her. She sparkled and blossomed and Jenny began to see the real person underneath the rather shy individual she had know up to this.

'I think your idea of involving Maria in the business is excellent,' Anna said when they had a quiet moment to themselves, and Guy was taking Maria for a stroll around the town. 'She's wonderful and would be great on the PR and marketing side.'

Jenny nodded.

'What does she do at the moment?'

'Office work of some sort. Although she is a qualified engineer, she would have to go back to study again here before she could work in her field.'

'Let me talk to Guy, I'm sure he'll agree.'

Chapter Twenty-seven

David was frustrated. Since being at St. Josephs, he had tried to think of some way to find Faye, aware that most of the legitimate routes were closed to him because he wasn't related. Then he had an idea which could get him into the hospital in another guise suggesting to the lads in the group that they perform a concert for the staff and patients.

On the night, they were put in the care of a middle-aged porter and as they made their way to the recreation hall, he engaged the man in conversation.

'How long have you been here, Bert?' he asked the large stocky man, who was an affable character and easy to talk to.

'Too long,' he laughed.

'I was hoping to trace a person who was through the hospital between the end of nineteen seventy-nine and early nineteen eighty.'

'Was it a patient?'

'She may have been an outpatient, I'm not sure. Do you know if any of the nurses who would have been employed at the hospital at that time still work here?'

'Very few.'

'The name of the person I'm looking for is Faye Brophy.'

Bert pulled a small notebook from the top pocket of his navy jacket and scribbled the name.

'It would mean a great deal to me if you can find out some information, anything at all.'

'Leave it with me. As soon as I see someone I'll ask.'

They swung through the doors of the hall which was well kitted out with a stage, green velvet curtains and dark blinds on the windows. The piano had been brought over earlier in the day and their tuner was working on it as they walked in. The rest of the gear and instruments were already in position. It was a strange feeling to be here, and they laughed among themselves feeling like they were schoolboys again taking part in an end of term concert.

The place was absolutely packed, it was standing room only. Everyone enjoyed themselves, and there was more than one encore, and loud applause from the enthusiastic crowd. When they finally played the last piece, they were invited for tea and had to stay just for politeness sake.

'God forbid any of mine would have to spend time here.' Cyril bit into a slice of crunchy apple tart.

'I've known a few guys who had to be dried out,' Steve added.

'Hospitals have improved a lot over the years, they make good cakes now anyway.'

David said very little. Just being here in this place was very disturbing, but he couldn't have explained to the lads what was going through his head.

He had a progress meeting with Breda the following morning, and as usual when they had finished working their way through the agenda, he asked about Helen. Breda was the one person who was friendly with her and his only contact, indirect though that was. Women shared confidences. 'Do you know if Helen has made any progress in finding her mother?'

'Apparently she died in England.'

'What?'

'So Chris told us.'

He was taken aback, and as soon as he had an opportunity he went over to the Brophy farm. He rang the doorbell and waited impatiently outside. There was no reply. He rang again, thinking they were probably watching him from behind the curtains. A dog barked from somewhere out back. He rapped the knocker. The sound echoed loudly. Surely they must hear that. He paced up and down. The dog appeared. A black collie which jumped up on him. David rubbed his coat, then turned sharply as a click from behind told him the door had opened.

'Chris?' he smiled.

She stared at him, her face expressionless.

'I'm David Taylor.' He put out his hand. But she kept hers in the pocket of the check apron she wore. 'Could you tell me how Faye is these days?' He made it seem as if it was simply a week or two since he had met her.

'No.'

'Is she still living here?'

'No.'

'I'd like to find out what happened to her after she left school, do you think you could fill me in on a few details, or perhaps your mother?'

'Mam knows nothing.'

'But I talked to her myself.'

'When?' She was suspicious. Her face drawn, curiosity etched there.

'At the time.'

'What time?'

'When Faye was pregnant, as you probably know, I was the father of her child.'

'That child drowned.'

'No.'

'I'm telling you it did.'

'Could I come in please.' He stepped forward.

She hesitated. For the first time uncertainty was in her eyes. He saw it and was pleased. Perhaps he was getting through to her at last. Silence hung between them laden with secrets. He pushed further. Into the house where Faye had grown up, lived, ate, slept and studied and thought about him. On mornings bright with anticipation and evenings sated with the pleasures of lovemaking in their place in the

138

woods.

'Thank you.' He placed his foot on the step. He would get in now, he was determined. Into her home. To smell her aroma. Sense her spirit. A ghostly presence still there. Waiting for him. Not in London now as he had imagined. In a concrete jungle. On a fourth floor apartment somewhere. Living out her life.

The door opened wider.

He saw blue-green eyes in a pixie face. That soft pink-lipped smile welcoming him. Vibrant red hair was soft. David? Her voice echoed all around him. He reached into her loveliness. To the girl he knew. His lips clasped hers and he breathed her into him.

The large square hall was painted cream, with old photographs on the walls. A tall mahogany hallstand held one lone umbrella. The shiny lino squeaked when he stepped on it. The stairs stretched upwards and out of sight. He could imagine her footsteps on it. Her hand on the banister. But it was as if no-one lived in this house now. Empty coat hooks waited for occupation. A brown gabardine. A blazer. A schoolbag.

A circular brass knob turned. The door of the parlour was opened.

'Sit down,' she said, 'can I offer you some tea?'

'Thank you, that would be nice.' He accepted, glad of any chance to extend the visit.

The room was still. The dining-table stretched away from him. The chandelier of glass reflected in its shining surface. The chairs set around awaiting guests. The sideboard heavy with silver plate. The curtain of red velvet protected. Only a chink of light penetrated. Truth fought with lies. He stood up. Uncomfortable.

After a few minutes she brought in a tray with a cup, saucer, teapot, milk jug and sugar bowl. He sat down again. She poured weak tea silently and handed the cup to him. Thick fingers picked up the milk jug and he let her pour, just raising the cup a little when he had sufficient. The sugar bowl was proffered. He declined.

She sat down then. Hands disappeared into her lap. Her shoulders were straight. Her face once again blank. Eyes shifted nervously. He sipped a little of the tea. The cup clinked against the saucer, loud in the silence. He decided to begin first.

'Why was Faye sent to St. Josephs?'

Her mouth opened and then closed, and opened again. A fish out of water. No-one questioned Chris. 'It had nothing to do with me.' The words escaped. There was no generosity there.

'And after that where did she go?'

'England.'

'Did she ever come back?'

'No.'

'Where was she living?'

'Don't know.'

'Did she write home?' He persisted. But realised by now that it was probably a losing battle.

'No.'

'I wrote many times. Do you know if she got my letters? I phoned as well. But the phone always sounded out of order.'

'She's dead.'

'How do you know?'

'I just do.'

'I don't believe you.'

She was silent.

To fill the void he sipped more tea.

Chris never moved. Their eyes never met. They were like two opposite banks of a river. He finished the tea. The clock chimed on the hour. It was a signal. Chris rose. He did the same.

'Thank you for the tea. If you ever find out anything else or hear from her, perhaps you would let me know.' He took a card from his inside pocket and handed it to her. She turned abruptly and led the way to the front door.

'Goodbye, give my regards to your mother.' He tried to be civil to the last.

But as he turned the jeep in the yard, carelessly he almost scraped the bumper against the wall, and recalled suddenly how he had put his bicycle against the very same wall on that summer day in 1979 when he had come looking for Faye. Since his own father had reacted so badly to the news of their planned marriage, he prayed she had not told her parents about the baby yet and that they could go away together quickly. He walked across the yard where fowl scratched, cackled and strutted. A dog jumped around him, barking. This was their place and he was the interloper. He took no notice of the dog who seemed to want to play more than anything else. There was a sudden roar of a tractor engine from the barn and he glanced over his shoulder to see Faye's mother walk towards him. Pale blue eyes gazed blankly at him. Large. Flat. The floral apron was spotless. The white blouse crisp.

David's mouth opened and closed. No sound came out until finally he managed to stutter her name.

'Yes?' Her tone was sharp.

'I'm David Taylor, a friend of Faye.' He stepped a little closer. 'I said I'd call around to see her about college, is she here?'

'No, she's gone away.'

At first he was unable to grasp the import of the words, only vaguely aware that she had moved slowly around him and positioned herself between him and the house. 'But I talked to her just a few days ago.' His voice sounded very loud to him as the tractor engine cut out.

'Well, she's not here now.' She folded her arms and moved towards him, forcing him towards the gate.

Images shot through his mind. Faye smiling. Her eyes soft. Hand holding his. Laughing. Loving him. His palms felt sticky and he rubbed them against his jacket. The smooth finish of the leather reminded that he had worn it the last time he had met her. That day she had told him about their baby. Words spiralled in his mind. Angry demands were on the tip of his tongue. Tell me where she is - I want to marry her - you have no right to stop us. But no words came from his mouth. His mind hypnotised by the vacant blue pools which stared at him.

'Mrs. Brophy, I really would appreciate if you could tell me where she has gone.' He managed to utter another few words, but the pale fleshy features dissolved and the face of his father superimposed. He blanched and felt the full force of their power, draining his confidence. He was a weakling. A coward. A nothing. Fight for her. Remnants of his courage urged, but the small voice inside his head was feeble. He tried again. 'Perhaps you could tell me her phone number?'

'Wait a moment.' She turned from him and walked across the yard. His heart leapt in the hope that she was going to call Faye and that she hadn't left after all. He stared up at the windows shrouded in white lace.

Mrs. Brophy reappeared. He waited.

'I think this is yours.' She threw something to him.

He tried to catch it, but it fell on the ground and rolled along, glinting, eventually coming to a halt in a crack in the concrete. It was his ring.

'Faye?' he called out. 'Faye?' But his voice was drowned out by the sound of the tractor which had started up again. Tears stung as he hurried away, his vision blurred, heartbroken.

Now, as David drove home, he thought about himself as a boy, saddened by the fact that he had never experienced such a depth of feeling about anyone since. His phone rang.

'Yes?'

'This is Bert from St. Josephs.'

Chapter Twenty-eight

After seeing David off, Chris came back into the kitchen and stared across at Pauline who slept in the chair, her mouth slightly open, giving a little snort every now and then. What if Faye came back? The possibility of that was horrendous. She knew enough about the law to be aware that her sister would have a greater entitlement to the farm than her own son Sean. She took down his last letter and smoothed the single page. The fact that it had arrived six months before and there had been no contact since then didn't register. She read the words again. A brief summary of life in New York. He was enjoying himself. He was very busy. The weather was warm. What was it like at home? How was Gran? Must close now he wrote. She turned it over and stared at the back of the crumpled paper. As always, searching for something there. But it was blank. And told her nothing else. She kissed it and put it away in her handbag.

Then she sat back on the couch and looked at television.

'We'll have to get the cattle in, it's late,' Pauline said.

'Yea, if we had any. Don't you remember we set our land to old Corcoran? We need a man to run this place. We need Sean back,' Chris retorted.

'He'll be here any minute.'

'I wish.' She rose and took down the whiskey bottle from the top shelf of the press. She poured a generous measure.

'I'll have one as well.'

'You will?'

'You're drinking too much. It'll be the end of you.'

Chris grimaced.

'Where is Faye, she's not home from school yet. Do you think anything's happened to her?'

Chris gulped the whiskey. 'Stop going on about her, will you? Give us some peace and quiet.' She lay her head back and closed her eyes.

There was a ring on the doorbell.

'That's her now at long last.' Pauline blessed herself. 'Chris, wake up.'

There was no movement from her.

'For God's sake, she must have lost her key again.' She pushed herself up from the chair and went out into the hall. The bell rang again with loud impatient jabs. 'Who's there?' Her voice quivered but she didn't answer the door and after a moment, she returned to the kitchen and shook Chris. 'Wake up, Faye can't get in.'

Chris opened her eyes, and looked bleary-eyed at her mother. 'Wha?'

The bell rang again.

'I told you she was there,' Pauline said.

Chris rose. She patted her hair into place. 'Better not be anyone else looking for her, they can take themselves off, I've no time for this,' she muttered out loud as she ambled down the hallway and opened the front door a few inches.

'I was wondering what's up with you women, I've been out here a good ten minutes and it's a freezing night, let me in there Chris.' Old Corcoran pushed past her as he was wont to do. She stood back and he made his way into the kitchen.

'What are you doing at the front door? Is the back not good enough for you?'

'Thought I'd come in this way for a change. How're you, Pauline?' He plonked himself on the couch, dressed in an old dirty anorak, jeans and wellies, soiled from the fields.

The old woman stared blankly at him.

'Who's he?'

'That's Mr. Corcoran from next door.' Chris gave him his full title.

The old woman nodded and smiled at him. This wasn't a good day. She had swung through a number of decades in her life today, already drifting from the present back thirty years, sixty years, and into the present again when she didn't even know her neighbour.

Chris was irritated, and not interested in sitting down and making small talk with old Corcoran. He had taken it upon himself to call occasionally of an evening and sit there for a couple of hours with them, and she had decided she would have to think of some way of shifting him. She knew what he was up to. Ever since he had suggested that they might join the farms and by that inference marry, he had been calling. It was awkward. But she couldn't get rid of him without being rude. And where a neighbour was concerned she had to maintain a certain level of civility so she was caught.

They sat watching television. Corry. The news. Prime Time. Pauline was asleep, and Chris longed to have another couple of drinks but she wasn't going to open the whiskey bottle with him there, so she suffered in silence, growing more and more frustrated, wishing that he would get the hell out of the place.

'You've had a few callers lately,' he said suddenly, a sly grin on his grizzled face.

What business is it of yours? She thought, and would have liked to ask him that, but swallowed the words.

'I know the cars, one of them belongs to Breda who works at that holiday place, and the black jeep is driven by the fellow who runs it, David Taylor. What were they bothering you for?' Small dark eyes peered under bushy grey brows at her.

'Nothing.'

'Come on now Chris, they weren't here for nothing.'

'I told you.'

'If there's anything about buying the land, I want to be in first. You can't sell to them.'

'It's nothing about land.' A dull red flush slowly moved upwards from her neck into her face.

'What's it about then,' he pressed.

'It's private.'

'But what have you to do with them all of a sudden, I've never seen anyone from that place over here before.'

'Maybe you shouldn't be noticing one way or the other.'

'I've an interest here. All my efforts are put into this land. That's why I asked you to marry me, Chris.' He shifted along the couch, nearer to her armchair.

'I don't remember.' She decided to play the fool.

'It was a few weeks back.'

'I'm sure I'd remember being proposed to.'

'But don't you know why I'm coming over to see you in the evenings?' A dribble of saliva drifted down his chin, which needed a shave.

'If a man was visiting me I certainly wouldn't expect him to come wearing his wellies.' She was enjoying this now, and placed special emphasis on the word "visiting".

He looked down at his feet. 'I'm a man of the land, I don't go around in fancy clothes, I've no time for that sort of stuff.'

'Maybe that's what I want.'

'You mean to say that Taylor man?' He coughed as if a crumb had gone the wrong way down his throat. He coughed again and pulled a grimy checked handkerchief from his pocket.

She shrugged.

'Has he made an offer?'

'Now that would be telling,' she smiled.

'You're not his type.'

'How would you know.'

'Christ, that bastard wants to take over the whole place, bit by bit.' He wiped his mouth. 'And he thinks by chatting you up he'll succeed.'

She leaned back in the chair, a look of satisfaction on her face.

'Chris, don't let him try to wipe us out. We've farmed this land for generations. Our fathers and grandfathers worked their backs off trying to make a living here. We can't let their efforts be swallowed up. Our names would be dirt anyway. They'd come back and haunt us. And what would my sons do?'

She said nothing. Let him stew, she thought, and shook a cigarette out of the packet on the broad arm of the chair, and lit it with her lighter. As an afterthought she held the packet out towards Corcoran. He took one and struck a match. They smoked in silence.

When the butts were squashed into the ashtray, he picked up his cap, put it on his bald head, and stood up. 'Chris, this shouldn't happen. We'll get together and prevent him putting a foot on our land. Think about it. Give me your answer soon.' He sized her up.

Hating his scrutiny, she opened the door and saw him off.

She poured the longed-for whiskey and her insides relaxed a little. If he only knew how close he was. If her mother died and Faye came back looking for her share, the farm might have to be sold and Corcoran would get his hands on it in the end, or at least some of it. To halve the acreage would mean it wouldn't be economic to farm, and her dream of Sean coming home to turn the place into a viable entity would never happen. As for David Taylor having any interest in her or their property was so ridiculous that she laughed out loud.

Pauline jerked upwards in her chair. 'What's wrong?'

'Nothing.'

'Was someone telling a joke?'

Chris shook her head.

'I heard laughing.'

'It's no joke.' Her mouth twisted with bitterness. Ugly.

Chapter Twenty-nine

David stared across the parquet floor of the foyer at St. Josephs. A sunbeam shone through a blue pane in the window. It was beautiful. But he couldn't relax and watched people come in and out of the automatic doors wondering from which direction the woman would arrive. He had been so excited when Bert told him that one of the nurses, Una Duignam, remembered Faye, and now within seconds of meeting the only person who could talk to him about her, his heart thumped erratically and he felt so emotional he wondered would he even be able to hold a logical conversation with her.

Time passed and more than once he glanced at his watch, impatient, until finally he heard his name spoken and looked up to see a woman standing in front of him.

'Una?' She was probably around his own age, but it was hard to tell, he wasn't a good judge of age in women. She had a pleasant open smile, fair hair, and was wearing her uniform.

'It's so good of you to meet me, thank you.' He stretched out his hand and she took it.

'My pleasure.'

At first they chatted about everyday things. It broke the ice somewhat and after a while he felt at ease enough to raise the subject of Faye.

'I remember her well,' she smiled at his first diffident questions.

'She was a beautiful girl.'

He was shocked at her choice of words and must have shown that in his expression. 'Was?'

'Is, I should say, but in those days especially so, and it was such a waste for her to spend all that time here.'

'How long?'

'It was about four years.'

He ran his hand over his forehead and could feel a film of dampness on his skin. 'What was wrong with her?'

'She was admitted in a traumatised state. Very withdrawn. We couldn't get a word out of her for a long time.'

'What was the reason for that?'

'As far as I know it had something to do with the death of her father.'

'Was there any mention of a baby?'

Her eyes widened. She shook her head.

'I know she was admitted in January 1980 and she was due to have a baby around that time.'

'I never knew that,' she seemed puzzled.

He went on to tell her about Helen.

'How sad for her to lose the baby.'

'I'm sure she'd want to meet her daughter, and I would love to see her again.'

She has never mentioned you or Helen.'

'I can understand why. What happened after she left the hospital?'

'She made a new life for herself.'

'Is she happy?' Above all he wanted to know that.

'Oh yes. She's extremely happy, successful, wealthy, and has had an amazing life when you think of what happened,' Una said, smiling.

'I'm glad about that.' He twisted his hands together, and tried to hide the emotion which he hoped was not too obvious to her. 'Would you be able to ask her if she would meet Helen? For myself I wouldn't want to put any pressure on her.'

'I could ask, but I don't know what her response will be. She's married and it could be difficult, her husband and family know nothing about her past.'

'I've written a letter.' He pulled a white envelope from his inside pocket and handed it to her. 'I'll be away on tour up to Christmas, but she can contact me anytime on the phone or by email.'

Chapter Thirty

It was Christmas but the season was eclipsed by the excitement of the wedding which would be celebrated in the New Year. Pearl was in the thick of it with Jenny, and enjoying herself hugely. But Eoin wasn't happy. He knew his father was not going to attend and had forbidden Jenny to be there either, and he really resented that.

Traditionally, Jenny always decorated Ballymoragh House for Christmas, something she really enjoyed. There was a huge tree in the main hall which needed a stepladder to climb up and place all the little novelties which they had collected over the years. There was another in the drawing room and Pearl liked to have a small one in her sitting room. Beautiful garlands encircled the banisters, and were arranged around mirrors and on the mantles, and there were candles everywhere. Finally, she set up the crib on the hall table, the porcelain figures lifelike. But the best thing of all was that she cooked the Christmas dinner as Maureen always went home. This year she managed to take a few days off, and spent the time preparing the food down to the tiniest detail. She loved it. There was never any change to the menu at Christmas. Turkey, ham, spiced beef, the usual vegetables, pudding, trifle. It had been the same as long as she had lived at Ballymoragh and there would probably be no alterations while Pearl was still alive. But she could choose to do what she liked as a starter, and that gave her a challenge, cooking something entirely different each year. That it might simply have been a small ruse by Pearl to make her feel useful didn't even occur to her.

On Christmas Eve, the immediate family always had a quiet dinner in a local hotel but this year Michael opted out as some owners were over from France and he had to meet them. The main talk that evening was of the Hennessy Gold Cup at the Leopardstown meeting which began on St. Stephen's Day, but inevitably as Michael wasn't there the subject of Eoin and Maria's wedding came up.

'Has anyone got an idea as to how we could persuade Dad to attend the wedding even at this late stage?' Eoin's mood was so down it affected everyone. 'We'd really like him to be there.'

'I've tried,' Jenny said. And she had too but he had simply refused to discuss it. Everyone in the family had made an attempt, Donal, Conor, Karen and of course Pearl, but it seemed he had dug his heels in and wasn't budging.

'I feel like thumping him,' Karen exploded, 'the way I used to do when we were kids.'

'Michael is stubborn, always was. He doesn't know how to back down. He probably wants to, but can't.'

'It must be tough on you, Jenny, pig in the middle.'

'It's my fault,' Eoin murmured, 'I shouldn't have mentioned anything until it was all over, although we're already married now we still have to go through this.'

'How's Maria taking it?'

'She doesn't really know what's going on. I haven't mentioned it. But she's all excited about her "real" wedding.'

'Well, we're going to celebrate,' Donal laughed, 'champagne for everyone.' The cork on the bottle popped and the liquid bubbled over. Glasses were filled. 'Wishing you a wonderful life with Maria, Eoin.'

'And that all this fuss with Michael will have completely disappeared by the big day.' Karen added.

At that moment, Jenny's phone rang.

'No phones allowed tonight,' the others chorused.

'Sorry, but I get calls from Pearl on the half hour and if I don't answer, she loses the head. There are more things going on in her mind than we could deal with in a month. Your mother is sharp, unbelievable for eighty-seven.'

She left the table and took the call. To her surprise, it was Fergus, one of the trainers at the stud.

'Jenny, Michael isn't well, we've called for an ambulance.'

She gasped. 'What's wrong?'

'Don't know, we've used the defibrillator, oh here's the ambulance now.'

Jenny could hear the siren in the distance. 'Is he conscious?'

'No. Must go. I'll get back to you.'

'What happened to Michael?" she asked Fergus as soon as she saw him.

'We were showing the buyers around and he suddenly got a pain in his chest.'

'He shouldn't be working this late, it's no wonder he collapsed,' Karen's voice held blame.

'You know Michael, there are no office hours with him.'

They looked at Jenny and Eoin put his arm around her shoulders.

She was shocked into silence and stood there, various emotions shouting at her. Michael could die. Could be already dead.

'He'll be OK, don't worry, they do wonders these days.'

Someone held her hand.

She nodded.

A doctor came out and explained that he had had a heart attack, and they were going to operate.

'Do you want to come in for a moment?' a nurse directed her question at Jenny. 'But I have to warn you, he's already sedated.'

She nodded and followed her. 'How is he?' she found her voice at last.

'He's comfortable.'

The others were close behind. Karen the most emotional of all, faced with the possible loss of her brother.

The nurse ushered Jenny into the cubicle, and pulled the curtain behind her.

Michael lay on the trolley. He seemed asleep. His face pale and drawn. He looked much older than sixty-seven. She touched his hand. Regardless of how she felt about him now, he was still the man with whom she had shared the last twelve years. She bent and kissed his forehead.

A porter came in and pushed the trolley out of the cubicle. The family followed in a tight little group.

'How long will it take?' asked Donal.

'It's impossible to say,' the nurse replied.

'Oh Michael,' Karen wailed.

They were not allowed to go any further. They stood watching the retreating trolley and the nurse wheeling the drip. When it disappeared through a doorway, they returned to the A & E and sat in the waiting room. Quiet now.

Jenny perched on the edge of a chair like a bird. Her hands clasped around the handle of her large black Louis Vuitton bag which Michael had given her last Christmas.

Chapter Thirty-one

This Christmas David felt his aloneness acutely, the first time that had happened in many years. They were in Rio coming up to the festive season and they only managed to get home on Christmas Eve, flying in from London late in the evening. Back in Lackenmore he walked into the studio foyer, and switched on the lights, the huge Christmas tree illuminated. It was unusual to find the place so quiet. But really Christmas was the only time when they closed down. It was just for a few days admittedly but for once he loved having his home to himself. He checked the post on his desk, quickly sorting through what proved to be mostly Christmas cards, hoping that there might be a letter from Faye. But there was nothing.

It took him back years to when he had first gone to college to study music. The flat he had in Rathmines was small and compact. Living room cum kitchen with a tiny bedroom and bathroom. He didn't want to share with anyone, needing to be alone until Faye made contact which he was hoping she would. Although the only way she could do that was to send a letter to the college. He knew his father wouldn't entertain her should she call to the house. During the day he was kept busy at Trinity with lectures and tutorials. There was so much happening it kept his mind concentrated and it was only when he went back to the empty rooms that he really missed her.

He remembered how he counted down the days until he returned home for the Christmas holidays, going over to the farm the first opportunity he got. Aware that their child might already have been born.

'Is Faye here?' he asked, smiling at Chris when she opened the door.

'No, she's in England.'

'Is she expected home for Christmas?' He moved closer.

'No.'

'Do you have her address? I'd like to write.'

The door was closed over a few inches. He could only see half of her face.

He pulled a package from his pocket. It was a present of a silk scarf for Faye. 'Would you give this to her please? Perhaps you'll be sending something over. I'd like her to have it even if it's late.' Deliberately he hadn't mentioned anything about the baby. Faye may have gone away secretly and told no one.

'All right,' she agreed, ungracious, took it from him and shut the door.

He remembered writing a letter which he hid in their secret mailbox behind a loose brick under the bridge, and sitting there pensively for a while, finally giving up and going home. He went back to college in the New Year, less confident that he would ever see her again. Perhaps she was already married to someone else. A stranger held their child in his arms, and he or she called him Daddy. Pain cut through him, and it was difficult for him to come to terms with the loss of the woman he loved, and the child he never knew.

His college experience was in many senses a blur. Friends, work, exams, coalesced. He remembered certain isolated events, but as time passed Faye and their baby drifted further and further away from him, stretching back into the past like a ribbon which floated in the wind. He longed to draw her with him into the present. Talk to her. Touch. Kiss. Know her again. But his hands were empty. His heart empty. Faye had been the centre of his life and for a long time part of him always waited to hear from her in the same way as he did now.

He wandered around his home. It had been built in the eighteen hundreds and he had had it refurbished in its original style. Even now he could hear echoes of the voices of his mother and father, his grandparents, aunts and uncles. He knew his father wouldn't have agreed with the establishment of Taylor Studios, or the marina development. He never approved of anything his son did.

David went down into the cellar to choose the wines for the Christmas morning drinks party he always held. The dark musty space was cool, and held an interesting collection. On the racks, bottles were covered with dust, the year hardly legible on many labels and now he wondered if anyone would ever even taste the wine, his enjoyment in picking up certain special years was purely a financial investment. He placed his chosen bottles on a trolley and took the lift back up to the kitchen. The company who did the catering for the studios had left a selection of finger food in the freezer and he only had to take it out. The tables were set with china and glasses and goody bags for everyone. It was the one day in the year when he entertained his guests personally. He wouldn't ask anyone to work during the Christmas holidays.

Everything done, he poured himself a glass of wine and went back to his own apartment. Piled up on the dining table were gifts for all his close friends he would see tomorrow. Most of them he had bought himself, the older kids received money which was all they wanted, and he had to ask his secretary to purchase a couple of the younger kids' toys. But he got a lot of pleasure parcelling and labelling, particularly when he came to Helen's. While he would have loved to give her something really special, jewellery perhaps, and had wanted to do the same for her birthday, he knew that such personal gifts would have to wait for another day. So he had given her a bottle of perfume, the same as he was giving Breda.

At about twelve the next day, people started to arrive. The place was packed, and the guests helped themselves to food and he was kept busy serving drinks. To his disappointment, Helen had gone to Dublin to her aunt and uncle, and he gave her present to Breda.

'She'll be delighted. And thanks a mill for mine, you always choose something really nice.' She kissed him. 'Now, can I go around and top up the drinks?'

Together, they kept things going, making sure no-one had an

empty glass. It was an enjoyable few hours, and by four everyone had gone. He dropped Breda back to her family home in the town on his way over to Steve's where he was always invited to dinner.

Arriving in the door with his bag of gifts, he was rushed by the kids.

'Uncle Dave, have you got presents for us?' The four year old threw his arms around his legs, followed by the three year old girl, and their cousins who were always there too.

'These have to go under the Christmas tree, Santa told me that.'

'But Santa came and he ate his pudding, and we heard Rudolph on the roof.'

'These presents fell off the sleigh and Santa asked me to give them to you.'

The kids jumped around him.

'Now, we'll put these extra presents under the tree until later.' Suzanne appeared, hugged him, and wished him a Happy Christmas.

'We want them now,' they screamed with excitement.

'It's been like this all morning.' Steve stood grinning at them, a glass of whiskey in his hand.

David was dragged into the lounge and forced to empty the bag of gifts.

The kids had great fun feeling each parcel, and trying to decide what it contained.

'Too much as usual, Dave, far too generous, but thank you,' Suzanne said as she watched the children begin to tear open the paper and giggle with anticipation when they found whatever was inside.

He got up from his knees. 'You know how much I enjoy them,' he grinned.

'You're lucky you can walk away.'

'I'd love to have them all the time, they're great kids.'

'Have a drink man, you'll need it. I'm worn out already.' Steve handed him a glass of whiskey.

'I'll drop them all over to you first thing tomorrow morning, you don't mind getting up at six I presume?' Suzanne grinned.

'Before you decide whether you'll be in a fit state to get up that

157

early come in and keep me company in the kitchen.' Steve was doing the cooking today for the large crowd invited.

They took their time over the delicious dinner, taking a break between courses so the meal lasted long into the night with interesting conversation and much laughter. Later, the music started and continued into the small hours, ending up with rowdy singing at some ungodly hour.

On St. Stephen's Day he was invited to Joe and Mary's, which was a repeat of the day before. Their children were teenagers, so it was cash in an envelope which was accepted with much delight, and they sidled out of sight as soon as the dinner was finished leaving the adults to themselves. But today David's mood was low. He received a few texts on his phone, and when he checked them some mad side of him expected to hear something from Faye. Just because it was Christmas. He had to make a supreme effort to hide his feelings from his friends, particularly Mary. But he didn't quite succeed and she cornered him later in the evening, and insisted that he sit beside her.

'You're not feeling the best, are you?' The expression in her blue eyes was shrewd.

'Tired I suppose, we've been busy. Maybe I'm not up to the touring any longer,' he smiled.

'What's up, Dave, you've been very down for months now, and while I've resisted saying anything up to now, I feel I must.'

'I suppose my life has proven to be a bit empty recently, I haven't met the right woman yet,' he grinned.

'You know lots of gorgeous women, and what about Vanessa, she's really something.'

'Vanessa is too much for me.'

'She'd whip you into shape.'

'Don't remind me, I live in dread of it.'

'That's what you need.'

He was very tempted to unburden himself to Mary. She was a lovely sympathetic woman and he was sure if he told her about Faye that she would have some very wise advice. But it wasn't the right time now, so he said nothing.

He stayed away from the marina, in dread of coming face to face with Helen again. His emotions so stirred now he felt sure that she would notice something different about him. Certainly he would be very much aware of the way she looked at him. How she smiled, or said something in that sharp Australian accent. He liked her voice and tone of phrase. It was musical and her sense of humour bubbled over at the slightest.

As it was quiet at the studios, he took the chance to travel to Italy for a few days. It was a while since he had been in Montepulciano and he felt the solitude of the place would help him sort out the confusion which dominated his thinking these days. His apartment was in an old house in one of those narrow cobbled medieval streets. The weather was cold and there was snow in the mountains. He spent his time walking and climbing. Long tough hikes which put him under extreme pressure. The air was sharp, the sky blue and the occasional bursts of sunshine were warm during the day. The beauty of the place healed and his heart ceased its mad rushing and calmed somewhat. His Italian friends made him very welcome, and he enjoyed their company when he got back from his day's walk, sharing a bottle of wine and dinner with the large extended family.

But he still couldn't forget Faye. She was there all the time and he remembered so much about the early days when they had first fallen in love. The excitement of their secret meetings. Those first tentative movements towards each other. Of fingers touching unfamiliar places, lips softly joining, hesitant explorations of tongues, kisses which developed into something so sensual it had to be satisfied. Although it was a slow build up over many weeks when they finally overcame their fear they entered into a new world and could never go back to the girl and boy they once were.

Chapter Thirty-two

Eoin and Maria's wedding went ahead in the New Year, and with Michael still in hospital the cloud which had hovered over the celebrations lifted somewhat, although everyone in the family was still worried about him. Jenny went to the hospital each evening, and even did so on that day, but she made no mention of the ceremony. Although he probably knew it was happening today he said nothing either. He was making a good recovery and was hoping to be discharged soon.

Knowing she would be tied to the house when Michael came home Jenny arranged to meet Una. She hadn't seen her in a while and was looking forward to a relaxed few hours with her old friend.

'I'd love you to see some of the designers we carry, so let's go into our store in Grafton Street, there's some lovely gear in at the minute,' Jenny said as they walked along St. Stephen's Green.

'I've passed by this shop many a time over the years but never went in, I suppose I felt I might put you into a difficult situation if you happened to be there, and anyway the clothes were always a bit out of my league,' Una laughed, 'upmarket cocktail wear, not everyday wear for a nurse.'

'I wish you had called in, I'd have loved to see you, I blame myself for not keeping in touch.' Jenny felt guilty.

'We'll make up for it now.'

They stood outside the shop. 'What do you think of the window display?' Jenny asked.

There was just one item. A two piece in a beautiful shade of aubergine, with velvet trim and matching accessories.

'It's lovely. But what price is it?' Una leaned down to see the figure printed on a small card.

'That doesn't matter, come on in.' Inside, the two assistants immediately came over, and she introduced her friend. 'We're just shoppers today, girls, no business to be discussed.'

They spent quite a time looking through the clothes and even Jenny tried on a few outfits, although she didn't choose anything. Besides she wanted her friend to enjoy the experience.

'Reminds me of the old days,' she murmured, slipped on a vibrant turquoise jacket, and stood in front of the mirror.

'Had you something like this?'

'No, but I remember that you did.'

Jenny looked at her, puzzled.

'It was one of the first things we bought, and you wore a tartan kilt, it looked great on you.'

She was taken aback. Suddenly reminded of the time when Una helped her step out into the world for the first time. Bringing her to live in her home in Galway, buying her a complete wardrobe of clothes, and then helping her to find that first job in Venus.

'You gave me a life. I can never thank you enough for that,' she smiled and kissed her quickly on the cheek.

There was an empathy between them. An unusual closeness which was almost spiritual, as if they were sisters.

'I have to have this jacket, it's fab.'

'And why don't you try the dress?' Jenny took it off the hanger and handed it to her. It was navy with turquoise detail and the cut suited her figure well. With matching shoes and handbag the outfit was really nice.

'I'll need my glasses to see the prices, the print is so tiny,' she said, anxiously staring at the label.

'Stop worrying about prices.'

'But I must, my whole salary could be swallowed up next month.'

'This is between you and me, and we'll sort it later.'

'We'd better,' she warned.

'Now let's look at the cocktail wear.' Jenny flicked through the dresses. 'Do you like black? How about this?'

'A little black number,' Una giggled.

'A must have.'

The girl wrapped the outfits in tissue and put them in bags.

'I'll have to pay you.'

'The clothes are a gift, Una, I've never given you anything much, I want to do this.'

'Yes you have, what about all the presents you gave me? Not to mention all the weekends away, lunches and dinners you treated me to in the old days. I can't accept it.'

'We're not going to talk about it anymore. Let me do this little thing for you. Please?' Jenny kissed her.

They had an early lunch in Fitzers and caught up with what had been happening in their lives.

'I'm glad to hear Michael made a good recovery from his bypass.'

'He's a bad patient though, can't wait to get back to his horses.'

'I'm sure you're glad to have him home, but warn him that he'll have to take it easy.'

'That's going to be the hard part.'

It was just after Una had paid the bill – she insisted on that – her tone changed. 'There's something else I want to say to you.'

Jenny waited.

'I don't know whether you'll be pleased or not, but I've promised someone that I would talk to you.'

'Who is it?'

'A person you haven't met in a long time.'

'Where did you meet him or is it a her?' Jenny was curious.

'He looked me up.'

'He?'

'Apparently he knew you when you were at school, and he asked me to give you a letter.' Una took a white envelope from her bag and handed it to Jenny.

A few days later, Michael came home from hospital and as she had expected, he was proving to be a very bad patient.

'I'm waiting to go for my walk, you're late.' He attacked the minute she arrived home from work, although she had taken a half-day to be here by three o'clock.

'I won't be a minute, I've just got to change. How are you feeling?'

He grimaced. It was a don't ask question. There were many of those peppered through the day and night. Cow pats on which she almost stepped. So she said as little as possible keeping her remarks to the simplest few words, hoping not to be misconstrued. But still a twist could be put on them.

'Can I get you anything before we go?' she asked.

He shook his head, and glanced at his watch. 'Just get ready.'

To her surprise, she was actually enjoying their walks. Bringing work home to accommodate the afternoon forays down by the gallops to watch the horses train. He had been instructed by the surgeon to take a certain amount of brisk exercise without fail each day. They were silent at first, watching the jockeys ride past.

'Where was I when I had the heart attack?' he asked suddenly, 'I can't remember. Did you bring me to hospital or was I in an ambulance?'

'You were with Fergus and he rang the medics.'

He nodded and said no more.

As they followed the path, Jenny stared at another group of horses which came into view. She would have given anything to feel Michael's hand take hers, but they were tucked into his pockets, and she felt he wouldn't appreciate her hand curling around his. She thought of how long it had been since they had walked together arm in arm and was saddened. Now she was expected to do whatever was demanded without demur. It was as if they were an old couple. No showing of intimacy or love between them.

The horses gathered speed and their hooves battered the ground the rumble growing in intensity as they came upon them, thundering so loud that Jenny stepped back nervously. Suddenly remembering another time when noise frightened. A time when she didn't know where she was. Who she was. All memory expunged in a distorted dream world of non-existence. In this place she stared at a dark square. A strange face looked back at her. She reached forward and put out a trembling hand and the person did the same, but the fingers which touched hers were icy cold. She drew back in fear, repelled, unable to articulate or communicate her feelings in any way to those around her. In the large room, the once white walls, stained with greenish patches of dampness, reared high above her. Sunshine poured through the top section of the window, the bright blue sky honeycombed by black bars which threw a trellis of shadow across the wooden floor. Everything frightened her, particularly the other women. Some spent their time staring at an old flickering television set in the corner of the room. Others swayed back and forwards unaware of where they were, many stared unseeing, almost comatose. All the time the clamour of voices rose and fell, rose and fell, and the noise deafened.

It was terrifying and Jenny's stomach churned as she was suddenly brought back to the present as a jeep driven by the trainer Fergus stopped beside them.

'Sweet Meadow's looking well,' Michael commented when they climbed into the jeep. Fergus drove along, following the horse which was galloping alongside, checking the time on a stopwatch and talking on radio to the jockey.

'That injury has healed up well, she should be ready for Leopardstown,' he said.

'I'm glad of that, her form is good, I'd hate to lose her.'

'No fear.'

'Hope so.'

'You haven't been riding Swift Eagle lately, Jenny,' Fergus said.

'No, since Michael came home from hospital I haven't had the time,' she patted his shoulder.

'Plenty of tender loving care, eh?' Fergus grinned.

'Yea,' Michael said, and glanced around at her. 'Why don't you take him out tomorrow?' he suggested.

It did her good to feel the wind whirling past. The rhythm of the horse beneath her. Cantering. Galloping. Across the meadows. Through the green woods. Dodging low branches. Sweeping into a clearing of fallen leaves. The horse jumping, his surefootedness clearing unexpected obstacles. It took her mind away from the things which had bothered her lately. Yesterday, those strange thoughts which came into her mind as she watched the horses had frightened her and she was glad now that she could put them out of her head. It was all a nothing. A meaningless jumble of nothing.

But to her surprise that evening Michael informed her that he was going back to work the following day.

'But isn't it a bit too soon? You've only been home for about two weeks.'

'Not for me. I'm bored witless and I need to be doing something.'

'Why don't you ask your consultant?'

'I have an appointment arranged in a couple of weeks, but in the meantime I have to get out of here. Mother drives me mad. On and on. And I'm much better than I was. You can see that. I need to be down there in the thick of things. Back to normal.'

'But I thought we might take a holiday before you go back, a nice leisurely break, perhaps down at Annabelle's place in France?'

'That wouldn't be much different to here. I suppose it would be a bit warmer but I'd be doing nothing. I can't stick that, you know how I am,' he snapped.

'We could go somewhere else. I want to spend some time with you, we need that. A romantic few days would be wonderful, how about Venice, we've always loved it.' She put her arm around his shoulder.

'For God's sake Jennifer, we're past all that stuff, romantic I ask you.' He shrugged her off.

So he did what he wanted, as usual, and life returned to normal for her too.

She was kept very busy travelling to see various fashion houses all over Europe ordering their collection for the following year. She didn't have to try very hard to put her devious thoughts out of her head while she was abroad, but once she was back home it was another thing altogether and they rushed back to torment her.

The letter had been pushed into the handbag she had with her that day she met Una. She hadn't wanted to open it. Reluctant to take a step into the past which was a vague shadowy place which terrorised. That particular handbag wasn't used often and she hoped that she would easily forget the letter. But that didn't happen. She thought about it too often, like it was someone who lived far away and she hadn't been in touch. But continuing to do nothing, guilt stalked in unexpected moments and lay siege. The demarcation line constantly shifted. Will I, won't I, will I?

'Why don't we sleep together in my room, I worry about you all alone.' She put her hand on Michael's.

'I snore,' he grunted.

'I don't mind,'

'I'm used to my own room, I've slept in there my whole life. Wouldn't get a decent wink in your perfumed boudoir,' he grinned.

'Come on, my love, just for tonight.' She kissed him, needing to be closer. Her resolution this New Year had been to make things better. Must try harder. She told herself constantly. Must make our marriage work.

'How did you get on in London?'

She was disappointed at his rejection, and surprised at his reference to the fact that she had returned from London today. He never took any interest in her business.

'We discovered who was stealing.'

'How did that happen?'

'We put in a private detective.'

'How bad was it?'

'By the time we caught her it was up to six figures.'

'You must be losing your touch,' he grinned.

'Me?'

'Don't get all prickly, I'm only joking. But the manager in that branch has a lot to answer for.'

'It was the manager.'

'Sure that it was confined to the one branch?'

'No, it's going to be difficult to ascertain whether she had any accomplices. We're checking all the shops, and the police are involved.'

'You'll have to keep an eye on things, I always felt you had expanded far too quickly. Once you take your finger off the pulse it can go out of control.'

'Guy deals with the UK, but I had to get more involved because of this.'

'Fancy name Guy - always thought he was a bit camp,' he laughed throatily.

'It's just his way.'

'He's much too young for Annabelle, more your style.'

'Not my type,' she smiled. They sat in front of the fire together and Jenny was glad Michael seemed in good form. They hadn't talked like this in a long time.

'What's he like to work?'

'All right. I try to keep out of his way.'

'Dimwit I'd say, any other ventures he's been involved in have failed miserably.'

'Where did you hear that?' It was a snap. She regretted it because she could immediately sense his hackles rise.

'What does it matter who told me. It's something you need to know.'

'I knew he had been involved in other businesses.' She was defensive.

'But you didn't know he lost a fortune in the process.'

'I can't do anything about it. He has a twenty-five percent share of the company.'

'I'd advise you to keep your eyes on him.'

'I do.'

'You're naive, Jenny.'

'I'm not,' she argued, although she didn't want to.

'Your head is in the clouds lately, I don't know where you are half the time.'

'I'm here.'

'Yea?' The word was sarcasm-coated.

'Of course I am.'

'Could have fooled me.'

'I'm sorry.' She couldn't explain how she felt. Did he think she was having an affair? 'I want to be with you as much as I can, but it's hard sometimes, I'm out there on the periphery of things, and when I suggest we do something together you never seem to have the time,' she smiled, trying to hide the accusation in her words.

'Maybe we don't want the same things anymore.'

She was shocked, and knew what she wanted to ask him, but didn't know if she had the courage.

He picked up the remote and changed the television channel.

'Do you still want to be married to me?'

'Don't be ridiculous,' he laughed.

'I need to know.'

'Sure what would I do without you?'

The phone rang. It was the stable manager asking him to come down to have a look at one of the horses. She wanted to continue talking, anxious to be reassured, and was annoyed at the interruption. He wasn't interested. Horses always came first.

But when the door closed behind him, her annoyance slowly diminished and disappointment took its place. She never felt quite the same again, and gave up trying to coax him around. Whatever they felt for each other, it wasn't love.

Chapter Thirty-three

'Another round?' Peter asked with a smile.

Helen and he were an item now. They were inseparable. He went through the crowd to the bar. Breda had been persuaded to join them for an evening out, and they had started the night in one of the pubs in Lackenmore, a taxi booked to take them home much later.

'Have to say Peter's improved, he's a different guy, I've never seen him so loving,' Breda said.

'He's great.' Helen glanced over towards the bar to see his figure standing among the crowd there.

'Maybe he needed someone different. He'd gone through all the local talent and was probably bored to tears. You've shook him up.'

'I'm used to dealing with the Australian men, have to keep them on a tight rein.'

'I'm sorry I mentioned that he might be related to you,' Breda was contrite, 'the chances are miniscule I suppose, the more I thought about it, the worse I felt.'

'Don't worry, I've decided not to go there. I'll take my chances I reckon.'

'It's good to see you so happy.'

'I am.'

'You'll be moving in with him next.'

'That won't be happening just yet.'

'It's probably the most sensible thing to do.'

'When I make that decision I'll be one hundred percent sure and I'll know when the time is right.'

'It's a difficult one since home is so far away, you might never go back.'

Helen thought of her Dad and a wave of nostalgia swept through her. So taken up with Peter and her genealogy work, Australia had drifted way out there, although she phoned and emailed regularly, suddenly she would have given anything to put her arms around her father and hug him tight.

'Here we are.' Peter returned and put the drinks on the table.

'Cheers.' Breda raised her glass.

'Where are we off to next?'

'How about that new club?'

It was a large place on several floors and was packed with people at that time on a Saturday night. The lighting was soft and the place throbbed with energy.

'This is great, isn't it?' Breda grinned, 'haven't been out in ages.'

'Imagine finding a place like this in a small town.' Helen gazed around, loving it.

'Let's dance, girls.' Peter swept them on to the floor and they joined the crowd moving to the music, twisting, turning, hands waving in the air, carried away with the fun of it all.

'We'll have to come here again, it's fantastic,' Breda giggled, taking a gulp of her gin and tonic. 'Hey, look who's over there.' There was a broad smile on her face. 'Imagine that, wouldn't have thought this would be his cup of tea.'

'Who?' Peter asked.

'David.'

'Oh yea, I noticed. He's with that group of musicians who were recording today, you know them, Inflections, they've made it big, number one.'

'I'd love to meet them,' Breda grinned, eyes wide and excited. 'I'm going over, now's my chance, are you coming?'

'No, I'm not fussed.' Helen shook her head.

'Come on, you'll never get the opportunity again.'

'You go ahead, Breda.'

She made her way through the tables.

'I thought you'd be keen to meet them as well,' Peter smiled and took her hand.

'No, I'd much rather be here with you, gives us a chance to be alone for a few minutes.' She kissed him.

'It's difficult with a third person here, I can't do what I want with you, frustrating.' He returned her kiss. But they were interrupted by David who invited them to join him.

'Well, we ...' Peter hesitated.

'We were just about to dance,' Helen added, standing up.

'Come over afterwards for a drink.'

It was a slow number, and they moved close together.

'He's still there,' Peter said.

'What do you mean?'

'David. I can't believe it, he's watching us.'

Helen glanced around but couldn't see him. 'Wish you hadn't said that, you have me all self-conscious.'

'Forget about him, babe,' he whispered in her ear.

She clung tightly to him.

After they had danced to a few numbers, Peter felt obliged to go over and join the other group where Breda was already enjoying herself hugely. They were welcomed by David and introduced to everyone.

'I believe you are kept very busy chasing all over the west searching up people's families?' He turned to Helen.

'Yea.' She felt shy.

'There's a lot of interest in genealogy, have you made any enquiries into your own family?'

'No, not yet.'

'Maybe I'll get you to research my own,' he smiled.

She felt immediately under pressure. She searched frantically for an excuse. 'I don't know when I could fit you in, I've an awful lot of enquiries to deal with first.'

'No problem, whenever. In the meantime I'll look up some information, there's a lot of old documents at the house so it will

171

give us a basis from which to work.'

The word "us" did something to her, and she looked around for Peter who was in deep conversation with the drummer in the group further along the bar.

David sipped his glass of beer. She stood there, nursing her lager, feeling awkward.

'Helen?' Peter waved.

'I'd better go over,' she murmured, 'see you.'

Peter took her hand. 'How are you, love?' He bent down and kissed her.

'I'm tired, could we go?'

'We won't stay that much longer.'

'Soon?'

'Helen, don't be a killjoy.' Irritation flashed across his face.

'I'm not.'

'You are,' he grinned then, put his arm around her shoulders and hugged.

'I need some fresh air, I'll see you later.'

'No, I want you here.' He tightened his grip, and his lips pressed hard against her cheek.

'My head aches.'

'Get a coffee or something,' he burst out laughing at a remark passed by the man beside him.

'I'm going.' She pulled from his grasp and pushed through the crowd, almost bumping into David.

'Are you leaving already?' he asked.

'Yes.' She tried to move past him.

'Is Peter?'

'No.'

'Let me drive you back.'

'It's all right, I'll take a cab.'

'At this hour of the night around here you could wait a long time.'

'I'm sure I won't have that much trouble.' She continued out of the club and stood outside. It was chilly and her arms hugged her body as she peered along the empty street.

David followed. 'I'll wait with you.'

'It's all right, you don't have to worry about me.' He was receiving the brunt of her annoyance with Peter.

'You can't stand out here alone.'

She walked away from him.

'Helen?' Peter appeared through the door.

'I told you I wasn't feeling well.'

'But you didn't say you were leaving with him.'

The cumulative effect of the amount of drink he had consumed was obvious.

'I didn't ask him to come out here with me.'

'What's going on?' He faced David, belligerent.

'Peter, I was concerned that Helen was leaving alone and I decided to wait until she got a taxi,' David explained.

'A likely story,' he sneered.

'I'll go, goodnight Helen.' David went back inside.

'Did he make a pass at you?' Peter demanded.

'Don't be ridiculous,' Helen snapped.

'I know he fancies you. I've seen him looking at you. I don't like him. Never liked him,' he muttered.

'You're imagining things.' She wondered in the back of her mind if there was a grain of truth in his accusation.

'No, I'm not, I'm going to have it out with him.'

'Let's tell Breda we're going.'

'Do you love me?' He swung her around by the shoulders until she faced him.

'Of course I do, you know that.'

He pulled her close and kissed her.

Chapter Thirty-four

For David the New Year brought the astonishing news that he had been nominated for an Academy Award. The film was entitled "Snow Blind" and he had composed the music. He had written a number of other scores over the years but this honour was something he could never have imagined and it helped chase away the gloom which had cast a shadow over his life lately.

The guys in the group, and their wives accompanied him to LA. Although they didn't have tickets to the main event, they accepted every invitation they received. On the night in question they crowded into the pre-ceremony reception, delighted to be sharing this night with David.

A journalist with a microphone and a television cameraman pushed their way through the crowd. 'David, are you feeling confident? Do you think there's a chance of winning all those awards?'

'As good as anyone else here,' he grinned.

'How's the film doing at the box office?'

'Here in the States it's broken all records.'

'Let's hope you'll sweep the boards.'

Joe raised his glass of champagne.

'Best of luck!' The others joined in the toast.

'Hey, I haven't got it yet,' David laughed.

'Here's Hal and Ronnie.'

The producer and director arrived with their wives, and some of the other people involved, all in great form as the film had been nominated for nine Academy Awards.

It was Cyril who first spotted Vanessa, a vision in a dramatic red gown.

'Darling.' She threw her arms around David and pressed her lips on his.

He returned the kiss lightly, he had no other choice.

'Guys, it's so good to see you all again.' She embraced each of them in turn with much air kissing and expressions of delight, while completely ignoring the women.

'Wow, that's some welcome,' Cyril laughed.

'David, you've been very cruel, no calls or texts or mails, I'm heartbroken,' she pouted.

'I'm sorry,' he smiled, a little embarrassed.

'Vanessa?' A young man pushed his way through holding two glasses of champagne.

'Josh, meet my Irish friends, David, Joe, Cyril, and Stevie – everyone knows Josh.'

They nodded.

The man was known to them all. One of that top coterie of actors who earned millions from every film they made.

'Josh has been nominated for Best Actor in "Tell me you need it", so we're keeping our fingers crossed.'

'David's been nominated for the music in "Snow Blind", Mary mentioned quietly.

Vanessa beamed. 'Two of my men win Oscars – what a headline.'

Josh looked at David over the rim of his glass – a cold calculating look in his eyes.

David was aware that he had immediately been viewed as a rival. If the man only knew the truth of it, he thought.

'Darlings, it's going to be a wonderful night. Come on, it's starting.'

He let them go ahead and continued talking for a while, leaving it to the last to go in with Hal, Ronnie, the lead actors and others involved. The huge auditorium glimmered with lights, and was crowded with well-known people in the profession, millions of dollars in the designer clothes worn by the guests. On the stage, a succession of very famous beautiful women and handsome men introduced the various films, and as the ceremony rolled on the anticipation was palpable. David had never been at the Oscar ceremony before and to be right there in the thick of it was a great experience. The film received the first six Oscars for which they had been nominated, and there was euphoria among the cast. He congratulated the others as they made their way to the stage, but unexpectedly he felt strangely out of it. He would have loved to have Helen here with him to share in this wonderful night, probably the pinnacle of his career to date. He had glimpsed red hair more than once and even here couldn't get the images of Faye and Helen out of his head.

'You're next,' Hal grinned, 'let's make it seven.'

David's fingers tightened.

'And now the nominations for Best Film Score.' The applause was deafening. He didn't really hear the words spoken and all the scores merged and when his own sounded - last of all – he hardly recognised it. 'And the Oscar ...' There was a tense waiting silence. 'Goes - to David Taylor for Snow Blind.'

The film won all nine Oscars, and it was a night of celebration. There were radio and television interviews, press photographers pushing for positions to take shots, asking him the same questions over and over. It was a crazy melee. At the party which followed, Vanessa appeared early on and made a beeline for them without Josh in tow this time.

'David, congratulations, it's wonderful.' She was excited, and gazed with wide blue eyes at the crowd of people around them. While he would have preferred if she had gone off with her actor friend - who it transpired hadn't won an Award - she didn't do that, and clung possessively to him. He tried to move away on a couple of occasions when she fell into conversation with someone else but it wasn't long before he felt her fingers on his arm again. He was becoming irritated with her, having assumed that over the last few months she had lost interest.

'Let's dance?' She took his hand.

'You know I'm not much of a dancer.'

'Come on,' she coaxed.

'I'm sorry but let's leave it until later.' He really didn't want to crowd on to the dance floor, it wasn't his scene, and he was more interested in talking to the people around him.

'Then let's slip away,' she murmured close to his ear, 'for a few minutes, just to be on our own.'

He pretended he hadn't heard and replied to someone who had asked him a question about another score on which he was working.

'Maybe we'll be here again next year.' The producer, a wealthy businessman, raised his glass. 'Cheers.'

'Darling?' She clung closer.

'I can't leave just yet.' He did his best to placate her, and certainly didn't want an altercation with Josh should he arrive.

'Come on,' she urged.

'I'm sorry, but I want to talk to these people,'

'You are so mean to me,' she sulked.

'I'm sorry but these are important contacts.'

'How dare you!' she shouted.

He looked at her, puzzled.

'I offer to spend some time with you and all you can do is refuse, preferring to talk to other people. Who do you think you are, no-one refuses me,' she glared at him, and raised her hand as if to strike him.

'Vanessa, please.'

'Hey, what's going on here?' Steve intervened.

She lowered her hand, and rushed away through the crowd.

'It's nothing,' David said, praying that not too many people overheard. 'She had too much to drink.'

'Too much cocaine more like.'

David didn't reply. He wasn't sure whether Vanessa used, but it was easily available and nothing out of the ordinary in LA.

'Let's have another drink, we don't need to drive home tonight.

But I've had enough champagne, I need something with a bit of a kick in it,' Joe said, 'I'm going to the bar, can I get anything for you lot?'

A few orders were called out as he left.

'She's some tigress,' Steve grinned.

'With a hell of a short fuse.'

'What did you say to her anyway, must have been something to receive that sort of reaction,' Phil grinned.

'She wanted to go back to her hotel, and I didn't,' David smiled, able to laugh at it now.

'Wouldn't have minded going back with her, don't think I'd have said no,' Steve knocked back the rest of his champagne.

'Don't let Suzanne hear that,' someone warned.

'I mean if I was his nibs here,' he laughed, 'how can you resist her?'

'She's not your type is she, Dave?' Mary asked.

'What is your type man?'

'That gorgeous leggy one he met in Paris, remember that, he couldn't keep his eyes off her.'

'Or the Italian, Juliana whatshername.'

'He's had too much choice that's his problem,' Phil teased.

'You're probably right. Why didn't I meet someone like Mary or Phil here?' He put his arms around the two of them.

'Well, we love you anyway, don't we, Phil?' Mary hugged. 'We'll always be there for you.'

They laughed.

'We're working on another script at the moment,' Hal said, 'and I'd like to talk to you about it. Can we meet while you're here?'

'I'd be very interested.' He was excited, the opportunity to be involved in another film project would be a challenge.

'I'll give you a call in the morning and we can set up a meeting.'

'Here we are.' Joe reappeared with the drinks and David swallowed the whiskey, the kick of the alcohol settling his stomach which had been in turmoil all evening. He was glad Vanessa had left, hoping that she would be so angry with him that she might never make contact again.

'No sign of the vixen, I'm sure you're glad to see the back of that mad woman,' Cyril said.

'Better off without her,' Mary grinned.

He smiled ruefully. Was Faye to be the only woman he ever truly loved. Would he spend the rest of his life searching for someone as beautiful as she?

Chapter Thirty-five

Jenny had had a tough morning, travelling to a few of the outlets, anxious to see for herself how business was going in these days of recession. The turnover was down, and she hoped that it wouldn't be necessary to let some of the staff go. They were all immensely valuable sales people and vital to the success of the Venus Group. She had taken the managers to lunch, which was something she did regularly, enjoying their company and making a point to avoid any discussion about business. But at the meeting afterwards, unfortunately there had to be some serious words about the sales figures, targets were lowered, and promotions examined.

When she arrived home, she continued working, but finally put aside the laptop, deciding that she would have to talk with their accountant in the morning. Difficult decisions would have to be made and she wasn't looking forward to it. She glanced at her watch, and hoped that Michael wouldn't be too late. He had gone out earlier to meet a client, and she knew he expected her to be still up when he came back, although she would have preferred to go to bed. She picked up the newspaper but didn't really take in what was written there. It was the name mentioned by the newsreader on the television which caused her to straighten up, eyes wide, back taut, her pulse hammering fast, and stare at the screen. He hadn't actually changed that much, being a little thinner perhaps, the longer hair replaced by a more fashionable tight cut. But it was still David. Her hands clasped, hot, and the newspaper in her lap crinkled as she leaned forward.

The door opened, banged closed and Michael flopped down into an armchair.

She didn't say anything.

'Do you want a coffee? I'm hungry, wouldn't mind a snack.' He asked the question first. It was his way. Michael was useless in the kitchen. Couldn't boil an egg. Never had to. Someone like Maureen always there to run after him and supply his every need.

She stared at the TV screen. David had won an Oscar for his music.

'What are you looking at?'

She shook her head, and sank back against the cushions.

He flicked the remote and the programme changed.

'How about getting me something to eat?'

She nodded and went downstairs to the kitchen, prepared something for him, and brought it up on a tray.

'That's a tiny bit of cheese, and what's with all that lettuce? Give us a decent slice will you.'

'You can't have too much, it's bad for you.'

'For God's sake,' he grumbled.

'I'm tired, Michael, I'll go on to bed.'

'You do what you want, don't mind me, leave me here like a mouse eating crumbs.'

'Goodnight love.' She dropped a kiss on his forehead.

He turned up the volume of the television.

That night she couldn't sleep. Finally getting up to sit at the window and stare out into the shadows of early morning, the sky a black mass of cloud not a star to be seen. Then a thought. She would have a look on the Internet. Shaking, she googled and immediately the website came up with the information about the current winners. She was in shock. She had not thought of him for so many years it was as if he was someone who had come back from the dead.

She remembered that when they had been parted, she had gone through every possible emotion. Love. Heartbreak. Frustration. Anger. Hatred. Fear. And a mix of all of those too forming new feelings for which she had no name. Mostly against David but also against her mother and sister. No-one understood how she felt. An image of the kitchen of her childhood home flashed across her mind. Suddenly, she could feel the warmth of the range always kept going day and night. The aroma of the turf smoke nostalgic.

Tears misted. She stood up. Needing something to do. She had a shower. Dressed. Did her face. But the memories came into her head unbidden, and she could not shut them out. Those of her father were very clear, and she recalled one particular day when the two of them were at home alone.

She had dried the last of the dishes and put them away. Wiped down the table, put a glass, knife and fork at her father's place. She opened the fire box on the range with the lifter, threw a couple of turf sods into it, filled the kettle with water and set it to boil. The door opened and her father came in. Once a tall broad-shouldered man, Dan Brophy was now bent from too much hard work and he looked older than his fifty-eight years. He smiled a greeting at her, washed up at the sink, and sat at the table. She took his dinner from the oven and put it in front of him, poured a glass of milk and cut two slices of brown bread.

'This looks good,' he smiled at her. Humorous blue eyes twinkled in the rugged features, bronze from outdoor life.

Suddenly she had an urge to sit beside him and talk. He always understood. But she knew her parents were keen for her to go on to do a business secretarial course in Galway and wouldn't be a bit sympathetic when she announced she was going to marry David. He was going to tell his father tonight, and she should do the same. But her courage failed, and she decided to wait until tomorrow.

'I'm sure you're glad the Leaving is over, soon you'll be spreading your wings and heading off into the big bad world.'

Their eyes met. Identical. She was her dad's girl.

She looked out the window, face cupped in her hands. The evening sun slanted gold across the land. Caught the dark water of the lake and turned it into a pool of shimmering light. But it was only for a few seconds. All too soon the blue spiked shadows lengthened, moulded, and the cloak of darkness spread and swallowed everything up. She prayed for tomorrow to come quickly, and remembered what she had been doing that afternoon. There was something so grown up about that. Her mother and father still thought of her as a child. But she was a woman now and knew it all. And she would be married in a few weeks and a mother herself by Christmas.

'You're back to the usual, coming in at all hours, even mother has noticed it.' Michael was peevish.

'I'm busy and you're back at work. You don't need me around.' Jenny kissed him.

'I have to deal with mother, go on up will you, she chewed my ear off earlier.'

Pearl was equally contentious.

'Is Michael all right? I don't like the look of him.'

'He's fine, don't worry.'

'He's very cranky.' Pearl leaned against a pile of white pillows. Her frail body sank into their softness dwarfed by the high padded headboard in gold silk which towered above her.

'It will take a while before he's really better.'

'It's a pity you have to work.'

'He doesn't need me.'

'I don't agree.'

Jenny sat on the side of her bed. She said nothing, her eyes fastened on the pair of pink slippers neatly placed on the floor. Pearl had small feet, she was petite in every way.

'He's not happy.'

Jenny looked up.

'And neither are you.'

She didn't know what to say.

'You were for a few years, but now I've noticed a change.' Pearl twisted a tissue in her fingers, it had begun to disintegrate.

Tears moistened Jenny's eyes. She knew it was true. Everything Pearl said was weighed up, and considered deeply before it was uttered.

'I always think of you as my second daughter,' the old woman murmured softly, 'I love you.

Jenny's heart began to throb erratically. The tightness which kept her emotions under control eased. Now she wondered how deeply she really felt about any of the Hallorans.

'I don't want you to leave us.'

'Neither do I.'

'Perhaps if you talk with Michael?'

'It's something we seldom do any more,' she admitted, and the lined face in front of her misted.

'I wish I could help.'

'No-one can do that.'

'We need you here.'

'Michael and I have been through a lot over the years, our relationship is not to be written off casually,' Jenny said.

'That's a very sensible way of looking at it. But, were you ever in love with him?'

The question came out of the blue.

She had no answer.

Chapter Thirty-six

'I've something to tell you,' Maria said.

Jenny looked up from the letter she was reading. 'What is it?'

'I'm pregnant, we're going to have a baby.'

'That's wonderful, congratulations,' Jenny stood up and moved around the desk to embrace the girl. 'You must be very happy.'

'We are, Eoin is excited, and of course he is hoping it will be a son, always the men, they want a boy.' Her eyes misted over.

'When are you due?'

'October.'

'Your life will never be the same again. All those night feeds, and nappy changes.'

'Would you like to see the scan?'

Jenny's eyes widened.

Maria pulled a brown envelope from her large handbag, took the scan of the newly formed baby and handed it to her.

She stared at the grainy image. Her hand shook. 'So beautiful, perfect – do you know if its a boy or a girl? Did they tell you?' she gabbled a little, her pulse racing.

'I don't want to know.' Maria moved closer to Jenny and ran her fingers along the surface of the photo, following the shape of the baby.

There was a moment between them. A sharing of what this child meant.

'I'm sure you are sad that you never had children?' Maria said softly.

Jenny was taken aback, and said nothing for a moment. Then she took a deep breath, and whispered. 'It just wasn't meant to be.'

Their conversation resonated with Jenny all that day and those following. The image of the baby had multiplied all those memories which had resurfaced lately. Now she gave up trying to push them to the back of her mind, and let the strongest image take over.

It was about twelve when Faye awoke. With horror, she realised that the bed was wet. She pushed back the bedclothes, heaved herself out as quick as she could and began to drag the white sheet off the mattress. Her mother would have a fit when she saw it. But just then the first searing pain shot through her and she dropped to the floor with a smothered scream. Clung on to the edge of the bed as the pain attacked. Unable to think coherently she cried for her mother like a small child.

'Where is the pain?' Pauline knelt beside her.

'Everywhere.'

'How often?'

'All the time, Mam,' she cried.

'It's the baby. Come back into bed and lie down.' She helped her up and tucked the bedclothes around her.

Pauline knew what she was doing. Her mother had been a midwife and she had assisted her when she was a girl. Now as her daughter's labour grew more intense, she showed an unexpected sympathy for the young girl, helping her through the worst of it. It was about five o'clock the following morning when at last the baby girl fought her way into the world. Pauline weighed her on the kitchen scales at almost seven pounds. When the tiny scrap of humanity was put into Faye's arms, she could not believe that she had been created inside her. With scrunched up face, and a tuft of reddish-fair hair, she took to her breast with such appetite it was painful.

'You'll get used to it, girl, once the milk starts flowing. Now give her to me, I've an old orange box here that will have to do for a cot.'

'No, I want to keep her here in the bed.' Faye clung to her.

'You'll have to let her sleep, she needs it and so do you. Don't you worry, she'll wake again for a feed in a couple of hours.'

'I have to give her a name.' Faye looked down at the baby.

'Time enough for that.'

'She must have a name,' she insisted.

'Well, you can call her Mary,' Pauline said, 'It might change later. Probably will.'

'No, I want to call her Helen.'

'It doesn't make any difference what you call her.'

'She's Helen,' Faye said softly as she handed the child to her mother.

Strong cries woke her a short time later and she stared over at the orange box where Chris sat on a chair looking down at Helen.

'Give her to me,' Faye demanded.

'She should have been my baby,' Chris whispered, 'I'm four years older than you.' Her fingers gently touched the delicate skin of the curled hand.

'Chris, why don't you go back to bed and get some sleep.' Her mother appeared.

'I just want to watch her.' Chris stared in awe, hugging the pink nylon dressing-gown around herself.

'She's hungry, bring her over, Chris, please.' There was an air of authority in the young voice.

'You can lift her,' Pauline said, 'but support her head.'

'Can I?' Chris put her hands around the tiny child, and carried her over to Faye.

She cradled the baby. Held her close to the breast. Her nipples hurt but a rush of love swept through her as the pink lips grasped and suckled. When she was satisfied, Faye held her close. She didn't want to let her go.

Pauline came over and stood beside the bed. 'Has she had enough?'

Faye nodded.

'Will I take her?' Chris reached down.

'No, don't disturb them.' Pauline's voice was unexpectedly soft.

Chapter Thirty-seven

Helen walked with Breda on the shore of the lake. There was a rough pathway which led through the rushes and she often went that way at night to take a few photos. Breda said she was mad to go out alone and tonight had insisted on keeping her company.

'The moonlight on the water is amazing isn't it?' Helen murmured.

'Beautiful.'

'I think I'll set up here, the path is quite straight, and we can sit on that bench.' She positioned the tripod, and took the camera and lens from the bag. 'I'll leave the aperture open for two minutes, I want to do a time lapse.' She sat beside Breda.

'It's chilly.' Breda shivered.

'We won't be too long,' Helen laughed.

'Thanks be to God.'

'You should have worn a heavier jacket.'

'Where's Peter tonight?'

'Out with his friends.'

'How's it going?'

'What?'

'Your relationship.'

'Fine.'

'You don't sound very enthusiastic.'

'We had a bit of a tiff last weekend, remember?'

'Surely you've made up by now.'

'Yes and no, there's still a slight coolness there.'

'Ah, the ups and downs of love,' Breda laughed, 'sometimes I think I'm better off out of it.'

At that moment the headlights of a car shone across the lake.

'Someone driving on to the jetty. Probably coming down to have a snog. There are often cars down here at night . Hope they can't see us, usually I'm not so close,' Helen said, grinning.

'We're well hidden from their angle.'

The car came to a halt, and the lights were switched off.

'I feel like a peeping tom, although I've been in the same situation myself,' Helen giggled.

There was a sudden burst of female laughter.

'They're getting out,' Breda whispered.

'I'll die if they spot us.'

'Come on Peter, it's not that cold, don't be such a wimp,' a high-pitched voice echoed. 'How about a skinny dip?'

'You're on your own there, kiddo, I have to be in the Med to enjoy that.' The male voice sounded very familiar.

Helen and Breda looked at one another.

In the moonlight, they could see him grab the girl around the waist, and kiss her. They clung together for a few seconds and then ran back to the car.

'The shit!' Breda burst out.

Helen stared at the car silently.

'Let's get back. We don't want to hang around here any longer.'

'I feel like going over there and asking him what he's doing with her,' Helen said furiously, 'in fact I think I will.' She ran towards the car.

'Helen, stop, it could be embarrassing for you.' Breda grabbed her arm.

'I don't care, it's him I want to embarrass, don't think he'd be too pleased to be interrupted right in the middle of whatever he's doing. Let go of me.'

'Are you mad going over there, you never know what he might do.'

'Or what I might do. I want to sock him one.' She pushed

through the rushes.

'Calm down, you can talk to him tomorrow when you've thought about it.' Breda followed.

'I don't have to think about it, I know exactly what I'm going to say to him.'

They reached the edge of the jetty. The car windows were in darkness.

'Stop, Helen.' Breda still held on to her arm.

At that moment a light appeared at the top of the jetty and another car turned down. The girls were illuminated.

'Come on, we can't stay here now. Let's get your stuff and go.' Breda dragged Helen back to the path and they ran together to where they had been sitting. She picked up the camera and lens and handed it to Helen, then she grabbed the tripod and pushed her ahead towards the marina.

'What a fool I was to have trusted him. I'm such an idiot.' Helen was full of self- recrimination.

Breda opened her mouth

'Don't say it.' Helen warned.

'I wasn't.' Breda threw her hands up in mock surrender.

'But you were right.'

'I'm sorry.'

'I could kill him. The bastard. And I'm not hanging around here any longer.' She ran into the bedroom, opened the wardrobe and began to take clothes off hangers.

'Why let such a low life force you to leave Lackenmore, you love it here?' Breda asked.

'I never want to see him again.'

Chapter Thirty-eight

Chris dipped the mop in a bucket of water, and wiped it across the kitchen floor energetically.

'There's dirt there on the floor.' Pauline pointed.

'Where?' Chris peered.

'Look.'

'I can't see it.'

'Don't worry, Chris will clean it up.'

'Yea, she will. Like she does everything else.' She rounded on her mother.

'You tell her what I said.'

'Look at me, mother, look at me. What's my name?' She leaned closer to Pauline.

'I don't know you.'

'I'm Chris, Mam, Chris,' she yelled.

'Don't shout. It hurts my ears.'

'It's me, Mam, me,' she bellowed.

'Get away.'

'You're driving me berserk.' She took one of her shoes off. 'Look, what size shoe does Chris take?'

'Seven.'

'What size is this?' She shook the black shoe in front of her eyes.

'I don't know.'

'It's seven. Isn't that what you said – seven?'

'And this is a size sixteen,' she dragged off the cardigan she wore and flung it at her.

It clung around Pauline's head. With a scream she pulled at it trying to remove it from her face.

'Is that mine?' Chris asked.

'I don't know, don't know.'

Chris turned away wearily.

'Faye wouldn't say that to me,' Pauline cried. 'Is she still in the store room?'

Chris looked at her.

'Is she?'

'She's long gone. She got off scot free. Although sometimes I wouldn't mind if she came back. Then she could take care of you. I'm very tired these days.' Chris was morose.

'I was sorry afterwards,' Pauline said.

'For what?'

'For putting her in that place.'

'Where?'

'St. Josephs. I remember it now.'

'You don't remember anything.'

'Yes I do.' Pauline drifted back to that time after the birth of Faye's baby her mind unable to cope with the dilemma she faced and which became more urgent as the days passed. She remembered one particular night in the kitchen, her husband Dan was slumped in the armchair, his old tweed jacket rumpled, one mud-stained boot off and one still on. A toe peeped through a large hole in the grey sock. His head lolled slack, mouth open, and he snored with low wheezy sounds. The television droned as a disjointed voice announced something. It irritated Pauline. She crossed the room and switched it off abruptly, angry at its innocuous presence. She went to her handbag on the dresser, took out a pack of cigarettes and lit one quickly. She smoked with quick anxious puffs as her mind grappled with the situation in which she found herself.

How would she get rid of this baby? It must be soon, she knew that. Couldn't keep a new born quiet. If anything was noticed by the neighbours, they would be the talk of Lackenmore. Shunned. Disgraced. Humiliated. How would they ever hold their heads up again? The awful consequences flashed through her mind with increasing clarity. She became more and more agitated and stubbed out the butt of the cigarette in the white china ashtray with vicious intensity. Vaguely she noticed the name printed around the edge – "Bundoran". She stared at it as if she had never seen it before, and then remembered that Chris had brought it back from holidays years before. The thought of her eldest daughter caused her to become even more distraught. What was this going to do to her? Her fingers trembled as she lit another cigarette. She reached up and opened a top cupboard door, searching among the bottles and jars until she found the one she wanted. The whiskey bottle was half full. She stared at it for a moment, then took a small glass and poured. With a jerk, she swallowed the liquid in one gulp, dried her lips with the back of her hand and sank into a chair. She sat there, running her fingers up and down the cool surface of the glass. It was comforting and she felt better. After a couple of minutes she poured another. Movements slower now, less frenzied, her need somewhat satisfied.

'Dan, I've decided. We'll have to put it up for adoption.' Pauline announced.

'But why? Can't they just stay here? We'll say Faye just came back from London. Who's to know different?' Dan argued.

'Don't be ridiculous. Why do you think I've kept her locked up all this time? If I was going to announce it to the whole country, then I might as well have done that in the beginning.'

'It's wrong.'

'There's nothing else to be done.'

'I don't like it.'

'It's not your decision,' Pauline said.

It was a shout from Chris which brought Pauline back to the present.

'You're senile.'

'I am not, I know what I know.' Her lips pursed stubbornly.

All that day they argued. Through lunch. After lunch. Before dinner. After dinner. It was never-ending. Pauline unable to recognise her own daughter and Chris trying to prove her identity.

Chapter Thirty-nine

'Are you going to talk to Peter before you go?' Breda asked.

'No.'

'He'll think it a bit odd if you just drop out of sight.'

'I don't care what he thinks, and I'd be physically sick if I had to meet him again,' Helen tried to speak clearly aware that the slightest thing would make her lose control.

'I have to say I'm not surprised,' Breda commented drily. 'Sorry, I'm being my usual smart-ass self, but honestly I'm glad you found out about him.'

'I should have listened to you,' Helen said slowly.

'He's not to be trusted where women are concerned, never was.'

'And I didn't really believe you, I thought it would be different with us. I was so sure he loved me.'

'He probably did, in his own shallow way. Might even have gone all the way, even married you.'

'No, don't think he'd have gone that far, but he wanted us to move in together.'

'Just as well you found out about him before you took that step.'

Tears suddenly welled up in Helen's eyes. 'I'd better go. I'll stay in Dublin until I book the flight.' She lifted her suitcase and carried it through to the front door.

'What if he comes up there after you? I know the nature of the beast, he won't want to let you go. No-one leaves Peter.'

'He won't.'

'He knows where your aunt lives, doesn't he?'

'Unfortunately. We called to see them that day we went to Dublin for the concert.'

'Maybe after a few days you might see things differently.'

'I'll never do that, Breda.'

'He can be very persuasive.'

Helen didn't reply.

'Hey, I'm going to miss you. Keep in touch.' Breda hugged her.

'Come up before I go back, will you. Or maybe we could meet somewhere else for a weekend, chill out.' Helen was emotional at their sudden parting.

'I will.'

'Say goodbye to everyone for me. Give them my apologies for leaving so quickly.' She sat into the car and started the engine.

'Look after yourself, see you soon.' Breda waved.

Helen drove towards the main road and stopped to look back. It was such a pity. Breda was the only good thing about Lackenmore and she regretted losing a good friend. But she was heartbroken over Peter.

Chapter Forty

To say David was shocked when Breda mentioned that Helen had left was an understatement. He stared at her silently.

'I'm going to miss her,' Breda admitted.

'Where has she gone?'

'Dublin first for a while and then home.'

'But I thought Peter and she were together.'

'No, that's finished.'

'I'm sorry I didn't see her before she left. Do you have an address for her in Dublin?'

'She's staying with her aunt.' She jotted down the details on a slip of paper and handed it to him.

He found it difficult to hide the sense of panic which raced through him. He had hoped that one day they would be friends although lately it didn't seem as if that would ever happen. Now everything had changed and he knew that he couldn't let her go back to Australia without seeing her once again.

A couple of hours later he was on the road heading for Dublin. On the way he rehearsed out loud. But it was difficult, almost impossible, to make it sound anything more than the crazy meanderings of a middle-aged man. It sounded so stilted. So totally improbable. There had to be a more subtle, gentle way to approach it. But by the time he arrived in the city he was no nearer a solution.

It didn't take long to find the house in Rathmines, but when he arrived he was surprised to see Peter's car parked behind Helen's rented Suzuki. He pulled in some way down the road and sat fuming. Obviously, their relationship was still going on and he would have no opportunity to talk to her now. He stayed there for a while wondering whether it might be better to come back later, but then they might head off together and his chance would be gone. He decided to go in.

A middle-aged woman answered the door. He introduced himself and asked to see Helen. She seemed to know who he was and asked him to wait for a moment in the front sitting room. He tried to get his thoughts in order, but he had no success and when she appeared, his mind was still in chaos.

'David?'

'Helen, I hope you don't mind my calling, Breda gave me your address.'

'Are you looking for Peter?'

'No, it's you I want to see.' His mouth was dry and he found it difficult to get his tongue around the words.

Peter followed behind. 'Bet you didn't expect to meet me here,' he smirked, 'and you won't see me for much longer Taylor, I'll be heading to Australia with Helen so you've wasted your time.' He put his arm around her possessively.

'I heard Helen was leaving and there was no chance to say goodbye.'

'You came all this way to do that?'

'Peter, there's no need for that,' she intervened.

'It's not what you think.' David felt very awkward.

'Then what are you doing here? You could have picked up the phone.' Peter's words were slightly slurred. On his arrival a few hours ago, Paddy had opened the whiskey.

David could see immediately that it was going to be difficult.

'Peter, please don't speak to David like that.' Helen seemed really annoyed.

He was very surprised at her reaction.

'Listen Helen. You don't know what Taylor's like. He thinks he's got it all. Money, success, everything. Feels he can pick and choose anyone he likes.'

197

'You've got it wrong,' David said quietly.

'I've always got it wrong, as you're so fond of pointing out.' Peter swaggered, his feet unsteady on the pink flowered carpet.

'Helen, I'd better go.' He felt the situation slip out of his control and made a move towards the door.

'And slip back later when I've gone?' Peter blocked his way. 'You can't muscle in here. Helen is mine and I'm going to make sure you don't forget that.'

'I'm not yours,' Helen said.

But neither heard and suddenly without warning, Peter landed a lethal punch on David's jaw and then leapt upon him, pummelling furiously.

Loathe to take him on, David fended off the blows and they struggled for a moment and then landed on the floor with a crash knocking over one of the chairs.

Helen tried to separate them but Peter seemed determined to continue the fight. They rolled about on the floor, although his drunken punches lacked accuracy and David was well able to hold him off.

'Hey, what's going on here?' Paddy appeared, followed by Noreen. Immediately he grabbed hold of Peter and pulled him off David.

'Get your hands off me, this is none of your business.'

'You're in my house and that makes it my business,' Paddy growled, 'now outside, Peter, outside.'

'I'm sorry Paddy,' Helen was visibly upset.

'Is everyone all right?' Noreen asked.

'You help your man there and I'll deal with this lad.' Although more than twice his age, Paddy, a broad six-footer, was well able to handle the intoxicated Peter, and dragged him out.

'I'm so sorry, Helen, if I thought this would happen, I'd never have called.' David stood up, dusted down his clothes and picked up the chair.

'It's not your fault, he had too much to drink.'

'He lands a hell of a punch.' He felt his jaw which was already beginning to swell.

'Come into the kitchen, you need some ice on that,' Noreen said.

'I should go.'

Noreen took no notice and ushered David ahead of her into the kitchen, where she made him sit down, wrapped cubes of ice in a towel and handed it to him. He pressed it against his throbbing jaw, the sound of a conversation outside quite clear.

'You deliberately attacked him, what possessed you? And he's your boss – what about your job, have you even thought about that?'

'Just lost my head. It's the whiskey. Can't take it,' Peter muttered, unapologetic. 'Didn't want him putting his hands on you, that's all he wants. Knew he fancied you from the start.'

'You're imagining that,' Helen snapped.

'Tell him to fuck off then.'

'This is my house, Peter, and I'll decide who goes or stays,' Paddy said.

'If he's staying then I'm not. Are you coming with me Helen?'

'No Peter.'

'Right, suit yourself,' he shouted, and David could hear the violent crash of the front door as he left.

'Are you all right?' Noreen asked.

'She's fine. Don't worry.' Paddy shepherded Helen ahead of him into the kitchen where David sat.

'I should never have opened that whiskey bottle,' Paddy admitted.

'Don't blame yourself Paddy, you couldn't have known. It was just one of those unfortunate things,' Noreen said softly.

'How are you feeling now, Mr. Taylor?' Paddy enquired.

'Please call me David, but I'm sorry I don't even know your full name.'

'Noreen and Paddy will do fine.' Noreen patted his shoulder as she passed by.

'You'll have a right purpler there tomorrow,' Paddy observed.

'It's not that bad.' Noreen gave Paddy a warning glance.

'Would you mind if I splashed some water on my face, then I'll be on my way.' David stood up.

'Not at all, upstairs, straight ahead, I'll just get you a fresh towel from the hot press,' Noreen said and they left together.

'I'm sorry such a thing should have happened to you in this house,' she apologised.

'Don't worry, Peter is a bit volatile, and anyway, I probably shouldn't have come in when I saw his car outside.'

'I'll leave you to freshen up.'

David came back into the kitchen to see Helen sitting alone at the table.

'Are you feeling better?' she asked shyly.

'I'm OK, thanks.'

He sat opposite. The clock on the mantle ticked softly, counting time through the questioning silence. 'I'm really sorry for coming up here and upsetting things for you. I hope that I haven't caused a problem. I only wanted to talk to you for a few minutes, and never expected Peter to react like that.'

'It doesn't matter,' she said abruptly, 'you wanted to see me for a particular reason?'

'Yes, but it's difficult to explain.' He reached into the inside pocket of his grey jacket and pulled out a black leather wallet. Then he took a plastic folder from it which he handed to her silently.

She opened it. 'Where did you get this photo?'

'I took it,' he smiled.

'When?'

'A long time ago.'

His brown eyes met hers, but she looked away unable to meet his gaze.

'I told you that you looked like Faye. When I first met you, I couldn't believe my eyes,' he spoke in a rush, almost tripping over his words.

Helen examined the photo closely. She searched in the pockets of her jeans for a tissue.

'But I didn't mention then that I loved your mother.'

'Did she love you,' she whispered.

'I think so, we were going to get married when she discovered she was pregnant.'

'She was your girlfriend?'

'Yes.'

'Why didn't you go ahead?'

'Our families didn't approve.'

'So you could be my father?' She stared wide-eyed at him.

'I hope so.'

'But you left her?'

'I had no choice, her family sent her to England immediately. I wrote many letters, but I never received a reply.'

'And it's too late now, she's dead.' She kissed the photo.

'No Helen, she isn't.'

'But Chris told me she had died.'

'She was lying, Faye is still alive.'

'Is she living in Lackenmore?'

'No, but I've made contact with a friend of hers and I've given her a letter for Faye, but so far I've heard nothing from her.'

'I'm not surprised she hasn't replied,' Helen said. A bitterness in her voice.

He looked at her, puzzlement in his dark eyes.

'You abandoned her. Left her to have her baby alone, your baby, just when she needed you most. Everyone else probably treated her as an outcast, wherever she was. And I was handed over to Carmel and Tom. Not that I wasn't loved. I'm not saying that. I was given everything I wanted and I loved them very much.'

David's face grew white and pinched.

'So for years you just sat on the sideline and did nothing.'

'I did try to make contact.'

'I can't understand how you didn't make more of an effort, it couldn't have been that difficult.'

'I feel so guilty.' He massaged his temple.

'And so you should, you didn't know her circumstances, and you never wondered about me, I suppose.'

'Of course I did, although I didn't even know whether you were even born, a boy or a girl.'

'Don't give me that. I didn't exist for you. So convenient. Men never deal with their responsibilities. It's always the women who

201

carry the can.'

'I'd have given my right arm to find you both,' he said passionately, 'believe me.'

'I can imagine.'

'I admit I should have found Faye no matter what, instead of dreaming about it,' he murmured.

'Well, what did you think had happened to her.'

'I assumed she had been sent to England and married to someone else. That was the usual thing in a small town like this. A pregnant girl had to be married as quickly as possible to save face, the whole thing shrouded in secrecy.'

'An easy scenario for you, wash your hands and romp on through life.'

'I'll try to make it up to you, and Faye as well, if only I could see her again.'

'Thanks a bunch, but I don't want anything. Don't need anything. I've my own life.'

'I'm sorry, Helen.'

At that moment, there was a soft knock on the door.

'Come in Noreen, Paddy, it's OK,' Helen said.

'We've taken over your kitchen, sorry.' David stood up

'We were just chatting,' Helen murmured.

'Don't you worry, David, will you join us for dinner?'

He looked at Helen questioningly, knowing that she probably didn't want him to stay.

'Of course you will,' Noreen said, 'you can't drive all that way on an empty stomach, you need a bit of sustenance.'

'Thanks very much.' He accepted in the hope that if he spent some more time in Helen's company she might change her attitude to him, but she was very quiet during dinner, and barely picked at her meal.

It was almost nine when David looked at his watch and insisted that he had better leave. 'Thanks for all your hospitality.' He shook hands with Noreen and Paddy.

Helen saw him to the jeep, and they made awkward small talk for a few minutes.

'I'm sorry about earlier. Everything you said was true.' He looked into her eyes.

She didn't reply.

'I'm going to make contact with Faye, find out what happened, if it's the last thing I do. Do you think you might come back to Lackenmore?' There was uncertainty in his eyes.

'I had planned to go home.'

'Don't go yet, come back with me, and you can stay at the house or at the cottages, wherever.'

She glanced back to where Noreen and Paddy stood in the doorway.

'I'll come up for you if you like and you can give back the rental, there are a couple of cars available at the studios,' he offered.

'I'll think about it.'

'I look forward to seeing you soon.' He felt suddenly happy. 'I'd better get going.' He opened the door of the jeep and climbed in. When he had inserted the key into the ignition and started the engine, he reached his hand out the window towards her.

'There is something else. I want you to have this. I gave it to Faye on the day I asked her to marry me.' He handed her a small black box.

She took it hesitantly. They stared at each other without speaking. Then he smiled and drove away. He didn't mention that Faye had been in St. Josephs. It would have been too difficult for Helen to deal with that, particularly if her mother didn't want to meet her.

Chapter Forty-one

'I can't get it out of my head.' Jenny gripped her hands together, the large solitaire diamond in her engagement ring glittering.

'Maybe it's time you faced it, Jen, you've a lot of baggage,' Una said softly.

'I don't want to do that, I just want to go back to where I was a few months ago when I knew who I was.' She gulped the gin and tonic.

'Hey, not so fast, you'll be pissed.'

'I don't care.'

'You'll have a hell of a hangover in the morning,' Una grinned.

'If I can just forget for a few hours that would be enough.'

'Maybe you should talk to someone.'

'I'm doing that.'

'But can I help you?'

'You're the only one who can, the only one who knows about what happened in the past.'

'And I don't know everything.'

'I can't remember a lot of it myself, the memories come in waves.'

'It's good for you.'

'I don't know about that.'

'I'll pour us another drink.'

Jenny was in Una's home in Galway, grateful to her old friend for once again giving her the chance to talk over days past. As Jenny spoke, she remembered more. Small insignificant details forced their way into her mind, random pieces of a puzzle which up to now it hadn't been possible to complete.

'We were in love, he was the only boy I knew. We thought we could run away, do what we wanted, we had it all planned. But I wasn't good enough for his father.'

Jenny remembered that the baby was the most beautiful thing she had ever seen. Perfect pale pink skin. Tiny pursed lips. Long eyelashes brushed crescent shadows on the little face. Dainty fingers curled around hers, unbelievably strong for such a tiny little girl. She had longed to show her to David, and fantasised about calling to his house, and asking his father where he was living in Dublin and go there. Demand. Order. That he just look at his daughter. Hold his daughter. Surely then he would not turn his back on them. How could he possibly resist her? But reality intruded and she remembered the money his father had given. David didn't want them. Faye realised that now. Her mother had been right. She tried to harden her heart. To build up a wall around herself so that she would be prepared for life without him.

The turning point came on that last night when her mother had switched off the light and the bedroom door closed. Her footsteps receded into the distance but Faye knew something wasn't right. She pushed herself up on her elbow and wondered. Then suddenly she knew. The key had not turned in the lock. She got out of bed and crept to the door. Held her breath as she turned the handle and it opened. Quietly she crept out on to the landing. At the top of the stairs she stopped when she heard voices from the kitchen.

'We'll take the baby to the adoption place in Dublin as soon as we can.' Pauline's voice was cold. 'I've arranged it with them.'

Faye rushed back into the bedroom and stared down at her daughter sleeping in the rough wooden box. Then she picked her up, held her close, and rocked her back and forth as the terrible words echoed over and over in her head. She panicked then, staring out through the window into the darkness wondering how she was going to save Helen. She tried to calm herself, got back into bed and pulled the clothes over herself and the baby. She must leave. Run away and find a safe place. She lay staring into the darkness, listening to the sounds of the house as it settled and prayed her mother would not remember that she hadn't locked the door.

It was still dark when she rose, fed and changed the baby. Threw on some clothes with frantic haste, blue skirt and jumper, her brown winter coat. She opened her purse and counted out the coins that lay inside, but there wasn't much and she could never manage on so little. But she snapped the purse closed with determination and refused to think about it. All that mattered was to get away from the house. Someone would help her.

She wrapped the baby in a blanket and over that the old black shawl belonging to her mother. As she walked towards the door, a sudden weakness came over her and she had to hold on to the bedpost for support, aware that she didn't have the strength to go very far. But after a few seconds, she took a deep breath, opened the door and walked slowly on to the landing. The house was silent at that early hour and she crept downstairs praying the baby would not cry. She opened the back door. Outside, a veneer of frost glistened on the ground and the cold night air caused her breath to vaporise. She shivered, and stood confused, unable to decide which way to go.

To her left a light twinkled in the distance. It was the McLoughlin house – Carmel and Tom. The possibility that they might help sent her heart throbbing with excitement. She broke into a run but after a short time she had to slow down, out of breath. She had so little exercise over the past months that her legs were weak. The baby whimpered as she skirted the barn, opened the gate and headed across the fields towards the farmhouse which was surrounded by a dark grove of trees. A fence loomed up in front of her, barbed wire wound around it. Frantically, she lurched along its length, in tears now with frustration as she searched for a gap. At last she knelt down and widened a section, the barbs tearing through the soft skin of her palms. Then she pushed the baby along the ground underneath, and crept under herself, but the barbs caught her coat and she couldn't move back or forward. The baby was crying now.

For a moment she panicked, struggling to free herself, but she was firmly caught. She was crying, the baby was crying, until at last she managed to get her mind around her predicament and opened the buttons of the coat, struggled out of it, lifted the baby and made her way towards the back door of the house. The coat hung on the wire fence, limp, lifeless. She banged on the door, praying they would answer, knowing that Tom was always up early. Then the door opened and he was staring at her, wearing a well-pressed navy suit, stiff white collar and dark tie.

'Faye, what are you doing here at this hour? Is something wrong?'

'Is Carmel here?' She leaned against the door frame, exhausted now.

'Yes, come in.' He ushered her inside. 'I'll get her.'

She stood in the middle of the kitchen and comforted the baby who had stopped crying now and slept. Two large suitcases stood in the middle of the room. A couple of smaller bags on the kitchen table. There was something bare about the place, cupboard doors stood slightly open to reveal empty shelves. She didn't know what to think. Carmel came in. She was dressed in her good clothes. A grey tweed suit which hung a little loose on the thin figure, the severity relieved by the pink lace ruffle at the neckline. Her short dark hair was carefully brushed and there was a touch of face powder on her pale cheeks. A synthetic blush. Faye assumed it was Sunday, she had lost all track of time.

'Faye? You don't look well. Are you all right?' Carmel was concerned. She made her sit down. Clucking over her, apologising that she hadn't anything to give her. Faye said nothing. Just clutched the baby to her. Carmel pulled up another chair and sat opposite, telling her that they were emigrating to Australia, and that very morning would travel to Dublin. Tears filled Faye's eyes and she buried her face in the bundle in her arms.

'What have you got there?' Carmel put out her hand and touched it.

Faye pulled back the shawl so that she could see the sleeping child.

Carmel gazed, astonished. 'Where did this baby come from?' she gasped.

'She's mine.'

'What?'

'She's just over a week old, her name is Helen.'

'But why are you here?'

Faye told her then, and asked her that one vital question.

'I thought you might look after her for me as you have no children.' She handed the baby to her.

Carmel put out her arms. She was awkward at first, but then managed to settle Helen comfortably in the crook of her arm. 'She's beautiful.'

'I know you've always wanted a baby, now you have one, and she is lovely and so good, she hardly ever cries unless she's hungry.'

'I can't, Faye, we're going away.'

'Please take her? If I bring her back home they'll take her to be adopted in Dublin, please, I beg you?'

'I'm sorry.'

Faye jumped up, rushed across the kitchen, pulled open the back door and disappeared. It swung closed behind her with a dull thump.

'I can't believe that ever happened, it must have been terrible for you.' Una covered Jenny's hand with hers. 'You should have told me, I could have helped.'

'I made a new life for myself and tried to forget. I thought I had succeeded.' She wiped tears from her eyes.

'Have you ever thought about looking for Helen?'

'I'm sure she wouldn't want to know me. I gave her away. Couldn't forgive me for that.'

'Many people want to find their natural parents regardless of the circumstances.'

'I couldn't look her straight in the face. No amount of apologies would be enough to make up for what I did.'

'You gave her to people you knew, not to strangers.'

'They went to Australia. Took her away from her family.'

'What if someone knew where she was?'

Una's words hung in the air and Jenny straightened up as an image of the white envelope in the black leather handbag flashed into her mind.

Chapter Forty-two

David waited for Helen. But she didn't come and made no contact. He was devastated. All his hopes were dashed. He had been over the moon as he had driven back to Lackenmore than night. To have finally opened up to her had been momentous although her reaction had been disappointing. Still, he couldn't have expected anything else. A man she hardly knew turned up out of nowhere and claimed to be her father. Crazy.

They were recording again, so he was glad he didn't have to travel, needing to be here if she should suddenly arrive.

'David?' Trevor was in the control box.

He nodded, and began to play the piece of music on the piano.

The base and guitar filtered in.

'The timing is off,' Trevor spoke on the studio talk back.

'Sorry. We'll do another take.' He tried to concentrate.

Next time David was still unhappy with the result. 'Sorry lads, it's my fault, can't keep my mind on it.'

'Let's try again.'

It improved.

They went on to something else.

He forced his mind to focus.

He wasn't a naturally gregarious person, being more quiet and reserved, and the lads didn't notice his preoccupation. He would have liked to talk with Breda but he didn't know if she knew anything at all so only discussed business with her. The studios were completely booked and they could only grab a few hours here and there for themselves. He couldn't have borne it if they had to spend all day every day recording so the short spells suited him.

Then on top of everything Vanessa turned up.

'I was in London and I had to come over.'

He didn't know what to say.

'How are you darling?' She advanced towards him. 'I'm so sorry about that night at the Oscars, I couldn't bear it if you were still angry with me. Are you?' She fluttered her long eyelashes at him.

'No, Vanessa, I'm not,' he smiled.

'Can I have one of your wee cottages?' She enveloped him in a white fur jacket.

'I'll see if there's one available.' He tried to get his phone out of his pocket and finally succeeded in pulling free of her grasp. 'Sit down while I check.'

She sank on to a couch and crossed her knees, long legs encased in white thigh-high suede boots. He checked with Breda and assured Vanessa that there was one available. Just as he turned back a group of people pushed their way through the doors, and he recognised a well-known German rock band who were booked in to record their latest album.

'If you don't mind waiting, Vanessa, I'll have to meet these people, Breda will be up for you in a few minutes.'

'See you soon,' she smiled, and blew him a kiss.

He walked across to the group and just out of the corner of his eye he noticed Peter come in. He hadn't met him face to face since their confrontation in Dublin and knew he hadn't been in work. Now he wondered what he was going to say. He welcomed the group, made sure their rooms were arranged, and turned back to see Vanessa and Peter in deep conversation.

'I've got company, David,' she beamed.

'I came over to see you,' Peter said and stood up.

He nodded.

'Hi!' Breda arrived and then it was all fuss, as Vanessa's bags were carried out to the jeep by the porter, and Peter.

'Make sure Vanessa is comfortable,' David said.

'Sure, gold card treatment,' Breda grinned.

'Exactly.

They saw her off.

Peter turned to David. 'Could we talk privately?'

David led the way to his office. Closed the door and sat behind the desk. He left Peter stand.

'I'm sorry for what happened.' The young man pushed his hands into the pockets of his jeans and stood awkwardly.

'You took your time.'

'I didn't know what to do.'

'I don't know if you fit in here any longer, Peter.'

'I had a few drinks that day and it had a bad affect on me, I don't even remember much about it.'

'You remember enough to come back here and apologise.'

'Well, yea.' He looked sheepish. 'But I just want to have another chance. I enjoy the work.'

'And there's not very much around at the moment.'

'It's not that exactly, I've always got a lot of satisfaction from the job, and the people are great.' He waved towards David.

'And the pay is good too.'

'Just give me another chance, I won't let you down,' he begged.

David could see the desperation in his eyes. Peter was pretty good at his job and he hated to hang him out to dry in this climate of recession.

'OK – a chance. I'll give you a month, but I warn you – any trouble and you're out.'

'Thanks David, I really appreciate it, you've no idea how much it means,' he grinned.

'Go on, get back to work before I change my mind.'

'Thanks.'

He left the room.

That was one problem solved for the moment. David wondered was he too soft. And decided that he was. Still if Peter moved out of line even an inch he'd regret it.

'Darling, I love my cottage, thank you so much.' Vanessa was full of the joys when he called to see her later. 'Champagne?' The bottle was already on ice.

'No thanks, not for me.'

'Come on, let's celebrate.' She handed it to him.

He gave in and opened it with a loud pop of the cork. She held out the glasses and he poured.

'Cheers.' He raised the glass.

'To us.'

He sipped.

They sat down.

'I was surprised to see you,' he began.

'I wanted to make an impact,' she smiled, 'just in case you'd forgotten me.'

'Difficult to do that.'

'You mean it?'

Unfortunately his words had given her the opposite meaning to what he had intended. 'What about Josh?'

'He means nothing to me. We had a row. It's finished. There's someone else in his life now.'

'I thought you were living together?'

'We were, until I caught him with that one who's starring in his latest film. She's a hopeless actress, useless, and it will be a complete flop.'

'What's your next part?'

'It'll be six months before we start filming, so I'm at a loose end. I might stay around here with you, honey, what do you think of that?' She leaned closer and kissed him.

'I'll be away on tour soon, sorry.'

'Maybe I'll come with you? Where are you going?'

His heart sank. 'We'll be in the States, and it would be boring for you, all those crowded little nightclubs, no big venues unfortunately.'

'I'd be company for you,' she smiled.

'Vanessa, it's not going to work.'

'But you said you couldn't forget me?'

213

'Not in a romantic way. You have to realise that we never really got off the ground, you could say we're friends, good friends, but no more than that.' He tried not to hurt her feelings too much.

'I thought you feel the same as I do.' She stared at him.

'No Vanessa.' He topped up her glass.

'You strung me along,' she accused.

'It wasn't deliberate.'

'It was too. Remember all those nights in LA when we had so much fun.'

'I'm sorry.'

'You're such a bastard,' she shouted angrily.

'Perhaps I am.'

'I hate you.'

'I deserve it.' He shrugged.

'And I travelled all the way from London to see you.'

'I appreciate that.'

'And this is how you show it?' She flung the almost full glass of champagne at him.

He wiped his face with a handkerchief.

'I'm not hanging around here for one moment longer,' she shouted, her eyes sparkling with anger.

Her phone rang. Flustered she searched for it. David saw it on the table and handed it to her. 'I'll let you take that call.' He went outside and stood there staring out over the lake pensively. Let her go now, he thought, once and for all.

A few minutes later she rushed through the door. 'That was Josh, he's finished with that one, he wants me back, I'll have to get a flight as quickly as I can, he's filming in Spain, do you think I could get there easily?'

'Yes, I'm sure you can, let's see if we can book now.' He went back inside and on the computer logged on to the airlines to see what was available.

'I can't believe it, I'm so happy.' She went into the bedroom and began to pack.

David couldn't believe it either.

Chapter Forty-three

At the farm things weren't going well.

Pauline closed the back door in Chris's face. 'I don't want you in here.'

'Mam, let me in.'

'No, you don't live here.'

'I've just taken the washing off the line, it has to be ironed, look out the window and I'll show it to you.'

'What washing?'

'I just put it out this morning, but it's raining now so how will I get it dry unless I come in?'

'I don't take in washing.'

'I don't want you to do it, I'll do it.'

'This isn't your home.'

'Of course it is, Mam, I've lived here my whole life.'

'I've never seen you before.'

'Open the door, please?'

'I told you I don't want you in here, Faye will be back later.'

Chris sank on to a stool, the pile of washing in her arms. She was getting very tired. Her mother was becoming more and more forgetful and it was unbearable.

'What are you doing out here, it's raining?' Corcoran strode across the yard.

'Just taking a rest.' She stood up and went towards the door.

'Let me open it for you.' He reached for the handle.

She stared at him surprised at his politeness.

'No, it's OK, I can get in.'

He turned the handle but the door didn't open. 'Have you lost the key?'

'No, it's stiff, I think.'

'Is your mother inside?'

She nodded, worn out with it now. He was the last person she wanted to know that her mother had deteriorated to such an extent.

'Pauline, are you there, Chris can't get in,' he called.

Her face appeared in the window.

The door opened.

Chris pushed in and dumped the pile of washing on the table. 'I must do something about that lock, can't have this happening,' she said.

'Do you want me to look at it for you?' Corcoran asked.

'No, I'll bet some oil will fix it.'

'How are you Sean?' Pauline asked.

'My name isn't Sean,' Corcoran said.

'He's definitely not Sean,' Chris muttered and began to separate the clothes. Towels. Pillowcases. Sheets. A Monday wash. She looked out the window again to check on the weather. It rained mistily now. No point in putting them out again. She unfolded the clothes horse and draped them over it.

'Who are you?' Pauline asked.

Corcoran looked at her, puzzlement in his eyes.

'Well?' she demanded.

'You know my name, Pauline, I've been around here for long enough, and I've every intention of being around for a long time yet. I might even be living here one of these days.'

'Why don't you stay for dinner? Faye cooks a good bacon and cabbage.'

'Mr. Corcoran is busy,' Chris snapped.

'I'll come back later, sounds good.'

'Where are you from?' Pauline asked.

Corcoran laughed out loud. 'Do you hear this?'

'Mother.'

'I like to know where people are from. My family all came from Lackenmore.'

'As did mine. We live on the next farm.'

'The McLoughlins?'

'No, they've long gone.'

'Their house is still there.'

'That should be demolished and the site cleared,' Corcoran guffawed.

'But where will Tom and Carmel live?' Pauline asked.

'Mam, you're forgetting again.'

'No I'm not.'

'I've got to bake bread, I'm sure you've something to be doing, Mr. Corcoran.'

'I'll be back later.'

'We'll be glad to see you, Mr?' Pauline put her hand out.

'Thanks.' He got up and shuffled towards the door.

Chris saw him off, her mouth a grim line of discontent. She closed the door and rounded on her mother. 'You're losing it altogether, now we're stuck with him all night again.'

'He's a nice man.'

'He's a disgusting old fart.' She put flour into a bowl, added bread soda, salt, a little sugar, and sifted.

'Such language, Faye.'

'And will you stop calling me that, I'm Chris, not Faye,' she yelled.

'Chris?' her voice faltered.

'Yes.'

'Where's my bag?'

'I don't know.'

'I want my money.'

'Get it yourself.' She poured buttermilk on to the mixture, and mixed it through.

'You've stolen it.'

Chris sighed. 'Will you just zip it.'

Her mother was silenced.

Chris didn't finish the bread. She just left it there and sat by the range warming herself, and drinking. The bottle emptied. Her eyes closed. She was unaware that the soda bread should have been in the oven. The bacon simmering. The cabbage cut and sliced. The potatoes peeled. And unaware too that the tip of the cigarette had fallen on to the green floral apron and was already burning a hole in it.

★

Corcoran was locking up his barn when he smelled smoke. At first he took no notice of it, but then he stopped what he was doing and walked out into the yard staring across the fields wondering who had set a fire. He could see a glow of light in the direction of the Brophys and jumped into his old truck and drove to the farm. The smoke was dense and he could see the flames roaring through the house. He parked and ran into the yard, getting as near as he could, but was beaten back by the extreme heat. Then he heard someone screaming and looked around to see Pauline in the doorway of one of the outhouses. He ran over. 'Thanks be to God you're all right, where's Chris?' he shouted.

She didn't seem to hear him.

'Did she get out?'

She covered her face with her hands.

'Come on, you can sit in my truck.' He ushered her ahead of him, tottering unsteadily, and helped her in.

A couple of neighbours appeared through the smoke, holding handkerchiefs over their faces.

'I couldn't phone the fire brigade, it would take me too long to go back to the house,' he was out of breath. 'Pauline is all right, but I don't know about Chris.'

'The brigade is on its way.'

'Let's see if we can get in,' one of them said.

They went around to the back but the heat was so intense they had to retreat again.

218

'I don't think there's much we can do.'

'I hope Chris is somewhere around. I'll have a look for her.' Corcoran went over to the barns and outhouses in search of her, but she was nowhere to be found. He checked on Pauline and moved his truck further down to the road. 'The fire brigade will be here soon,' he reassured the old woman.

But it wasn't quite soon enough.

Chapter Forty-four

Breda passed the Garda Technical Bureau van which was parked in the lane as she drove into the town, and it was only then that she noticed the burned out roof struts sticking up through the trees. She pulled up sharply, parked, and asked the Garda who sat in the car what had happened. He gave her some vague information about a woman being in hospital but very little else, and it was only when she arrived in town that she found out all she needed to know. Everyone was very upset about the tragedy as she was herself. Only just back from Dublin where she had spent the weekend with Helen, now she had to ring and tell her what had happened.

She was shocked.

'Will you come down for the funeral?' Breda asked, 'maybe Faye could be here, you might see her.'

'I can't imagine that, although I hope I don't bump into David.'

'He's away again.'

'You've no idea how I feel. I couldn't bear to come face to face with him again.' Still angry, she didn't see how there could ever be any relationship with him after what he had done in the past. She blamed him unconditionally for the loss of her mother.

'I understand. It's a very difficult situation.' Breda nodded.

The old church in Lackenmore was beautiful. With stained glass windows in vibrant colours depicting scenes from the bible. Candles flickered and there were pink and white flower arrangements on the altar.

'I wonder would you recognise your mother?' Breda asked when people began to walk up to sympathise with the family.

'I don't know.' The question shook Helen. Her mother was Carmel. Who should be still at home in Australia. But who wasn't. Who wasn't anywhere. But she knew Breda was referring to Faye. Who could be sitting with the family in the front row of seats, and with whom she might come face to face at any moment. She was terrified at the possibility.

As she knelt there, she didn't want to let go of the image of Carmel and Tom. And imagined them standing on the altar as they might have looked on their wedding day. There was a photo at home which had been taken outside the church. Her mother looking particularly beautiful wearing a white dress and her Dad in a dark suit.

'We'd better go up to shake hands anyway, it's the done thing,' Breda whispered.

'Do I have to?'

'No, of course not, but I will. You stay here and I'll join the queue.' She walked up the centre aisle.

Helen waited, feeling very self-conscious. The church was slowly emptying. Once people had sympathised with the family they left in silent groups. There was a pall over the place. Tragedy does that to small communities. A combined regret which was almost tangible. Helen felt guilty. The person who lay in the simple wooden coffin up at the altar was a member of her family. Her aunt. Her mother's sister. And the mourners were connected with her as well. She couldn't understand why she didn't feel more emotion about them, the only person who mattered was Faye.

Breda returned and sat beside her. 'I didn't see anyone who looked like you. I knew none of them except Chris's son Sean. Pauline's still in hospital.'

There was a heavy thump of disappointment in Helen's stomach.

'Maybe she'll come later. Sometimes family can't make it in time. And then who would have let her know about it? Chris told us she had died, and probably told everyone else the same.'

Helen nodded.

'If David knew he could have sent her a message, you said he's in contact with a friend of hers. Maybe I should have told him. I'll phone.'

At the church the following morning a large crowd was gathered, and Helen was introduced by Breda to a few people. The Mass was quite lovely, the local choir singing hymns some of which were vaguely familiar to her. The priest spoke about Chris, and how much she was loved by the community, and her family. She was such a great loss. Helen didn't know what to think. She probably was all those things but the woman she had met at the farm was very different.

'Do you want to go to the cemetery?' Breda asked.

'No.' She shuddered.

'I suppose it would be better not.'

'I don't want anyone in the family to notice me, couldn't bear having to answer questions.'

'Perhaps someone might know about Faye? It might be worth going. Funerals are great places for filling in the gaps in family trees.'

'Maybe we should.'

'Right, I'll ask the questions. You needn't say anything.'

They drove to the cemetery outside the town and joined the people. It was the tradition that neighbours dug the grave and family members carried the coffin on their shoulders along the narrow entrance path. A soft misty downpour soaked everything. Many gravestones were in bad condition, the names obliterated by weathering. Dark trees overshadowed. They stood around the grave as the priest said the prayers and the wooden coffin was lowered by ropes into the deep dark aperture in the earth. Helen shivered. There were other people in that grave belonging to her. According to the headstone, her grandfather – Daniel Michael Brophy – who to her surprise had died just weeks after she was born – was buried here. Chris's husband – Seamus Aherne. Her great-grandparents – Agnes and Cornelius Maher. It was strange to stand there and realise that all of these people were her family, and she hadn't known any of them.

Afterwards Breda spoke to a couple she knew and introduced Helen.

They shook hands, and it transpired then that they had known the McLoughlin family.

'A few years later we were thinking of emigrating as well but decided against it,' the woman smiled.

'My parents were still alive at the time and as my two brothers had gone to England I had to stay,' the man added.

'It's sad to hear that Carmel died, she was a good friend of my eldest sister. They were at school together.' The woman patted her arm.

'Are you coming around to the pub?' the man asked.

Breda looked at Helen.

They had something to eat and Helen relaxed a little, and strangely felt more like herself than she had for weeks until Breda mentioned the Brophys again.

'How many were in the family? I only met Chris's son, Sean.'

'She had one sister, Faye, she was a lovely girl, but I think she died many years ago. And you know the oddest thing, when I saw you in the church earlier, Helen, you reminded me of her. Your hair is the same colour, and I was immediately reminded of those days when we all fancied her,' the man grinned.

'Have to watch him,' the woman quipped.

'I'm past all that now.'

They laughed.

'That was interesting about Faye, and you obviously do look very like her,' Breda said as they made their way home later.

'I'd have liked to stay and talk with them.'

'And probably more open than David. Remember that night we were at his place for dinner and he told us he had known Faye.'

'I was always uncomfortable in his company.'

'He was in a very awkward situation. A bit difficult to come out straight with the fact that he thought he was your father.'

'Selfish bastard.'

'That's a bit hard. He's really an OK person.'

'Don't mind me, I'm just angry with him. I know you like him a lot and I suppose I have to admit I don't know him at all.'

'I wish I didn't. It's awful to feel the way I do about my employer. Particularly when there isn't a hope in hell. There's times I want to leave. Go somewhere else. Get another job.'

'Why not do that?'

'I'm not keen to leave Lackenmore, the family are here, and my friends. So I'll have to put up with it. Anyway, I don't see that much of him. But I wonder if he met your mother again would they get together?'

'She's married.'

'People break up, who's to say,' Breda mused.

'Why don't you go out and get another fellah, there's plenty around. Forget about David.' Helen advised.

'That's easier said than done. What about you and Peter?'

'No sign of him I'm glad to say. No texts or phone calls.'

'Can you put him out of your head?'

'Tit for tat,' Helen grinned.

'I think it will have to be Australia.'

'Plenty of men out there,' she smiled, thinking of Jim.

Chapter Forty-five

Una told Jenny about Chris's death.

'How did you find out?'

'I had a phone call from that person who gave me the letter for you.'

She was silent.

'You never even opened it, did you?'

'No.'

'Do you think you might ever read it?'

'I hadn't planned to. You know how I feel about the past.'

'What will you do now?'

'I don't know.'

'You've missed the funeral unfortunately, he didn't know about it in time. Your mother has been moved to a nursing home now, she has Alzheimers.'

'Then she won't remember me.'

Jenny put down the phone and found herself in a place she hadn't known for a very long time. Its faded contours slowly came to life, shadows retreated to reveal vibrant colours, and in her mind it was once again the way it used to be.

She went to her wardrobe, and took the white envelope from the handbag. Her hand shook as she opened it. So deep in the past now there was no escape.

'My dearest Faye,'

She closed her eyes and tears squeezed. So long since anyone had called her by that name. It was as if he was just beside her, his voice whispering. His lips on hers, warm, soft, his hands gentle, loving. She brushed the tears away and continued.

'It's been so long I don't know where to begin. To say how sorry I was that we never fulfilled our dream to be together is only a tiny part of the pain I suffered in those years following. For you too, having our baby alone in what were no doubt unimaginable circumstances and losing her to adoption must have been heartbreaking.'

She continued reading. He explained how he wrote many letters. Telephoned. Called to the house. But could not find out where she was. Anger spurted. Her eyes spun through the lines now when he talked of how a girl named Helen had come back to Lackenmore to look for her mother. Her pulse rate soared. Helen?

Suddenly, she remembered leaving the tiny child with Carmel and Tom and running into the darkness. Her coat still hung on the fence like a scarecrow, and she crawled underneath and made her way across the fields towards the lakeshore. Then stumbling back to tear it from the barbed wire, afraid her mother and father would see it and know. Exhausted, she walked slowly down to the shore of the lake dragging the coat behind her. Dawn was breaking now and the light from the east caught the stillness of the water, the surface glimmering. She pushed through the reeds. Breathing heavily. Weaker now. She sat down to rest. What was she going to do now? How could she continue on without her baby. Her Helen. The thought of a life of loneliness was something she couldn't contemplate. She looked back at the house. Prayed that Carmel and Tom would take the child somewhere other than back to her home.

She stood up again. The ground was soft and marshy. She pushed through the reeds into the shallows. It was icy cold. But she didn't really feel it, her legs numbed as she lurched across the uneven floor. She continued on, slower now as the water deepened. Waist-high. Shoulder-high.

Chapter Forty-six

His eyes closed, David's fingers chose the keys on the piano, the music tumbling around in his head. He was writing a new piece. Every now and then the melody surfaced and he smiled. Then it disappeared again and he had to concentrate harder. He wrote a scribbled notation in a pad on a side table, his fingers gripping the pen tightly. He had been working on the piece for months now and was frustrated that he couldn't get it quite right. He threw down the pen, got up from the piano, and stood staring out of the window into the grounds. The lawn stretched ahead, flanked by the old oaks, and he walked outside suddenly needing a breath of fresh air. It was a dry day, and a gentle breeze swayed the branches of the trees as he walked underneath. Since he had returned from the States and heard the news of the fire from Breda, he had been tormented with thoughts of Helen and Faye. Really disappointed that he hadn't been here when Helen came down for the funeral. He had phoned Una and asked her to tell Faye just in case she didn't know about Chris.

What was he looking for, he asked himself, time after time. He argued the case. How could he expect Faye to feel the same way. If she was anything like Helen, who certainly wasn't impressed with him, then she would have no interest in seeing him. That would explain her lack of response to his letter. She probably hated him. The way he had hated his father.

He clearly recalled that day he had made his decision to give up his plan to go to Trinity. He would still have Faye and their child – and his music. When his father had gone out that day, David went to his room and took a suitcase from the top of the wardrobe and packed all his best clothes. Then he snapped the locks shut, opened the window and heaved the case out. It landed at the side of the house in a flower bed.

It took him a while to find his Post Office book, and he was disappointed to see that there was only ninety-two punts left. He realised that it wouldn't get them very far and regretted he had not saved more. He put it into his pocket and slipped out the back door. Strapped the case on to the carrier of the bicycle and set off. Excitement gave his legs strength and he pedalled furiously down the drive humming a tune. He couldn't wait to see her. At the gate, he stopped to make sure that the case was secure, but before he had a chance to get going again, his father's car drove in and stopped with a screech of brakes. He climbed out of the car and stood in front of him.

'Where are you off to? '

'I'm going over to see Faye.' David summoned all his courage and stared defiantly at his father.

'Oh, indeed. And the suitcase?'

He glanced at it and turned back to his father. 'We're going away.' For once in his life he was standing up to his father. The tall man laughed and walked towards him, but David stood firm. Suddenly something connected with his stomach, his knees crumpled and he hit the ground, winded.

He didn't manage to sneak out of the house and go over to the farm for a couple of days, but by then it was too late. He left a letter in the space behind the stone under the bridge. Checking every day for a reply until he was sent to college in Dublin. Each time he came home he left another. Over autumns, winters, springs and summers the envelopes grew dry and brittle. Marked with dust and dirt. As the packet increased in size over the years, he wrapped it in plastic, making the space behind the stone bigger. And finally, one last time before he emigrated to Canada.

Now he continued walking across the fields. His shoes were

soaked and his jeans damp from the long grass which was still wet after recent rain. He had only come this way once before in recent times, that evening when he had been swallowed up by memories of Faye that he had hurried away from the place without even thinking of the letters.

The level of the river was a little higher after a wet month and he crept underneath the bridge his hand searching in the darkness for the stone. Some loose gravel fell into the water below as his fingers probed, and his heart leapt when he felt the plastic package still tucked into the place he had put it so long ago. It was brown, and damp, and as he cleared the dirt away from it, he thought perhaps that he would have been happier if it had disappeared, as it always left the possibility that Faye had picked it up. He took it home and later that night he opened it. To read those letters a boy had written. Such innocence. He sighed. Trying to imagine how he had ever been that person. Their notes to each other they had left in behind the stone had been brief arrangements to meet and had not been kept for fear that their parents would find them. These letters held all of his love for Faye. His pain at her loss. And as he grew older the realisation that he would never see their child.

The next day he went to the river again. To put the letters back where they had been for thirty years, and forget that he had ever read them.

But he couldn't escape. The memories wore him down like a woodpecker stripping bark from a tree, until he stood exposed. That part of him which he had thought dead still throbbed, very much alive. With friends who might have remembered, he dropped her name. A tiny pebble falling into a deep pool. But there were no ripples of recognition. No recollections of a day when – a night that – not even a glimpse on the street. Her name sliced through the minds of people with barely a what was that? Who did you say?

.

Chapter Forty-seven

'Have you thought about going to see your grandmother,' Noreen asked.

'I have, but as she's never met me I'd feel a bit awkward.' Helen scribbled on the border at the top of the newspaper. Bits of words. Possible answers to crossword clues which Paddy barked at her every now and then.

'Would you like me to go with you?'

She shook her head. 'But thanks anyway.'

'Five across "who's the man behind the wall rubbish"?' Paddy asked.

They ignored him.

'Have you decided how long you'll stay?'

'Well, I've got quite a lot to do here over the next while, and if I go home then I'll be back to my usual – looking for any story which will appeal to the newspapers. But I hope that's OK with you? '

'Paddy and I are delighted to have you. We need someone around the place now that our own two are in the States.'

'Thanks,' Helen smiled and hugged her aunt. 'But I'd like to pay my way. How much do you think?'

'Look, you hardly eat a thing, and the bedrooms are empty, I don't want to hear another word about paying anything. We want you to stay as long as you want.'

'You're too kind to me.'

'No more about it now, tell me, have you heard from Peter?'

'I haven't had any contact with him since that day he was here.

And I'm glad of that. There's been some stuff which I can't take.'

'But you still like him?' Noreen smiled knowingly.

'I suppose, but at least one of my worries has been cleared up if David is my father.'

'If?'

'I hate to suggest this but sometimes girls can be friendly with more than one guy, even I knew people like that at school. I don't see why it would be any different then. It's not that long ago.'

'But he seemed to think he was the only one.'

'I'm not suggesting my mother was promiscuous, but every guy thinks he's the only one.'

'It's a pity she has cut all ties with home.'

'Thirteen down "cartload can be overfull" eight letters? Ah yes.' Paddy filled in the answer himself.

'I'd give anything to find her.'

'Has David heard from her?'

'I don't know. Anyway, I suppose he'd tell me, although I don't want to have anything to do with him.'

'It's a pity, he seems a very nice man.'

'He may be now, but he wasn't when he was young, I can't stop thinking of how he deserted us, I can't forgive him for that.'

'Maybe in time.'

'I don't know,' Helen murmured.

'And you will, I'm sure of it.' Noreen stood and kissed her. 'Now I'd better get on with the day.'

'Nineteen down? Hey, someone give me a hand here,' Paddy asked,

'Let's have a look.' Helen moved over to where he sat at the table, and together they worked on the cryptic crossword. Paddy was very good at solving the clues, but it took Helen a while before she was able to contribute any ideas.

There was a ring on the doorbell, and Noreen bustled through from the kitchen

'I'll get it,' Helen offered.

'No, you stay where you are.' She disappeared through the door.

'What do you think?' Paddy asked pointing to another clue.

She stared at it.

Noreen came back inside. 'Helen, you have callers, they're in the hall.'

'For me?'

'Yes.'

'Who is it?'

'Go on, you'll find out.'

Helen pushed open the door and stared astonished at the two men who stood there.

Chapter Forty-eight

'Now Pauline, it's time for your lunch.' The nurse helped the old woman sit up. 'Do you think you might be able to go over to the table with the others?'

'No.'

'It'll do you good to get a bit of exercise.'

'No.'

'Come on now, put one foot in front of the other.' She got her into a standing position and drew her towards the table, surprised to find Pauline suddenly agreeable although she had been adamant that she would not go over to join the other patients.

'There you are now, sit beside Mary.'

'I don't know her.'

'Of course you do, she's your friend. She's in the next bed.'

The woman smiled. A little younger and not quite as forgetful as some of the other patients.

'I'm going home,' Pauline announced.

'Of course you are.' The nurse brought a bowl of soup closer to Pauline and handed her a spoon.

'I'll have my dinner at home. I don't want this.' She pushed it away.

'Have a little, just in case you get hungry on the way.' The nurse moved it back.

She looked at her and then took a spoonful. 'This is horrible.'

'Try a little more, it'll taste nicer then.'

'It'll never be nicer.'

'This evening we'll try something different.'

'I won't be here this evening. I told you. I'm going home.'

'Of course I forgot. Have another spoonful.'

She sipped the thick vegetable mixture.

'Good girl.' She patted her on the shoulder and went to take care of someone else.

Pauline hadn't settled well. After she had been assessed as needing institutional care, and transferred from the hospital to the nursing home, all she wanted to do was to go home. The staff were aware that this was something she could never do, unless she had someone with her for twenty-four hours. And there was no family support, and no visitors so far. Then one day someone came in. A young man. Dark-haired. Well-dressed.

He sat beside her chair and talked to her intently.

She didn't seem to understand. Repeating her usual mantra. 'I want to go home. Why am I here?'

'I can't take you home, Gran, I live in America.'

'Where?' She was puzzled.

'America.'

'You must know Sean.' She immediately delved into her bag, pulling out tattered pieces of newspaper. 'This is his letter. We asked him to come home.'

'I am Sean, Gran.'

'Faye sent a letter.'

'Who?'

'Faye.'

'I don't know her.'

'She's waiting for me.' She stared at the papers in her hand.

'Gran, I want to ask you something.'

'Take me home.'

'I will if you tell me about Mr. Corcoran.'

'Old Corcoran?'

'He says he has held title to the land for many years, some special arrangement with Mom.'

'He liked me.'

'Did you agree to this title.'

'What's that?' She played with her frizzy grey hair.

'To let him have access to the land?'

'Who are you to come questioning me. Away with you.' She brushed him off.

'I'm your grandson.'

'Take me home,' she begged.

'I promise I will as soon as you tell me what I want to know.'

'Faye told me never to breathe a word,' she whispered.

'For God's sake, who's Faye.'

'Your mother.'

'Chris was my mother.' He was becoming irritated.

'I don't know anyone called Chris.'

He sighed and stood up, arms folded across his chest.

'Is everything all right?' The nurse appeared at the end of the bed.

'She doesn't understand.'

'Well, you know she's become a little forgetful.' She turned to him as she spoke, then back to Pauline. She smiled at her. 'Later I think we'll do your hair, and maybe put on some lipstick and perfume.'

'Oh please, I love lipstick,' she smiled and rubbed her hands together. 'Do you want some?' she asked Sean.

'No.' His expression was grim.

'I want to look beautiful.'

'We'll have you looking beautiful in no time,' the nurse assured.

He grimaced.

'Then you can take me home. I must find Faye. She went into the lake.'

Sean stared at her for a moment, then turned on his heel and left, as Pauline's mind swept her back to that morning when Dan and herself had found Faye walking into the dark water.

'Faye, Faye, come back, don't go any further,' they shouted.

'Merciful Jesus.' Pauline crossed herself. 'You'll have to go in after her.' She pushed Dan ahead. 'I can't swim.'

The dog had followed and now jumped up and down in the shallows.

Dan trudged into the water. Falling almost immediately and flailing about as he tried to swim.

Pauline screamed, her voice bouncing back eerily from the mountains on the opposite side of the lake. 'Faye, stay where you are.'

Dan drew near, swimming stronger now. He reached her, his fingers clawing at her clothes. But she slid underneath, just let herself go like a stone, and her body disappeared with a quiet ripple.

'Faye!' he roared, diving below the surface, hands searching until at last he pulled her head above the water. Going under but recovering and under again as he dragged her through the icy depths, his arm around her shoulders. He swam slowly until he reached his depth, but the lake didn't want to let them go, the softness of the lake floor holding his feet in a vice, sucking him down. Lulled by a strange miasma which drained the last ounces of energy from his body, he almost gave up more than once but the weight of the still form of Faye forced him on until after what seemed like hours he pulled her up on to solid ground where he collapsed beside her coughing and spluttering.

'Is she all right?' Pauline fell to her knees. 'Faye, wake up, wake up.' She patted her face, softly at first, then harder.

Faye moaned and coughed up water. The dog nuzzled.

'Thanks be to God.' Pauline took off her cardigan and put it around her. 'Let's get her back to the house. I'll take her legs, you her shoulders.'

Dan pushed himself to his feet and between them they made their way across the fields to the house. In the kitchen, Pauline wrapped Faye in a blanket, and pulled the armchair close to the range which was always kept going day and night.

'Change your clothes, Dan, or you'll get a chill.'

He poured water into the big pot on the range, and replenished the turf, then turned and stared down at his daughter. 'You're going to be all right, Faye, don't you worry.' His hand cupped her face and he kissed her forehead. 'Oh my God, Pauline, where's the baby?'

'Have a look in the bedroom.'

He hurried upstairs, and back quickly.

'She's gone.'

'What?' She stopped in the act of trying to pour a little whiskey into Faye's mouth and stared at him.

'She must have put her somewhere.'

'Or dropped her in the water.' Pauline compressed her lips. 'You'll have to go back, search, now before anyone finds it. Quickly!'

He threw on dry clothes and went quickly to the lake. He still felt shaken, his legs weak and unsteady. He searched along the shore in the brightening morning light. In and out of clumps of shrubbery and among the brown reeds. He took the small wooden boat out and rowed slowly along parallel with the shore. His eyes scanned the dark green depths intently, searching for a small white body caught in the grip of the long training weeds which twisted and churned like reptiles with the flow of the water. It was hours later when at last he gave up and slowly made his way home.

'God's will.' There was no emotion in Pauline's blunt remark.

Dan's body was hunched in grief at the loss of his first grandchild. 'She was such a beautiful baby. A life barely begun suddenly cut short and returned to God, unwanted,' he murmured sadly.

'Maybe it's just as well,' Pauline muttered.

'How is Faye?' Pauline stacked the plates in the dresser.

'Seems all right.' Dan slumped into the chair suddenly shaken by a fit of coughing.

'You don't look so well yourself, your face is all flushed.'

'It's just the end of that cold I had, hasn't cleared up yet.' He coughed again.

'Better get to bed early tonight.'

The next morning he was up as usual to attend to the animals, but felt weak and dizzy. He lurched back into the kitchen for breakfast, but couldn't eat, almost stunned by a violent headache. For the first time in his memory, he stumbled upstairs to bed in the middle of the day. It was just after twelve and he couldn't go on any longer.

Pauline came up later. She called his name but he didn't seem to

237

be aware of her presence as he lay in the bed, drenched with sweat. Suddenly, she was worried. If anything happened to Dan, who would run the farm? She sent for Dr. O'Sullivan.

'Pneumonia,' he pronounced.

'Should we get him into hospital?'

'Dangerous, the journey is too long. You'll have to look after him here. It's his only chance. The heart is weak. He should have been to see me before now.'

Pauline made the sign of the cross.

The doctor returned the following day, and the day after that, but Dan grew steadily worse. Pauline and Chris prayed on their knees. Said countless rosaries. Neighbours called to see him.

Faye stayed in her room, where she had been for months. She washed and dressed herself, and ate her meals obediently. She had almost recovered physically but her mind was in another place.

It was the week after Christmas, and Dan still lay in bed, a thin wasted man. He had changed out of all recognition and had no energy left to fight the final battle. Nor was there any love here to encourage him to make the effort. No warm arms wound around him. No intimate whispers. No lips on his. Nothing except Pauline's eyes, dark and irritable, resenting the position in which she now found herself. He tried to whisper. 'I'm sorry for giving you all this trouble.' He called for Faye but she never came. And he gave up the fight somewhere in the small hours, just closed his eyes and slipped away without another word.

Pauline seemed inconsolable, but the tears were for herself. She blamed Faye for his death. It was all her fault. At the funeral, Faye didn't seem to understand what was happening. Her eyes deep pools of loss. People were respectful and sympathetic. They all came back to the house afterwards. Drank whiskey, cups of tea, ate sandwiches and cake. Someone played a fiddle, and the wake went on long into the night until eventually it was over and they were left alone at last.

The following morning Faye's door was thrown open.

'Get up.' Pauline shook her daughter who stared at her with

vacant eyes.

'Come on, get up, this instant.'

Faye cowered.

'There's nothing wrong with you. You'll have to pull your weight around here now. Your father is dead, do you realise that. She drew closer to her face and glared at her. 'And he died trying to save you. It's all your fault, do you hear me? All your fault.'

'You say she never speaks, and doesn't seem to know you?' the doctor questioned Pauline after he had made a cursory examination of Faye.

'I'm sure she's putting it on.'

'Why would she do that?'

'Because of Dan, his dying and all,' Pauline stuttered.

'Perhaps the shock.'

'It must have been that.'

'How long has she been this way?'

'Since he died.'

'I think perhaps we had better refer her to St. Joseph's, I know a good man there.'

'I don't want anyone to know she's gone to a place like that.'

'You needn't worry, no-one will find out.'

Chapter Forty-nine

Jenny sat staring at the laptop screen, their latest set of accounts detailed there. She went through the various sections. Balance Sheet. Profit and Loss Account. Expenses. It was almost three o'clock in the morning, and while she had managed to sleep for an hour, after that she twisted and turned in the bed, her mind clear as a bell, questions shooting through it. She had got up eventually, and did some work. She felt so alone that she would have been glad of Michael's company. But he was the last person in whom she could confide. In the small hours, when the imagination runs riot and takes you to places you never thought for one second you would ever visit, there is no-one but yourself.

The darkness of the night yawned. Endless seconds, minutes and hours until she had to face the day. To put on a face which would be acceptable to the family, to the people she worked with. To cream beige foundation into the contours, over high cheekbones, across the forehead, on the chin and neck, making sure there was no white skin visible at the line of her blouse collar. Soft grey eye line contrasting with blue green iris, brown mascara, and lastly a slight touch of blusher. A camouflage. But that was all a very long way away. Now her eyes were red-rimmed with tiredness, shadows emphasising the classic features, spelling trauma there. She clicked the mouse and another page came up. She tried to concentrate. Succeeded for a couple of moments but lost the focus again, swept up into a myriad of images. One in particular dominating.

She sat in an armchair. An uncomfortable plastic covered metal thing. Her limbs awkwardly splayed as if they didn't belong to her but were mere appendages without purpose. Her large blue green eyes were fixed expressionless on the blacked out window in front of her.

'Faye, dinner time,' a voice ordered and she obeyed automatically. To scoop brown stew into her mouth from a bowl with a plastic spoon, and drink milk always warm and slightly sour.

'Faye, exercise.' Wasted muscles forced to move the slight frame up and down the long room until she stumbled and flopped, exhausted, into the chair again.

'Faye, medication.' Tablets administered three times a day kept her mind dulled, her emotions depressed, caught in that place between consciousness and sleep, a distorted dream world of non-existence.

So it was, day in, day out, for over two years. Faye didn't know where she was, or who she was, all memory expunged.

Suddenly one day the noise was louder, much louder, every sound magnified. As usual she stared at the blacked out window, but now she could see a strange face looking back at her. She reached forward and put out a trembling hand and the person did the same, but the fingers which touched hers were icy cold and she drew back in fear.

'Where am I?' The question screamed in her head, but she was unable to articulate or communicate her feelings in any way to those around her, suffering wave after wave of pain and nausea which kept her confined to bed. But slowly it receded and she became more aware of her surroundings. Seeing the large high-ceilinged room which was her home clearly for the first time. The once white walls stained with greenish patches of dampness reared high above her. Sunshine poured through the top section of the long narrow windows, the bright blue sky honeycombed by metal bars which threw a trellis of shadows across the wooden floor.

Everything frightened Faye now, particularly the other patients in Ward 6 Female. Dressed in a mixed bag of hand-me-downs, the brighter ones spent their time staring at an old television set in the corner of the day room. Others seemed quite unaware of their surroundings. But all the time the clamour of voices rose and fell.

That was the worst thing. The level of moaning, shrieking and wailing was so loud at times Faye shook her head from side to side and covered her ears with her hands in an effort to block it out.

★

'I'm worried about her.' Una, the nurse, stared through the small square glass pane in the door between the office and the ward. 'If she would only tell us how she feels.'

'The medication has been changed, that's something,' the other nurse, May, counted out tablets into individual containers on the trolley.

'I know, but she needs more than that.'

'The wheels grind slowly here, you can't expect miracles overnight.'

'I don't expect miracles, just more interest.'

'There are a lot of changes planned apparently.'

'But when? Faye seems so agitated, I don't know whether the new meds suit her.'

'So would you if you'd been on the same drugs for a couple of years, withdrawal is tough. She needs to get used to the new levels, then maybe, hey, are you going to do any work around here today?' she laughed.

Una produced her keys and unlocked the door. Together they pushed the trolley through and she locked it behind them. Immediately they were surrounded by some of the more agile women.

'Now girls, sit down, otherwise no sweeties.' May gently shepherded them back to the chairs which stood around the walls. It was difficult to control them. Always more excited and intractable when the drugs had worn off somewhat. It was then that Una could glimpse the real people hidden beneath. Grandmothers, mothers, daughters, sisters, aunts.

'Nurse, nurse, when am I going home?' A middle-aged woman plucked at her sleeve.

'Tomorrow.'

'Nurse, I want my dinner,' another demanded.

'Later, put your shoes on.'

'I can't find them.' The old woman pointed down to her bare feet.

'We'll have a look in a minute.'

'Nurse, she took my money.'

'I did not.'

'You did.'

'I didn't.' They started to tear at each other's clothes, pulling hair, scratching and screeching invective.

'It's one of those days,' Una laughed as they separated the two.

'Let's get on with this otherwise World War Three will break out.' May placed a yellow capsule into a woman's mouth and helped her sip water from a paper cup.

'It's so bloody pathetic,' Una muttered.

'What is?'

'Drugging them up to the eyeballs.'

'They have to be kept quiet.'

'I know, but keeping them incarcerated inside, never to see the light of day or feel the sunshine on their faces is so cruel.'

'Can you imagine trying to control this lot outside?'

'They could be taken out one at a time.'

'Are you mad, we can barely manage to get everything done as it is.'

'I'd love to take Faye out of this room for a few minutes.'

'Rather you than me. God only knows what she might do, particularly now she's on new meds. Anyway you'd never get approval from Dr. McNamara.'

'One of these days I will, I promise you.'

★

Faye's mind was bombarded with impressions. Colours so strong they blinded. Sounds incredibly sharp. Pictures of other places, other people, haunted her day and night. One face in particular. A boy's face. With brown eyes. He smiled, laughed, and called to her. The sun shone. She picked daisies. Made a chain. A baby cried. The brightness darkened. It was icy cold. In the nightmare she cried out but no-one came.

She liked Una, and would do anything she wanted without protest, jealous of the time the nurse spent with the other patients. Today, she watched her in the office. Wanting to be in there too she pushed herself out of the chair and walked slowly over to the window. She leaned her head against the glass and rapped with her knuckles. Una and May stopped talking instantly and gazed in astonishment at her.

'Faye?' Una came through the door.

She smiled.

'May, look at her eyes, her face, she looks normal. I can't believe it.' She threw her arms around Faye and hugged her. 'Are you feeling all right?'

She nodded.

'She understands me, May.' There were tears in her eyes.

'It's amazing after all this time.'

'I must tell McNamara,' she gasped, 'now I'll get her out of here.'

Chapter Fifty

Helen rushed down the hall and threw herself into her father's arms. They hugged close. Their tears mingled. She pulled back a little and stared into his face, at the square weather-beaten visage that she knew so well, so glad he hadn't changed. That was the great thing about it. He was still her Dad. Her only Dad.

'I didn't mean for you to come all this way, the funeral is over.'

'It gave me the excuse I needed, I've been thinking about it for too long. And Jim seemed keen as well.'

Helen turned to him.

Jim smiled.

She reached out and brought him into the circle. 'It's great to see you.'

'I can't believe I'm here.'

'Neither can I,' she laughed, and kissed him. Full on the mouth. It was by accident and the first time she had ever done so. But it felt good. And she was very aware of the softness of his lips. The warmth of his breath.

His arms encircled her body and they clung together. A sudden knowing taking them to another place. Somewhere they had never been before.

'Tom!' Paddy put his arm around his brother.

'It's been too long.' Noreen kissed him.

'We should have come back to see you all before Carmel died, it was sad that she never saw Ireland again,' Tom said.

'It's good to see you now and about time,' Paddy grinned.

'And you haven't introduced this young man, but I know you must be Jim,' Noreen said.

'Yea, that's me.'

'How did you leave the store, you two, who's looking after it?' Helen asked.

'Since Jim's become a partner, we promoted Nigel, so he's in charge. About time I had a bit of time off. Maybe one of these days I might even retire,' Tom grinned at Helen.

'And come back home for good,' Paddy said.

'I'll have to get to know my family all over again.'

Jim smiled. 'And I'll have to get to know Ireland. Someone will have to take me on a tour. Although I've been reading those articles by a certain well known journalist and I'm really keen to see some of those places she mentions, as I know a lot of other people are as well.' His hand rested briefly on Helen's.

She felt suddenly shy at his touch and hoped the others hadn't noticed.

'We might all go back to Lackenmore, we've been threatening that for a long time.'

Tom planned to stay for over a month, but Jim had only two week's holiday, so they were keen to make those days as full as possible. Helen was so happy. It was wonderful to spend time with her Dad and they talked endlessly. He was always there at the kitchen table watching them prepare meals, following them around the house, touching Helen every now and then as if to reassure himself that she was real.

'Hey, give me a hug,' he asked as she passed by the couch where he sat. She was carrying a tray of glasses and quickly put them down and turned back. She leaned towards him and he pulled her down beside him. 'My girl.'

She buried her face into his shoulder. 'Dad, hold me tight, hold me.'

'I will my love, always.' Faces touched, and there was moisture on their cheeks. She sat there, loving the warmth of his body. Drawn back to her childhood when they were father and daughter and there was no doubt in the world that it was so. She sat up and kissed him. 'Better get my chores done.'

He laughed, and held on to her hand for a few seconds.

'I don't know if I really want to go back to Lackenmore again. David could be there and you'll want to meet him and I can't bear that you might like him because I don't,' Helen murmured.

'We don't have to meet him, if you don't want to go, I'll just take a quick trip down and back.'

'I feel guilty.'

'Don't be.'

'I want you to really enjoy yourself.' She stared into his eyes. 'That's the only thing I want, but he's in the way.'

'Forget about him.'

'I can't disappoint everybody, take no notice of me.'

'So you'll come with me?'

'I reckon I will,' she grinned.

'Thanks.'

'While we're there, maybe you might come with me to visit my grandmother? I've been thinking about it but hadn't the courage to go myself.'

They headed off the next day in two cars. Jim travelled with Helen and as they drove along, they talked of home in Alice Springs.

'I miss everything, everybody,' she confessed.

'And we all miss you.'

She smiled.

'Some of us more acutely than others.'

'Yea,' she laughed.

'When are you thinking of coming back?'

'I don't know yet. I'm enjoying the work and I can't do that at home, so I want to stay on a bit longer.'

'You remember what we talked about before you came back to Ireland last time.' Jim was looking at her but she stared straight ahead, glad of the excuse not to have to meet his eyes as she drove.

She nodded.

'I haven't changed. I still feel the same and always will.' He reached his hand across and ran it along her shoulder to the back of her neck, where he massaged the soft skin.

A shiver went through her. Since the day he had arrived and their lips had somehow inadvertently met, she had not known what to think. How was it that her previous disinterest in Jim had been replaced by this heightened feeling of excitement every time she saw him. Now that they were alone it was nerve-wracking. They continued on the motorway, a monotonous drive which usually made her sleepy, but now there was no chance of that, her mind was fully focussed on Jim.

'Tell me if I'm being too pushy. It's just there's so little chance to see you these days I have to make the most of my time. You know, if you hadn't kissed me when I arrived I never would have said a word. I really only came to keep Tom company, it's a long journey, and I think it was a bit daunting for him.'

'That's why you came?' She was suddenly disappointed, and her stomach churned.

'It was the main reason. I had given up on us. That last time we talked you made yourself very clear. Now I'm like a boy in love.'

'A boy?'

'I know, sounds crazy, doesn't it?'

She wondered if she was in love too. Could it happen so quickly? She had thought she loved Peter. He was everything she wanted. All during her twenties she had waited for someone to come into her life and love her so much she would be perfectly content, never looking beyond to some other horizon, prepared to give up everything for him. Now her heart was telling her different. You didn't love him at all. He was just a passing fancy. Feelings which faded almost as quickly as they had begun. A glittering light in the night sky which died after a brief existence like a falling star. This was different. She knew Jim as long as she could remember. They had grown up so close he was like her other half. A twin brother. Always there in her only child life. A shadow following close behind.

His fingers ran through her hair. Her scalp tingled sensually.

'If you keep doing that I'll crash the car.' She had to say it.

'Do you want me to drive for a while?'

'I don't know what the situation is with the insurance on a hired car.'

'We should have checked it out. I could have shared the driving and then you wouldn't be tired.'

'You don't like me driving, go on, admit it,' she grinned.

'You're a very good driver.'

'It's the male ego, even worse in Australian men,' she teased, 'you have to be the one behind the wheel making all the decisions.'

'You think I'm domineering?' he quipped.

'Oh yea, master and slave.' She could josh with him. His personality easy-going. That was the nice thing about their relationship. She could say anything to Jim.

Tom and Paddy had taken all of them around every inch of Lackenmore's streets, and its hinterland. Out to the old ruined homestead which sadly still stood there, a reminder of times past. Tom talked about how he had met Carmel. Courted her. Married her and brought her back to the farm. But there was a sadness in his eyes as he talked about their efforts to have a child, all those miscarriages, each one a terrible tragedy in itself. Something they had to keep quiet. No-one talked about it. It wasn't done. No burial in consecrated ground. No grave. No headstone. No-where to grieve or say a prayer. But then he smiled and put his hand out to Helen, and the sadness was chased away.

It's wonderful to be back.' Tom raised his glass, and they all joined with him in the toast at the dinner they arranged to celebrate their visit. They were staying at the new four star hotel in the town, a private room booked for their celebration. Some of Tom and Paddy's cousins were invited along, and Helen asked Breda also. 'Helen saved our lives. She made everything worthwhile. And Australia gave us the chance of a new start with her. Thank you my love.' He kissed her.

She returned his kiss.

Everyone clapped.

Then Jim stood and put his arm around her.

And they clapped again. And whooped. And cheered.

She blushed.

'Have you something to tell us, Helen?' Breda beamed.

'No, I haven't, curiosity box,' she laughed.

'I'll tell you,' Jim said, 'I just want to announce that I love Helen McLoughlin, and I hope one day to share my life with her. I don't know whether she loves me or not yet, but ...' he smiled down at Helen.

They were all quiet for a few seconds then the applause burst out again.

'Hey, this is wonderful. I'm so happy for you,' Noreen smiled.

'It's too much for me,' Helen smiled, tearful also.

'We're all a bunch of cry babies,' laughed Breda, wiping her eyes with a tissue.

The following days were glorious. Helen hadn't been so happy in a long time. While she didn't talk to Jim about her feelings, she hoped that as time passed she would be able to tell him what he wanted to hear. She left him to Dublin Airport at the end of the week, still afraid of ultimate commitment just yet.

'Don't forget me, promise me that?' he asked, and kissed her before he went through.

'No, I won't, you'll see me soon.'

The nursing home was a large sprawling building, and seemed a nice enough place, quite comfortable and cheerful. They enquired at reception about Pauline, and were directed to her ward. Helen found it quite tragic to see that many of the patients were unaware of their surroundings.

'Pauline, you have visitors today. This is Tom and Helen, won't you say hello to them? Take a seat here.' The nurse pulled two chairs nearer.

Pauline sat in an armchair, dressed in pink blouse, cardigan and grey skirt. Her white hair was combed neatly, but she stared beyond them, her hands holding on tightly to a large handbag on her lap. There were other patients there as well, some sitting in chairs, others in bed.

Helen sat down, while Tom stood behind her, his hand on her shoulder.

'How are you today, Pauline, it's good to see you after all this time,' Tom said, 'and this is Helen.'

The woman raised her eyes and looked at her with a vague puzzled look. Helen was unsure what to say.

'We've spent a long time in Australia, and I'm sorry I never managed to come back before now. Sadly, Carmel died earlier this year.'

She ignored him.

'Faye?'

Helen glanced around at her father.

'No, I'm Helen.'

'You're Faye. Who else could you be? Haven't you got her eyes and her face and who else ever had hair like that in our family? Tell me that,' she rapped angrily.

Helen couldn't say anything.

'Right, I'm ready now.' Pauline stood up shakily and opened the door of the small wardrobe beside the bed. She pulled clothes down, and began to stuff them into an empty plastic bag.

'Where are you going?' Helen asked.

'Home of course. '

The nurse came back in. 'Pauline, are you packing?'

'Yes.' She struggled with the bag which wasn't big enough for her things.

'You're going with Helen and Tom, is that it? Well, I was just about to make tea, wouldn't you like a cup before you go?'

Pauline stopped what she was doing. 'What have you got to eat?'

'I think we can rustle up some apple pie and custard.' The nurse winked at them.

'All right then, I'll wait.' She sat on the bed, her hands still clinging to the handbag.

'We'll go into the small dining room. Come on now.' She helped Pauline up and walked slowly with her out of the room.

Helen looked at Tom, and they followed.

They shared apple pie and custard, and hot cups of tea. Pauline said nothing as she ate. Scraping the bowl of every last morsel. Drinking her tea slowly, two hands around the cup. When she had finished, she put it down and wiped her hands with the paper napkin given to her by the nurse.

'He died.'

'Who?'

'Dan.'

'That's sad.' Tom said.

'I didn't know him.' Helen shook her head.

'You don't know your own father?' Her eyes stared at Helen.

'This is my father,' Helen leaned towards Tom.

'No, he's not.' She shook her head vehemently.

'Yes, he is my Dad,' Helen insisted.

'You're lying.'

'No, I'm not, this is Tom McLoughlin, my father. Dad, tell her I'm your daughter.'

He looked uncomfortable. 'Dad?'

Chapter Fifty-one

Jenny went to the office early the following morning. Annabelle would arrive from Paris later and there was a lot to do before she left for the airport to pick her up. She tried to concentrate but it was difficult. She made coffee and drank two cups. It helped a little. She had to get herself together before her friend arrived. But she couldn't get her mind to stay in the present. It strayed away constantly dragging her with it like a naughty pup on a lead. Chris was dead. Her mother in a home. The farmhouse a burned out shell. The knowledge cast a noose around her neck. Her childhood consumed by flames.

Maria arrived, looking incredibly beautiful. She kissed Jenny. 'You look tired, had you a late night?' she asked, concerned.

'I didn't sleep very well.'

'Me neither. Up and down to the loo,' she smiled as she eased herself into the chair.

'You look well.'

'I suppose it's the excitement of the baby coming. Both of us are looking forward to it so much. I pray my child will be healthy, that is all that matters. It is so wonderful to feel this little being inside me. Oh, there's a kick, feel it, Jenny, feel, here.' She reached for her hand and drew it down on her bump.'

Jenny almost dissolved in tears at the unbelievable longing which swept through her as she felt the movement through the soft velvet top Maria wore.

'Isn't it amazing?' Maria smiled.

She nodded.

'I can't imagine having a son or a daughter.'

Jenny's mobile phone rang.

'Excuse me,' she flicked it open, and listened.

'We're making the bookings for the Breeders Cup in Santa Anita, are you coming this year?' Michael asked.

'I'm not sure.'

'We'll take the jet so the numbers are important.'

'I'll check my diary.'

'I want you to come, try not to be doing anything else,' he said.

'I know.' He needed her these days. His clash with mortality had done that to him. Her role was now a carer, a mother figure, someone who would always be there for him. Her wife/lover status had ceased altogether. The times when he demanded that she oblige him didn't happen any more. While she had hated the almost impersonal conquest at the time, that hurried searching for sexual satisfaction, now she missed the intimacy. The chance to communicate. To renew the love they had once felt. He didn't seem to need that any longer. Their marriage was only in name.

She clicked off the phone. 'Right, I'd better get on with things, I'm meeting Annabelle, so will you check the listings?' She changed the subject taking her mind back to business, to the place where she felt most comfortable. Her safe zone.

'You should see next year's Spring designs, Jenny has excelled herself.' Annabelle was full of enthusiasm at dinner that evening.

'Thanks,' Jenny smiled, pleased.

'Our fashion guru,' Michael grinned.

'I wish I could go to Santa Anita,' Pearl sighed.

'It's far too tiring for you.' Michael topped up his wine. 'I might go, I'm not written off yet,' Pearl retorted, feisty.

'Won't you be travelling together?' Annabelle asked.

'We could arrange for a wheelchair at the airport,' Jenny said, 'that's if I can go, I'm not sure yet.'

'Make your mind up.' Michael cut into his fillet steak.

'I will,' she smiled at Annabelle, and Pearl, anxious to dissipate the tension which had suddenly crept into the atmosphere.

'Imagine the shopping. It's so long since I was able to enjoy a good browse. Now stuff is brought over to me, someone else's choices, it's not the same.'

'Pearl has very definite preferences,' Jenny put her hand over hers, 'haven't you?'

'I like old fashioned things.' Her eyes met Jenny's. There was a meaning there, and she was reminded of the white dress.

'So do I, some of the twenties and thirties dresses are wonderful, I have a few in my wardrobe,' Annabelle smiled.

'There was nothing like them, nowadays there's no attention to detail.'

'It's all about money.'

'It was then too I suppose, but time was given to everything.'

'Time means different things to different people.' Michael had already finished his meal. 'I have to make the most of mine, don't know how much I have left.'

'Well, if you keep on the way you're going, eating and drinking so much, then you'll be on the way out before you know it.' Pearl's remark was acidic. He was put down and he didn't like it.

'Mother, I'm not your boy any longer,' he flashed.

'Look at me, this family always had longevity, most of us have lived long lives, keep that in your head before you commit suicide.'

'Mother,' he raised his voice.

'Michael, she has a point.'

'Are you on her side now?'

'No-one's on any side,' Jenny murmured softly. This was getting a little out of hand and she was embarrassed in front of Annabelle.

'Ah, for God's sake, bloody women.' He stood up and marched out of the room.

'I'm sorry, Annabelle.'

She shook her head and smiled.

'Can't talk to him at all these days, he's got a very short fuse,' Pearl said.

'He hasn't been well,' Annabelle murmured.

'Should look after himself properly. Takes no notice of either me or his wife. We might as well be talking to the wall. Isn't that right, Jennifer? As for me, I feel the same way as I always did about my children. Doesn't matter what age they are. Although I don't suppose either of you understand that, having no children yourselves.' She wiped her lips with a napkin. 'I'm tired now, I think I'll go up.'

'I'll help you,' Jenny offered.

'Maureen will look after me, you take Annabelle into the drawing room.'

'I'm sorry, but things spin out of control these days at the drop of a hat, Michael's not in good form,' Jenny murmured, embarrassed.

'Neither are you. Although I don't know how you put up with Pearl, that was a caustic comment about children if ever there was one,' Annabelle seemed slightly miffed.

'She can be sharp, I suppose.'

'And your mind is somewhere else I've noticed. Even today when we were looking at the designs you didn't seem to have your usual focus. Is there something wrong?' Annabelle was very concerned. 'Can I help?' Her still beautiful face was anxious.

Jenny shook her head, suddenly emotional. She had always been so good to her.

'What can I do?' Annabelle was insistent.

'Nothing.'

'But there must be something, you've changed so much since the last time I saw you, remember you brought Maria down to the villa, you were in great form then, what has happened since?'

'With Michael being so ill, life has been a bit stressful.'

'But he's getting well, full of enthusiasm for work, the horses, surely you must be relieved about that.'

'I'm still concerned.'

'You're probably worrying unnecessarily. Although I suppose he's a bit tetchy. Maybe difficult to live with these days?'

'Yea.'

'But he has his life back, surely that's the main thing for now.'

'He pushes himself too much.'

'Sure I could say that about Guy, but men don't listen, don't you know that?'

'I suppose you're right,' Jenny was morose.

'But you seem so down. In the early years when you first came to work for me you were always such a live-wire. So passionate about everything. Now I'm really worried about you. Tell me what's going on, and don't hide it, I want to know.' She put her hand on Jenny's.

'There's nothing in particular, it's just life in general.'

'Are you ill, is it something like that?' Annabelle pressed.

'No, thanks be to God. Annabelle, you're losing the run of yourself.'

'You know I love you, you're probably the only family I've got, my surrogate daughter. Maybe I should have told Pearl that.'

'She's not as bad as she seems. There's another side to her.'

'I'd want to see that, otherwise I don't think I could stand living here.'

'It can be difficult,' Jenny admitted.

'Come over to me for a couple of weeks, you'll feel better.'

'We're very busy, you know, even though there's a recession we have to do twice as much to keep everything going.'

'Promise me you'll come as soon as you can?'

They kissed, and hugged.

'I miss you, sometimes it's a bit lonely.'

'Want me back in the office?' Annabelle grinned.

'Wouldn't mind.'

'Let me tell you that you'd hate it. You're the boss now. Imagine how it would be if I was stepping on your toes again?'

'We've always worked well together.'

'I'm too old now, couldn't keep up the pace, believe me.'

'No way, I'm going to take you out tomorrow to inspect some of the outlets. You'll get hooked again, won't be able to resist that feeling of having it all at your fingertips.'

'I'm looking forward to it.'

'But I have to warn you, the level of client interest is low, sometimes we don't have a person in all day looking to buy. I'm concerned about the figures.'

'I know sales were down in 2008, but we've been through ups and downs before, we'll come out the other end.'

'I'm keeping a close eye on the turnover. I've asked the accountant to let us have weekly figures.'

'Good idea. How's the horse business?'

'Couldn't really tell you, Michael doesn't divulge very much information, although I know Conor and Eoin are worried.'

'There are a lot of businesses closing.'

'We're reducing everything. Fifty per cent off. We have to do it, everyone else is, and some of our regular clients have been badly hit themselves, orders have been cancelled.'

'It will be OK.'

'I was going to tell you tomorrow, I'm sorry I wasn't able to hide it for longer.' Jenny was glad the conversation had taken this turn. It had covered up Annabelle's searching questions about her mood. She couldn't have told her friend about her past. 'When I last talked with Guy he wasn't terribly confident about the UK either.'

'No, and it hasn't improved. We're just hoping that there will be a bit of an upturn soon.'

'We'd better start praying,' she laughed, although she wasn't too confident that God would be listening, she hadn't talked to Him lately.

Chapter Fifty-two

'I know that you find it difficult, Helen, but I would like to meet David. You needn't come along. I'll just buy him a quick cup of coffee – that's if he agrees to see me. It's something I've wanted to do since you told me about him,' Tom said.

She felt suddenly nervous. That feeling which started somewhere down in the pit of her stomach and swirled upwards set her heart racing.

'I'm sorry to upset you.'

'I'm sorry too, if it's important to you then I think you should, take no notice of me.' She hated making things difficult for her Dad.

'How will I contact him?'

'I have his number.'

Her father arranged to meet David at the Four Seasons Hotel, in Ballsbridge, but in the end Helen insisted on going along to keep him company. She couldn't let him go alone. She was edgy but tried hard to keep it from him. As they walked into the foyer, he put his arm around her shoulders and she felt a little better, although she was thrown into panic again when David came towards them, his hand outstretched. Awkwardly, she made the introductions, and they went to the bar.

'It was very good of you to fly back from Germany especially to see us, I really appreciate it,' Tom said.

'I had a break between Berlin and Hamburg so it gave me something to do.'

The coffee arrived. They busied themselves with that for a few minutes.

'I wanted to meet you, although I can't say I remember you particularly when you were young,' Tom said.

'You might have known my father.'

'I knew him a little, we rented some pasture from you in the old days.'

'We didn't work the land, Father was an engineering professor in Galway University, an academic.'

The conversation was stilted, and Helen felt out of it as they went on to chat about Australia and Alice Springs. It was all general stuff and she was relieved at that. As the men talked, she found herself watching David. Wondering if he really was her father were they alike in any way. It was then she noticed his hands as he gesticulated. Thin with long fingers. You have piano fingers she remembered her mother used to say when Helen had taken those early lessons. She might also have been a pianist, but the discipline of practice was something she didn't possess and she always wanted to be somewhere else when the time came to go inside the house for half an hour. She studied for a couple of years but then gave up.

'We toured the main cities. Melbourne. Sidney. Perth. Brisbane. It was back in 2002.'

'At least you saw some of the country,' Tom said, with a grin.

'Not really. It was a flying visit literally, just a few weeks. But at the time I did intend to return, I tried to plan a trip but unfortunately it never happened.'

They finished their coffee. Tom tried to pay the bill but David insisted on doing that. It signalled the end.

'I want to thank you for what you did for Faye and Helen,' he said.

Tom nodded.

'Helen was lucky to have you and Carmel as her parents. Otherwise, perhaps we would never have met if you had been adopted in the normal way,' he smiled at her.

'And we were lucky Faye gave us Helen. Carmel and I had a new life, happiness, all we ever wanted,' Tom said.

Suddenly she felt emotional and tried hard to hide it.

They stood up to go. David walked out to the car with them. He shook hands.

'If I'm ever in Australia I'll definitely look you up. I'll try to persuade the others to fit a tour into the schedule, although we're already booked up for the next two years, so it will be some time away.'

Tom took his business card from his pocket and handed it to him. 'We'd be very glad to see you.'

Helen drove out of the hotel silently, aware that Tom had waved to David, and that she hadn't. They headed for Rathmines.

'He seems like a very nice man,' Tom said.

'You've only seen one side of him,' she snapped, 'and he has our address now.'

'I realise that.'

'I can't forgive him.'

'Maybe in time,' Tom murmured gently.

Those last couple of weeks flew by in a whirl, and when her Dad went back to Alice, she felt very isolated and wished she could have gone with him. But something kept her here. Waiting. It made her go back to Lackenmore, knowing that David was touring and would be away for a couple of months. She was less sensitive about Peter now, and had actually glimpsed him driving by a couple of times but wasn't bothered. Breda was delighted to see her, and they picked up where they had left off, good friends as ever.

She came with her to visit her grandmother and Helen was really grateful, needing the support of her friend.

'It's pathetic to see them, isn't it,' Breda said as they walked into the ward. 'If I ever get like that will you make sure that I'm given an injection or something to knock me out. Or arrange for me to go to that place in Switzerland where they will help you through the whole thing. I just couldn't bear it.'

'If you're like the people here you won't even know what's happening.'

'True, but I could contract an illness of some sort and know all about it, promise you'll be there for me?'

'OK, promise!' Helen laughed.

Pauline was crotchety and took little notice of Breda.

'You haven't been in to see me in a long time,' she barked immediately.

'I'm sorry, but I was away for a while,' Helen smiled, 'I've brought you some flowers, we'll get a vase for them.'

'And biscuits, you have a sweet tooth haven't you, Pauline?' Breda produced the bag and put it on the locker.

She looked at her suspiciously, and picked it up, peering inside. 'Don't like them,' she grunted.

'We'll get something different next time, what sort do you like?'

'Custard Creams.'

'Right, that's what you shall have.'

'What's your name?'

'I'm Breda.'

'Where are you from?'

'Just outside Lackenmore.'

'Where?'

'Lisroan.'

'Oh, I used to know a family there.'

'What was their name?' Breda asked, and grinned at Helen.

Pauline stared at her. 'What's your name?'

'Breda.'

'Where are you from.'

'Lisroan.'

'Would you like to come for a walk, Pauline?' Helen intervened. She immediately began to push herself up.

Breda reached out an arm to help, but she shrugged her off.

'I have my walking frame.' She leaned on it, and slowly they made their way to the day room. It was a pleasant bright airy place, with wide windows through which they could see the gardens, the lake beyond and the blue sky reflected.

'Was it cold in the water?' she asked suddenly of Helen.

'What do you mean?'

'It was December I think, very late in the year, icy.'

Helen stared at her, puzzled.

'You were soaking wet. I gave you whiskey. It was a pity you let it fall.'

Helen still said nothing.

'What are you looking at?' Pauline pointed at Breda.

'You,' she said, smiling.

'It's no laughing matter.'

'I'm sorry.'

Helen changed the subject. 'You have a beautiful view from here, look at the lake.'

'I'm going back now.' Pauline pulled herself up.

Breda positioned the frame.

'You go on ahead,' she said, 'Faye will be with me.'

They walked back slowly and Helen helped her settle into her chair. As she moved away, Pauline gripped her hand and looked up into her eyes. She said nothing but there was something so beseeching about her expression, Helen felt very close to tears.

'She's definitely for the fairies,' Breda laughed as they left.

'I'm sorry, she repeated herself a lot, and she was a bit cranky,' Helen smiled ruefully, 'must have driven you mad.'

'Sure she can't remember from one minute to the next. God, I'd hate to be living with someone like that, it must be difficult.'

'It's sad.'

'She thinks you're Faye.'

'I know, and all that about water and cold, I couldn't understand it.'

'God knows where her mind is.'

God knows where Faye is. Helen thought unexpectedly.

Chapter Fifty-three

Jenny tossed and turned, the sky still dark through the gap in the curtains. She glanced at the clock radio to see that it was still only four twenty-five. Two more hours until she needed to get up. These disturbed nights were exhausting, and as the weeks passed she grew more and more tense and irritable from lack of sleep. She sat up, and bent her head in her hands, suddenly aware that she couldn't continue like this. She would have to face her fears.

The first thing she did was to make a phone call. A cautious reaching back. It was the family solicitor. She remembered the name and checked the number with directory enquiries. That number which rang a phone which sat on a desk in an office in Lackenmore. It was picked up quickly.

'My name is Faye Brophy.' To her surprise, she found herself using her old name automatically. She had to wait a short time before being put through, and shook with fear as she wondered what she would say. What Faye Brophy would say.

'Ms. Brophy?' The voice sounded friendly, and had a dark velvety tone.

She hesitated. Swallowed. Ran her fingers over her forehead which felt clammy. 'Yes.'

'What can I do for you?'

'My family were one of your clients years ago, and I'm wondering if you have had any contact recently. They live in Lackenmore. There was a fire - and my sister died.'

'Ah yes, Faye, we do indeed represent the family, and I must offer my condolences on the tragic loss of your sister, it was a terrible thing to happen.'

'I wonder could I come and see you?' Even as she said it, a sense of dread rippled through her.

'Of course, let me look at the diary and we can set up an appointment.'

The day arrived far too quickly, and she left mid-morning anxious to give herself plenty of time. Her appointment was at two-thirty and on no account did she want to be late. She was nervous, and tried hard to stay calm but the nearer she came to the little town the tighter her hands gripped the steering wheel, and the muscles in her neck grew stiff, sending darts of pain into her shoulders. The car seemed to eat up the kilometres. She didn't have control over it. Thirty became twenty which became ten and finally it was only a matter of metres as she took the last turn in the road and could see the twin spires, and the old ruined castle on the hill. A sign welcomed her to Lackenmore. She slowed down for once glad of the speed limit to delay her arrival. She tried to control her emotions, blinking rapidly to prevent the tears building up, so glad that she was arriving on the side of town opposite to where she had once lived. She drove down the main street and had a few seconds of panic as she searched for parking, but someone pulled out and she took that space. She was here at last.

In the outer office she had to wait while Mr. Curran finished off a phone call, and then the secretary told her to go in. She sat on the chair in front of the desk, in an office which was full of files. Walls of them. Cabinets of them. Bursting with papers. Elastic bands. And dust. She didn't know how he could find anything in the mess.

'I don't think we've met before?' he smiled.

Somewhere around her own age, he was attractive, with fair hair and friendly eyes.

'No, I haven't been here for many years,' she admitted.

'My uncle left me the business, so I'm a blow in you could say.'

She nodded.

'Now what can I do for you?' He leaned his elbows on the untidy desk.

'I have to admit I've been estranged from the family for many years. I don't know whether my sister was married or not, or had a family, do you happen to know?'

'Her husband is deceased, but her son, Sean, was in to see me. But you must understand that I can't divulge our conversation, it's confidential.'

'And my mother?'

'She's in the nursing home. I'm sorry to say she isn't very well.'

She nodded.

'Would you like to give me your address and phone numbers, so that I can get in touch with you.' He held his ball-point pen poised over a sheet of paper.

She bought a bouquet of flowers and drove out to the nursing home, the only one she remembered. It was a large rambling place run by the State, and the woman at the desk gave her the ward number. She took the stairs but stopped suddenly at the top unable to go any further. Fear swept through her. She felt hurt. Vulnerable. All confidence drained away, and left her like a child dreading punishment. She stood at a window and looked out. Time passed, and suddenly she knew that she couldn't leave without seeing her mother. Even if it was just at a distance. But now she couldn't remember which corridor to choose. She met a nurse and enquired again as to her mother's whereabouts.

'I'll take you.' The nurse walked with her. 'She will be delighted to see you.' She turned into a room which had six beds positioned around the walls. Jenny hung back, thinking that perhaps she mightn't recognise her mother. The awfulness of that possibility made her stomach sick.

'Now Pauline, look, you have a visitor today.' She stood by the elderly woman who sat in a chair by her bed, and looked up at Jenny.

She had short white hair, and wore earrings and a diamante

pendant around her neck. Her pale face had been brushed with powder and her lips were painted with bright red lipstick. But it was the eyes which drew Faye. Large, blue, they stared at her through gold-rimmed glasses.

The nurse pulled another armchair over beside the bed.

'You're looking very well today, Pauline,' she smiled down at her, 'our Pauline loves bling, all the glamour.'

Jenny was too scared to move closer. Tense hands gripped the flowers tightly. Her heart beat uncomfortably, the rhythm like a drum which she was sure could be heard by everyone.

'Did you bring it?' Pauline demanded.

She didn't answer, just laid the flowers on the end of the bed.

'Aren't they lovely, I'll get a vase for them.' The nurse swung past her and out the door.

'You said you'd bring me some perfume, where is it?'

'I couldn't get the one you like,' Jenny managed to say at last.

'Comb my hair will you, I love the way you did it the other day.' She rooted in her handbag. 'And sit down will you, I've a pain in the neck staring up at you. Here, beside me.' She patted the seat of the other chair, and continued to search for something in the handbag which she held on her lap.

Jenny sat on the edge.

'Here it is, now. I want nice long strokes.' She held out the large brown plastic comb to her.

Jenny took it. Her mother turned away.

'Come on, I'm waiting,' she said, irritation there.

Jenny's hand shook. Her body shook. She didn't think she could do this. It was too intimate. Too close. In seconds she would be drawn back into that whirlpool which she had thought had long been buried. Caught in its power, unable to escape. If she didn't do it right then she would be in trouble. She would be blamed. Told it was her fault. A shadow threw darkness over her, and guilt walked in tandem. Inexplicable thoughts slipped through her mind.

She lifted the comb, and drew it through the short white hair, using a slow gentle movement. Her other hand rested on her mother's shoulder, keenly aware of the warmth of her body through the pink cardigan which she wore, and how close they were after so long.

'That's lovely, keep doing it,' Pauline sighed.

A strange delight surged through Jenny. That feeling of satisfaction at doing something right for once.

She continued on, silently combing.

'Stop, that's enough,' Pauline barked.

Her hand did that of its own accord, half way through a stroke.

Pauline's head swung around and she stared at her.

'He insisted on going into the lake for you, and it took him to his end. Who was to blame for that?' She peered at her, eyes squinting through her glasses. 'You killed him.'

Jenny couldn't say anything. Tears moistened her eyes, and she tried to control them. She didn't want to break down here.

'Left me to run that farm on my own. Hour after hour, morning until night, day in day out. I worked as hard as any man. Harder, the truth be told. It was all your fault.'

Jenny put down the comb on the bed.

'What are you doing? My comb has to be put back in my bag.'

Jenny handed it to her.

'Now here we are.' The nurse appeared carrying a glass vase. 'These are going to look really lovely, what beautiful flowers.' She took them out of the cellophane and arranged them. 'Where will we put it?'

'Here.' Pauline waved her arm towards her locker.

'I don't think there's enough room there, Pauline, with your Seven-Up and the water jug and tissues.'

'I want them here, they're mine.'

The woman in the next bed said something. Jenny couldn't understand but nodded and asked her how she was.

'Stop talking to that one, you're my visitor, not hers,' Pauline muttered.

The nurse put the vase on the window sill.

'I told you to put them here, they're mine,' Pauline cried.

'All right.' She made room for the flowers on the locker.

'Where are my biscuits?'

Anxiety swirled through Jenny.

'You were to bring them.'

'We'll get you some tomorrow, Pauline.' The nurse patted her shoulder.

'Yes, next time.' Jenny rose. She had to go. She couldn't stay any longer.

'When will you be back?'

'Soon.'

'Make sure you do.'

'Goodbye.'

Pauline said no more and started to rummage in her handbag again.

The nurse walked with Jenny. At the door she looked back to see her mother still intent on examining the contents of the bag.

'This is a good day,' she said softly, her eyes sympathetic.

'There are worse?'

'Yes.'

'It's sad.'

'They don't realise it, thanks be to God.'

Jenny was very disturbed. She just wanted to put her head down and pretend this had never happened. Meeting her mother had not been part of her plan. Now she found herself driving through town towards the farm. It was like she had been taken over by another personality. She drove through the town, staring straight ahead, concentrating on not seeing anything. Out in the countryside again, she was even more tense. At last she was going home. Like she had done hundreds of times, thousands of times. A homing instinct drew her over the hill and down into the valley, the fields bordering the lake, the blue sky reflecting, the sunshine glimmering the way it always used to do.

But suddenly stark black struts protruded up into the sky and she slowed down, turning in through the gates and bringing the car to an abrupt halt. The house was gutted. The fire had roared through it and destroyed everything. The glass in the windows had splintered from the heat and exploded outwards, but someone had brushed most of the shards into piles against the wall of the house. The roof had partially fallen in. The red paint on the front door was still visible under the dark unforgiving stain of fire.

She opened the door of the car, and stepped out. A terrible sense of loss swept through her. The life she had known, all those early years, was bound up with this place. Memories of her father were suddenly fresh and raw. She turned sharply. His tall figure stood in the doorway of the barn. Dad? She moved towards him. But he had disappeared. A ghost, conjured up by her imagination? She looked through the door to see his tractor inside, and the tears came then as grief swept through her. Who had killed him? Her mother's reference flashed through her mind. She tried to remember what had happened but she couldn't recall the circumstances exactly. Those days were full of shadow.

She walked slowly towards the house. Her black leather shoes crunched on tiny pieces of glass which still littered the yard. She stood at the slightly open door immediately assailed by the smell of fire. That bitter acidic aroma caught her breath and she began to cough, holding a tissue to her face. She pushed the door but it stuck on some debris behind it. She tried again and it allowed just enough room to squeeze through into the hall.

Immediately she looked for the hallstand which used to be there. But now the only thing left was the square metal tray which stood at the end to take the dripping points of umbrellas. Twisted hooks on the scorched floor were those on which her schoolbag used to hang. The door into the sitting room was gone. The remnants of curtains, still hung like black sculpted stalactites from the metal rail which had been twisted out of shape from the intense heat.

She continued on into the kitchen. The hub of the house. The destruction even more apparent in here. The ceiling above and beams of the roof had fallen in and she had to pick her way through the rubble, the only thing recognisable was the range which still stood there defiantly. She looked out the window and the view outside was so beautiful she cringed, remembering how she used to sit at the kitchen table doing her homework, that image of the lake something which was always there, every day of her life.

She looked upward but all she could see was sky. There was nothing left upstairs. She turned to leave but a sudden thought brought her into the store room. Strangely, it hadn't been damaged quite so badly, the remains of the bed and wardrobe still visible under a coverage of soot. She ran her finger along the metal struts, the black residue staining as dark as her most recent memories of this room. The day she left St. Josephs Hospital to come back home after four years away was suddenly clear in her mind.

'You look really pretty.' Una stood back and smiled at Faye who stood in the entrance hall of the hospital dressed for going home. She was wearing a soft blue jacket, cream polo-neck sweater and jeans. The colour scheme suited her colouring, her skin softly flushed, vibrant shoulder-length red hair silky again.

'I'm going to miss you.' She hugged her.

'And I'll miss you too,' Faye whispered. She had changed out of all recognition. During therapy a clever imaginative person had been revealed, someone who could think and speak, beautiful in every way.

'This is the happiest day of your life, no tears now.' Una touched her cheek.

'Nurse we have to go.' The heavy set woman said.

'Sorry for the delay Mrs. Brophy, everyone wanted to say goodbye to Faye.'

'Is this her suitcase?'

Una handed it to her. 'There's not very much, just some clothes and a few gifts.'

Faye's mother took her arm and led her towards the car. Una followed. Faye suddenly stopped and turned back to her.

'What's wrong?' she asked, and reached for her, arms outstretched. They hugged tightly.

'Stop this nonsense, Faye,' her mother snapped.

'Don't worry, you're going home,' Una assured.

'Come on now, we've a way to go.'

'Perhaps she's a bit nervous. It's a big change.'

'Nervous? Of what?'

'It's been a long time.'

'Rubbish, she's as difficult as she ever was, no different. Now come on Faye, I've no time for this carry on.'

As they drove it began to rain. The soft misty downpour soddened the landscape which was enveloped in low cloud. Faye sat in the back seat watching pictures whizz by. Fields bordered by stone walls. Houses. People. Animals. Images without sound.

She was home. The car slowed and drew up outside the farmhouse, its gaunt lines relieved by the shadow of the red-roofed barns behind. A thrill of excitement fluttered through Faye, like the wings of a bird. She moved closer to the window and smiled in anticipation. She climbed out of the car, stood in the yard and watched the hens peck busily in the dirt. A brown and white collie bounded around the corner. He padded close to Faye and jumped up on her. With pleasure she stroked him. His soft fur was warm and comforting. It was Rex.

'He remembers me,' she exclaimed, delighted.

'Go on in, and don't be encouraging that mongrel.' Pauline marched around the corner of the house to the back door, opened it and disappeared inside. Faye followed slowly. She ran her fingers along the embossed wallpaper like a blind person reading Braille. Everything was so familiar.

The blackleaded range.

The large wooden table set for tea with the blue willow patterned ware.

The picture of the Sacred Heart with the little red cross shining in front of it. She touched the back of a chair. Her thin fingers caressed the smooth warm wood. But then she felt the walls begin to close in as fear gnawed at her insides, and she flinched at some dimly remembered pain.

'We've put you in here,' Her mother flung open a door off the scullery and dumped the small brown suitcase on the cracked lino. 'It was used by a labourer we had working here, so you've everything you need.' She indicated the single bed, the cheap dressing-table, wardrobe, and wash-hand basin, partly hidden by a collection of old boxes, paint tins and broken household implements. 'We'll burn some of this stuff, and make space.'

Beside the fireplace, there was an old armchair, the horsehair stuffing protruding in places like a hedgehog. The green baize top of the rickety card table was spotted and stained. Faye looked around her.

Her sister Chris walked in.

'Oh, you're back.'

Faye smiled at her.

'That's a nice bit of material in that jacket.' She fingered it. 'Wonder would it fit me Maybe I could let it out? You won't be needing it. Let me try it on.' She pulled at the sleeve but Faye resisted. 'You haven't changed, always so selfish.'

'Yes Faye, let Chris try it on.' Pauline interrupted.

Faye was forced to stay inside all of the time. Her mother muttered something about the doctor having said that she should not be allowed out until she went back to the hospital to see him. But she was happy to be home. Pauline and Chris kept her busy. Hoovering. Dusting. Scrubbing. Washing. Ironing. Cooking. She didn't mind so much, glad to be doing something normal. Everyday things which she used to do when she was young. She loved when the clothes came in from the line. Folded neatly ready for ironing, sunshine or rainfresh. The aroma of the outdoors so sweet. She would bury her face in them and breathe deeply, sucking fresh air into her lungs like a drug addict needing a fix. She enjoyed ironing. The satisfaction when she held up a blouse without a single crease, the fabric smooth as if it was bought new that very day. And cooking too, particularly baking. But it was hard to please her mother and sister. When something wasn't to their liking then fear jumped and swamped.

You're too slow.

Too lazy.

Trying to cut corners.

Lazy man's load.

There's a wrinkle around that button.

That collar should be perfectly flat.

The back is as important as the front.

The litany of do's and don'ts grew longer. Every day a new transgression added. So she tried harder but couldn't seem to satisfy them. She was glad to climb into bed at night, and lie there in the dark. She felt safe then. When the house grew quiet, and she could think clearly. She made plans. To get away from Lackenmore, where her life was bounded by the walls of the farmhouse, the outside world non-existent. The past was a rustle of dead leaves. The future dark and secret as buried treasure.

She couldn't understand why she wasn't allowed to visit friends she knew in the past, or go for a walk, or into the town. Although she had thought it would be wonderful to come home, she found the farmhouse to be a prison, and all she wanted now was to leave. But she couldn't go without money and searched the house when her mother and sister were out. But all she had collected was a small cache of coins. Found at the back of the cushions on the couch. In a jar. At the bottom of a drawer. In old boxes. A china jug in the cabinet.

As she foraged that Sunday morning when her mother and sister were at Mass, she was startled when the doorbell rang, immediately sent into a quandary as to what she should do. At first she was scared and ran back into the store room. When the bell rang again, curiosity took her down the hall and into the sitting room, to peer through the heavy lace curtains in an effort to find out who was there. A red car was parked outside. It looked familiar. Her heart began to thump. She flattened the lace in order to see more clearly. A woman walked back to the car, and opened the door. As she turned her head Faye

274

knew her immediately, banging on the glass to get her attention.

It was wonderful to see Una. Faye was in tears as she opened the front door and clung to the woman who had once been so close to her.

'You've lost weight. There isn't a pick on you. Are you well?' Una stared at her.

'I'm fine.'

'You don't look it.'

'Come in. They'll be back soon.' Faye ushered her in anxiously.

'I've rung a number of times but you never returned my calls. I was worried.'

'They didn't tell me.'

'What?'

'I'm not allowed to use the phone.'

'Why not?'

'They don't let me do anything.'

'That's so awful.' She was very concerned.

'Except the housework and cooking.'

'You should have told me.'

'I couldn't, my mother doesn't want anyone to know I'm here.'

'It's disgraceful.'

'They'll be coming back after Mass.' She glanced out the window nervously.

'You can't live like this. It's not right.'

'What can I do? I've no money. I've been searching the house for coins, but it will take me ages to save up enough,' Faye explained.

'Listen, would you like to come and live with me for a while?'

Faye stared at her in astonishment.

'You're over twenty-one, you can do what you want.'

'I'm not sure.'

'Come back to visit, but don't stay here if you don't want to, there's more out there for you.'

She couldn't think straight. The very idea of leaving was something which she had only dreamed of.

'Do you want to make a life for yourself?'

She nodded.

'Then let's go. Get your coat.'

'I don't have one.'

'What about the one we gave you?'

'Chris had it altered for herself.'

'Have you a heavy cardigan or something, it's a bit nippy.' A sudden uncertainty flashed across Una's face. 'Maybe I'm putting you under too much pressure, I'm sorry, would you like to think about it?'

'No, I've prayed for this chance, I'm going.' Faye rushed into the store room, and returned a few seconds later with an old jumper.

'Are you sure now?'

'Yes.'

'You'd better leave a note, otherwise they'll be ringing the police,' she suggested.

It was enjoyable shopping for those first clothes. While they bought most of them in the cheaper stores, it was like Faye had a makeover. And when Una took her to the hairdressers and her hair was cut and blow-dried, she felt a new person.

'Wow, you look amazing.' Una stood back to admire when she came down that evening dressed in one of her new outfits. A casual pair of jeans, a pretty green striped shirt, and matching sweater.

'Thanks so much for everything, I don't know how I'll ever thank you. I'll pay you back, I promise.'

'Just to see you looking so good is all the thanks I need, I can't believe you're the same person who was in St. Josephs.'

'That seems like another life.'

'And one you want to forget.'

Through a friend of Una's, Faye got a job in the Venus Boutique in town. For the first couple of years she worked in the stockroom at the back and gradually was promoted to the main salon. It was the beginning of her career.

Jenny came out of the house, unaware that her pale grey jacket had smears of black along one side where she had brushed against the door. She stopped once again to look back, and was startled by the sound of footsteps coming behind her. She turned.

'What are you doing here?' the man demanded.

'I used to live here.' She recognised him immediately. It was Corcoran who lived on the next farm.

'You did?' He peered at her.

'Faye.'

'Well, I'll be damned. I thought you had died.' He pushed his cap back and scratched his bald head.

'No.'

'Well, it's been a long time since you've been home, pity you had to come now to see the place like this, and Chris gone.'

'Yes, it is.'

'While you're here, I want to ask you what's going to happen with the land?' He pulled on a cigarette, exhaled, and then kept it cupped in his hand. 'Your mother being in the home and all that. I've rented the land for the past few years, but I'd like to know where I stand. I could make an offer for the place if you're open to that, you're hardly going to take over,' he said, grinning, his teeth brown and stained.

She didn't reply.

'I was talking to Sean, he's here at the moment. He's keen to sell, has no interest either.'

'It still belongs to my mother.'

'But she doesn't know her head from her arse as I well know, although I suppose she could still sign on the dotted line.'

'I don't know what's going to happen.'

'Look, I've a lease until the end of the year, and if I can't buy then I want to continue with that, I've put a lot into this land and my two sons as well, so we can't lose it.'

'Have you a copy of it?'

'It's up at the house.'

'I'd need to see it.'

'Sure thing, do you want to come up now.'

Jenny didn't but felt she had to.

She drove to his farm after him.

It was still much the same way she remembered when Mrs. Corcoran was alive. Although now the walls were brown stained with smoke. The old lino on the floor was cracked. Clothes were thrown around. The dishes from previous meals still stood on the table, there were empty beer cans on the floor, and in the corner a dog chewed on a bone, his eyes watching her suspiciously. Corcoran rooted among a pile of papers on a shelf. 'Where is it now, I only saw it the other day,' he grumbled.

Jenny waited.

'Sit yourself down, you could put on the kettle there for a cup of tea if you want.'

'No thanks.' She sat on the grimy kitchen chair.

It was a good ten minutes before he finally located the contract which he handed to her.

She read it through. 'This is the only copy you have?'

'Yep.'

'Could I borrow it to make another, I'll bring it back.'

'I don't know about that.'

'I'll just go into town.'

'I can't let you have it.' He grabbed it back from her, and held it close to the dirty old jacket.

'Maybe you'd come with me and we can have it copied?'

He considered that for a moment, the deep-set eyes in the lined face squinting. 'All right,' he agreed, folded the sheet of paper and shoved it into his pocket.

He climbed into the passenger seat of the car. A large lump of a man wearing mud-splashed Wellington boots.

'Could you put on the seat belt, please?' she asked, as she buckled on her own.

'Never bother with them,' he grunted, in a coarse gravelly voice.

'Please, I'd prefer if you would, I don't want you going out through the windscreen if I have to brake suddenly.'

He pulled it out but it didn't fit him, being short by a few inches. He jerked it, and it stuck, he did it again. 'Jaysus.' He tried again, and finally managed to get it into the receiver. 'Bloody hell, I feel like a trussed chicken. Hate these things.'

She pulled out on to the road and drove towards town. There was a smell from him. A smell of the farm. Animals. And that sharp aroma of the unwashed. She opened the window a little and breathed easier.

'Nice Merc.'

She didn't say anything.

'You must be doing well to have one of these, and it's a new model.'

'I need it for my business, I travel a lot.'

'And what would that be?'

She could feel his eyes on her. Accessing. And storing all the information in his little gossipy mind.

'I'm in fashion.'

'You're going to be affected by the down-turn. Could be selling up everything if the government have their way. Crowd of shysters up in Leinster House.'

They had arrived in town now, and she drove along Main Street searching for the stationery shop.

'There it is, on the corner,' he said, pointing.

She parked, and both of them went into the shop where the girl made a copy of the contract.

They went straight back to his farm.

'Now you won't forget what I said to you. I'd be willing to make a good offer for the place and the whole thing could be done in no time, and all of you would be happy.'

'I don't think that's going to happen, not while my mother is still alive.'

'But you'll have to make decisions for her, she's not capable. Any solicitor will agree with that, particularly my man, he knows all about it.'

Chapter Fifty-four

Helen began to visit her grandmother regularly. She felt very sorry for the old woman incarcerated in that home with all those other poor souls with no hope of ever getting out again. Breda kept her company sometimes, but was always subjected to a barrage of questions.

'What is it about me? Bet you anything that she'll give me the usual third degree and won't listen to any of my answers,' she laughed as they walked down the corridor to the ward, where one of the nurses was plumping the pillows tucked behind Pauline.

'And here are some visitors for you, aren't you the lucky girl.'

'Did you bring it?' she asked immediately.

'Guess what that is?' Breda laughed.

'I have it.' Helen handed a small bag to Pauline, who smiled excitedly and took out the bottle of perfume.

'How does this work? Show me!'

Helen sprayed some of the perfume on her wrists. 'Do you like that scent?'

'Lovely,' she smiled.

'You know how to please her,' the nurse smiled, 'there was a woman here the other day and she persuaded her to comb the hair, you know how you do it. Now I even have to stop work and do it as well. She has us all running rings around her.'

'Who was that person?' Helen asked curiously.

'I don't know her name, but now that I think of it she looked a lot like you.'

There was a shocked silence. Helen stared at Breda.

'I like this smell.' Pauline squirted the perfume into the air which was heavily laden with the scent.

'You're looking well today.' Breda took the second chair.

'Who are you?'

'I'm Breda, Pauline, I was here the other day.'

'You were not, it was her.' She stared at Helen.

'OK.' Breda gave in.

'Comb my hair, she did it.'

Helen took the comb from the locker and began to do her hair. She was very quiet.

'I think I'll bring a scissors the next day, and trim your hair. I'm good at that, should have been a hairdresser,' Breda grinned, 'who did your hair the other day?'

'Faye did it, she always does, I like that. Give me the mirror.'

Breda took it from the locker and handed it to her.

She rooted in her handbag, and pulled out a lipstick. Pursed her lips and spread it unevenly. Licking it as if she really enjoyed the taste.

'Going to a ball?' asked Breda.

'Don't be cheeky. I've been to many a ball in my day.'

'What are you going to wear?'

'I've plenty of clothes.'

'But have you a boyfriend?'

'There are lots of them too. What age am I?' She turned to Helen.

'You're young.'

'But what age am I?'

'I think you're about fifty maybe.'

'Fifty?' She didn't look pleased.

'I think so, but I'm not sure. You don't really look your age.'

'Don't I?' She took up the mirror again and stared at herself.

'Not at all, you're as young as you feel.'

'I'm going home tomorrow. Will you come and collect me?'

'Sure I will,' Helen assured.

'What time will you be here?'

'I'll have to check that with the nurse, she'll tell me when to come.'

'Don't be late, I hate anyone to be late.'

'I won't be, don't worry. See you then.' It was their chance to leave, although it was always difficult to choose the right moment. They rose and Helen put the mirror back on the locker. The lipstick was on the quilt and she picked that up also and replaced it in the handbag.

'Bye Pauline.' Breda waved.

'I feel sad leaving.' Helen was gloomy.

They said goodbye to the other patients, and again a special wave to Pauline as they stood in the doorway, but Pauline wasn't taking any notice. They walked down the corridor.

'I can't believe that Faye might have been here,' Helen murmured, 'it's more likely to be another relative who looks like me.'

'Imagine if it was her.'

'I don't want to think that, I'd just be fooling myself. Anyway, I'm heading home soon.'

'Have you decided on a date yet?'

'Well, you said David is due back in a couple of weeks and I don't want to be here then. Anyway, I'm looking forward to going back to Alice.'

'To Jim?'

'Yea,' Helen said, smiling.

Chapter Fifty-five

The phone call came as Jenny drove home from Lackenmore. She still felt very emotional after the events of the day. Meeting her mother for the first time in so long had been a shock, and she couldn't get the vision of that pinched face out of her head. Pauline's aggressive nature hadn't changed, and her voice took Jenny back to her youth, especially her words about her Dad.

She lifted the phone automatically forgetting that she wasn't in a fit state to talk to anyone. But she didn't have to say very much.

'Jenny, it's a girl, it's a girl!' It was Eoin on the line, over the moon that Maria had given birth to a seven pound, two ounce, baby girl. 'We're going to call her Elena, and she is the most beautiful thing you've ever seen.' His voice broke.

'I'm so happy for you.' Jenny was choking with tears.

'You'll have to come in to see her, although we'll be home soon, they don't keep you long these days, and she's perfect, absolutely perfect, I think she even looks a bit like our family, Maria says she's got my chin, and her eyes, I can't believe it.'

Jenny remembered another baby girl. In an orange box. She was beautiful too. But there was no father there in tears because he was so happy. No-one was happy. It was the worst tragedy which had befallen the Brophy family. She had disgraced them. So much so both of them had to be hidden away. Out of sight of the world.

She knew her daughter for two weeks only. She held her for that short time. Suckled the tiny baby at her breast. Cuddled her. Kissed her. Marvelled at the exquisite beauty of the small child. The tiny head with a soft cap of reddish hair. Blue eyes. Even then so blue. The most delicate of soft pale pink skin. The little fingers with those perfectly formed finger nails. The pain of that recollection stabbed through her, but she still couldn't imagine that Helen would want to know her now.

She took a bath. A long leisurely soak in very hot water. It was refreshing. She made some tea and toast and sat staring out of the window trying to get her mind in order. She did some work. Read through a report. Signed some papers. There were various sections. Her handwriting was neat. She always used a fountain pen with blue ink. But as she flicked over the pages the name that stared at her wasn't what it should have been. No-one would recognise it. No-one knew who this person was. Faye Brophy was a nobody.

Chapter Fifty-six

'It's so good to see you.' Jenny threw her arms around Una.

'What's wrong?'

'Everything,' she sighed.

'Come in.'

They talked long into the night. It was good for Jenny. Una was the only person in her life who knew who she was. She could talk truthfully to her. About the person who had grown up in Lackenmore, and spent those years in St. Josephs. Faye Brophy had shed her identity when she left the prison in which she lived with her mother and sister. She began to use her second name – Jennifer – and tried to persuade herself that she had ever been known by any other name. Una had given her freedom. Freedom to forget the past.

'I'm like a person with dual personalities, each one struggling to oust the other.'

'I think you have to decide who you want to be.'

'Jenny Halloran is diminishing and Faye is taking over. Sometimes I sign my name, and even call myself Faye. It's crazy. I don't know who I am.'

'Maybe you'll have to go back to being Faye.'

'Imagine just announcing that, do you want Michael and Pearl to collapse?' she smiled in spite of her mood.

'You must let her in. She is the real you. Jenny is a fiction.'

They talked then of Helen.

'Do you want to meet her?'

'I do, so much. But she would never be accepted by the Hallorans.

If Michael knew my real past I wouldn't be accepted either. So I can't put her through that. If I make contact, then I'll have to know where I stand myself. Who I am.'

'Have you read the letter?'

'Yes.'

'What about David?'

She raised her eyebrows.

'He would also like to meet you.'

'I know.'

'He needs forgiveness,' Una said slowly, topping up their glasses with the last of the red wine in the bottle.

'I don't know that I could.' Jenny twisted the glass in her fingers. The red wine swirled. 'Too much happened. I can't forgive him.'

'It's been a long time, you were both very young.'

She shook her head.

By the time she arrived home the following day she had made her decision. Driving up the avenue, Ballymoragh House came into view, and she slowed down. Suddenly it didn't seem like home any more. She was someone who didn't belong.

Later she saddled up Swift Eagle and rode out across the paddocks, loving the smooth movement of the horse. It did her good. And for that short hour she forgot about her troubles, but as she trotted back in, the unpleasant thought that this could be the last time she would ride him came into her mind. She was saddened and spent quite a while brushing down the shiny black coat until eventually she had to leave him. He whinnied as she walked away, and she turned back to look at him once more, and whispered goodbye.

That evening. Right after dinner. She told Michael.

'What are you on about?'

'I can't stay any longer.' She hated herself for doing this to him. He wasn't the worst.

'At Ballymoragh?'

'With you.'

He jerked up in the armchair. A puzzled look on his face.

'Things have changed between us.'

'You keep on saying that. I'm sick of listening to you.'

'You won't have to listen to me any longer.'

'Ah, for God's sake, give over, will you, you're driving me nuts.'
He pulled a cigarette from a packet, and lit it with his lighter.

'I thought you'd given those up?'

'See what thought did.'

She sat down opposite.

'We have to talk about this – properly.'

'Want all my assets split down the middle, that it?'

'It's got nothing to do with money.'

'Don't want your share? No alimony? Thought you'd take me to
the cleaners, as they put it.'

'Why would you think that?' She was hurt.

'Because you're a woman. Remember Colin and Valerie. She
ruined him. Took him for millions,' he sneered.

'I'm not looking for anything.'

'Maybe not now, but wait until you get talking with your
solicitor. He'll encourage you to look for as much as possible so that
he'll get his cut.'

'I want for nothing. I'm comfortable. You needn't worry.'

'But how will I manage? I'm not well. I need care.'

'Why don't you employ a nurse.' She couldn't resist it. If he was
going to persuade her to stay then it certainly wouldn't be that way.

'Well, you can fuck off then.'

Chapter Fifty-seven

Jenny moved out the next day. But before she left she went up to see Pearl who was having tea with Karen. She joined them and they chatted for a short while.

'I'll head on down, I've a lot to do before I go.' Karen rose.

'I've always wanted to visit India, it sounds fantastic,' Jenny smiled.

'Come out to see me. I'll be staying in Kerala.'

'Maybe I will.'

'I spent some time in India when I was a girl, but I didn't like it, far too hot,' Pearl said.

'Before you go, Karen, there's something I want to tell you both. Would you mind waiting a few minutes?'

She sat down again on the couch, her face puzzled.

'I hate to give you such a shock but – I'm leaving Michael.'

'What?' Pearl paled.

'It's been coming for a long time, I think you already knew.'

'I'm glad you made up your mind finally, you haven't been happy lately.' Karen put her arm around her shoulders.

'Where are you going to live?' Pearl asked.

'I'll stay in a hotel at first.'

'How awful. What am I going to do without you.' There were tears in Pearl's eyes.

'I'll come and see you.'

'It won't be the same. You've always been there for me. Now you'll be gone as well as Karen, the house will be like a morgue.' The old woman looked from one to the other, obviously distressed.

'I'm sorry.' It was the worst that Jenny had felt since she had made her decision.

'You can't stay in a hotel, why don't you come down to me and then stay on in the lodge after I've gone,' Karen offered.

'Thanks for the offer, but I don't want to see Michael driving by every day, I need to make a complete break.'

'Maybe that will do you good, both of you. You might feel differently after a while,' Pearl said.

'I don't think so.'

'Let me hope,' the old woman murmured, 'without hope there is nothing.'

Jenny clasped the thin lined hand. 'You're right. I'll always have hope for the future, maybe my life will take a new direction, maybe not. But I've got to give it a try. There's something inside forcing me on.'

'Don't forget us.'

'You probably need to get away for a bit, shake him up,' Karen said, grinning.

'He neglects you, I've seen it,' Pearl added.

'Mother, he'd neglect everyone if he got away with it, you just seem to manage to keep a hold of him, can't imagine how you do it.'

'I know him best.'

'And you made him what he is - a spoiled brat. You didn't give Donal and I the same attention. All that love was expended on the eldest son who didn't appreciate it in the least. Dad thought the sun moon and stars shone out of his backside as well.' She stood up. Suddenly angry now. 'You were pathetic.'

Pearl stared at her. 'I didn't mean to be that way. I didn't realise. I'm sorry.'

'Easy enough now to say that, what about all those days and nights when you never even noticed us. Michael was the star. The one who was to take over everything. The one who was going to make a huge success of the business.'

'It wasn't like that. I loved all of you - equally.' Pearl pulled a white lacy square from the pocket of her soft blue wool cardigan.

'Like hell,' Karen retorted.

As always, Jenny felt in the way. And regretted that her situation had caused this row to erupt between Pearl and Karen. What was it about this family? Suddenly she was glad she was going.

'You know, Mother, Jennifer's got the courage to stand up to Michael so I think I'm going to do the same.'

Pearl sniffed into her handkerchief.

'I'm going back to Kerala, and I'm going to live with my partner.'

Jenny listened, surprised. She hadn't known that Karen had a man in her life.

'And just for your information, my partner happens to be a woman,' she grinned.

Pearl's face paled.

'I hadn't the courage to tell you. So I'm taking a leaf out of Jennifer's book. I was a wimp. All the time I've wasted on my own when I could have been with the only person I love in the world, but now it doesn't matter to me what anyone thinks.' She turned to Jenny, and hugged her. 'Thanks for everything.'

Jenny went to see the solicitor in Lackenmore again. Forced to step back into her old self, she was Faye once more.

'The next door neighbour, Mr. Corcoran, wants to buy the farm.'

'He can't do that.'

'I believe my nephew is keen to sell, according to Corcoran. He's home from New York at the moment.'

'He doesn't have a claim on the farm, your mother still owns it.'

'I'm worried in case Sean might try to force her to agree to give it to him.'

'I'm sure the nursing home wouldn't allow something like that to happen.'

'They don't watch everything that goes on, and maybe she wouldn't realise what she was doing.'

'You're thinking he might force her to give him Power of Attorney?'

She nodded.

'That's pretty drastic. Anyway, a solicitor would have to be present. It won't happen.'

She felt more relieved.

'I want to rebuild the house.'

'You're next in line, so I suppose you could.'

'Am I entitled to live there.'

'Yes.'

'Not that I intend to, but I'd like someone to be there. I might bring my mother home, arrange for people to care for her.'

'The insurance should cover most of it, and prices have come down, so it's a good time.'

'It's something I really want to do.'

'It would be good to give some jobs locally, there are so many builders out of work.'

'Can you give me the name of a reliable one?'

'I'll get back to you.'

'And could you arrange for me to meet with Sean. I'd like to talk to him.'

She met him in the foyer of the local hotel. A young man in his twenties who came straight over to her when he walked in.

'Curran told me I'd recognise you. Couldn't mistake that red hair.' He stretched out his hand and took hers.

He was a genial relaxed character with an American twang already in his voice. 'I have to admit I'd forgotten about you, I only have a vague memory of Mom telling me you had died.'

'No, I'm glad to say I'm not dead,' she said, smiling. Surprised that there was nothing in his features that reminded her of the Brophys.

They talked a little of the family, he told her of his father, a man she had never met. Then he brought the subject around to the farm. 'I'll never come back, I have my job in the States, my life.'

Faye nodded.

'But I could do with money. I had hoped the farm might be sold. Corcoran is keen to buy.'

'Unfortunately, it still belongs to your grandmother.'

'But she's senile, and can't make a decision one way or the other. She didn't even know who I was when I went over there,' he said with derision.

'Legally it can't be sold without her permission.'

'But my father always thought he owned it.'

'It was willed to Chris by my mother, but since she has died I'm next in line.'

'But it should come to me, I'm her son.'

'The law doesn't work like that.'

He was angry. 'So I'll get nothing.'

'You could live there if you want, I'm going to rebuild it.'

'I'm not coming back here for a few acres,' he retorted.

'I'm sorry.'

He stood up. Angry. 'My mother always promised me that I'd get the farm. You didn't even exist.' He turned on his heel then, and left without another word.

Chapter fifty-eight

'Hi boss,' Breda was her usual breezy self when David met her in his office. 'I'll go through the schedule, give you an idea of how business has been since you've been away.' She opened the file. 'The studio bookings are good, but the tourist accommodation is down. It's the recession, everyone is being affected. But I thought of offering a special autumn rate. Three nights for the price of two. And a reduction on the weekly rate. It's been on the website and there has been some uptake.'

'That's good.' He was vague. Aware somehow that it didn't matter too much to him.

He wanted to ask about Helen. But held back. She had made her feelings quite clear to him that last time they had met. He might be her biological father, but Tom was her real father in every way. Had known her since she was a baby. Lived through all the ages of her life, her sicknesses when she was a child, schooldays, teenage years, growing up trials and tribulations, young adulthood, failures, triumphs. He knew every nuance of the person who was Helen.

'How are bookings at the marina for next year?' he tried to force an interest.

'It's not looking so good. I know we're normally booked up way in advance, but with the times that are in it people are going to wait before they commit themselves.' She flicked through the diary. 'Oh by the way, I'll be looking for holidays soon, I'm going out to Australia to see Helen, so you might let me know your schedule.'

His heart thudded with shock. She had gone.

'That guy she knew at home turns out to be something special after all. I think it's a case of absence makes the heart grow fonder.'

He nodded.

'Anyway, I'm looking forward to going out there soon, need to see how the other half of the world live, and what the men are like out there. Might grab myself a sheep farmer with thousands of acres,' she said, grinning.

'It's a great place, you'll enjoy it.' He managed to speak at last.

It was the end for him. The end of a dream which had begun on the day he met an Australian girl and life as he knew it was radically changed. A dream of making amends for the mistakes he had made when he was young.

He went back. Walking across the fields in search of something which was like a mirage drifting ahead of him, tantalising. In his heart a crazy hope that she would do the same thing through some telepathic link between them. He removed the loose brick from under the bridge, checked that the letters were still there and then replaced it. He walked on into the clearing under the trees which swayed softly above him. They whispered to him. Persuasive. Telling him to hope. Never to give up. He stared at the majestic oak which towered above. His fingers swept across the bark until he found the place where he had cut their initials – "FD" – remembering how he had promised Faye that this impression in the great tree would, like their love, last forever. He leaned against it, feeling the uneven surface of the bark through the thin jacket he wore, and stayed there thinking that this would be the last time he would ever return here.

In his memory her soft voice whispered on the breeze. A fragment of words told him that she loved him. Her lips framed the sound. Her eyes persuaded. But time slipped away. And took her with it. Into the past.

Chapter Fifty-nine

Before going to the nursing home, Faye went shopping for some things for her mother. A soft wrap in a shade of dusty pink. A couple of nightdresses, a dressing gown, and some toiletries. She was anxious to do as much as she could for her now. Would have liked to arrange a private room, have the hairdresser come in regularly, a beautician to manicure her nails, and do anything else she might like. Faye was surprised at herself. All the anger against Pauline had disappeared. Suddenly.

As she walked down the corridor she met the same nurse as before.

'Your mother is good today, bright,' she said, as they reached the door. 'And when I tell her she has another visitor she will be so excited.'

Faye stopped suddenly, her heart thudding when she saw the person sitting by the bed. She stepped back, and stood outside the door, leaning against the wall, her breathing uneven. It was the sight of the red hair. Rich, shining, shoulder length. Could it be Helen? Was it possible that her daughter was inside that room combing her own mother's hair? Her brain spun into shock. It refused to function. To give instructions about what to do. She was in a nightmare. A crazy dark place where things were skewed and nothing made sense.

'Are you all right.' The nurse stared at her with concern.

The voice was broken, vague, and came from a long distance away. Faye couldn't understand. She felt hot, but cold too. She bent her head.

'I'll get you a chair.' The nurse disappeared into the ward, came out quickly, and insisted that she sit down. Went inside again and was back in a few seconds with a glass of water.

'You look very pale. Do you have a condition? We need to know. Are you a diabetic?'

'No, no.' She shook her head. 'I'm all right, really I am.'

'Would you lie down? There's a room free.'

'I'll go outside, maybe the fresh air will help,' Faye pushed herself up.

'Wait a little longer. You don't look well.'

She balanced with a hand on the back of the chair. But the weakness rushed over her again. She sat down. Her head was pushed between her knees. She stayed in that position and after a while began to feel a little better. 'I'm sorry.'

'Don't you worry.'

'I'll get some tea.'

'No thanks, I'd better be going.'

'You can't go yet, we have a responsibility. We'll see how you are when you have the tea, relax there for a while.'

Time passed. Faye held a tissue to her forehead. Her stomach felt sick. She wanted to get away before Helen came out, but her legs just had a mind of their own and refused to support her.

The tea was hot, and sweet, and although she didn't like it, she drank it anyway. It strengthened her, and gave her the energy to stand up at last. 'Thank you for everything, you've been so good to me.'

'But can you drive? I wouldn't like to think the same thing would happen on your way home, there could be an accident. Helen will take you and you can always collect your car tomorrow.'

Faye was in shock. Her pulse raced. She couldn't meet her daughter here. Not in a place like this. She wasn't prepared.

The other nurse reappeared. 'I mentioned to Helen that you were here. Is she your daughter, or perhaps your niece? You're so alike,' she asked.

'I must go, thank you very much.' She was unsteady in her black suede stilettos.

'Won't you wait a little longer?' The nurse walked with her.

She hurried on.

'Faye?'

A soft voice called.

Bounced off the sides of the long corridor.

Whirled.

Dived.

Darted.

Around her.

She stopped and turned around. Unable to see properly, her vision clouded by tears.

'Faye?' A woman stood in front of her now.

'Helen?' she whispered.

Chapter Sixty

'I'm nervous,' Faye stared out the window of the small plane.

'You shouldn't be, it's going to be great. I'm really looking forward to seeing Dad and Jim,' Helen said, smiling, 'and they will be so happy to meet you.'

'We're starting to descend.' Below them, the land stretched away, a wilderness, as far as the eye could see. The arc of brilliant blue sky above. The mountains in the distance shadowed red.

'Alice Springs here I come!' Helen said, laughing.

'It's going to be wonderful to see where you grew up. Now I can imagine you as a little girl, with that red hair tied up in bunches. I hope the other kids didn't tease you?'

'No, not really. Just the occasional carrot-top remark. Didn't bother me,' Helen smiled.

The smallest thing was of concern to Faye now. She watched her daughter constantly. Revelling in the sound of her voice. The warmth of her smile. The excitement in her blue green eyes which clearly showed how much she loved her Dad and Jim.

For Faye, it was astonishing to find herself here beside her daughter after so many years, and all she longed for now was that some day Helen would love her too.

'Before we land, there is something ...' Helen took a small black box from her handbag. 'I wanted to give you this.'

Faye opened it. The signet ring lay on its bed of black velvet, shining. Tears filled her eyes and she closed the box again without a word, holding it tight in her hand.

THE END

TO MAKE A DONATION TO LAURALYNN HOUSE AT THE CHILDREN'S SUNSHINE HOME HOSPICE PROJECT

Children's Sunshine Home/LauraLynn A/c.
AIB Bank, Sandyford Business Centre,
Foxrock, Dublin 18.

A/c No.32120009
Sort Code: 93-35-70

www.lauralynnhospice.com
www.sunshinehome.ie

CYCLONE COURIERS

Cyclone couriers – who proudly support LauraLynn House – are the leading supplier of local, national and international courier services in Dublin. Cyclone also supply confidential mobile on-site document shredding and recycling services and secure document storage & records management services through their Cyclone Shredding and Cyclone Archive division.

Cyclone Couriers
The fleet of pushbikes, motorbikes and vans can cater for all your urgent local and national courier requirements.

Cyclone International
Overnight, next day, timed and weekend door-to-door deliveries to destinations with the thirty-two counties of Ireland.
Delivery options to the UK, mainland Europe, USA, and the rest of the world.
A variety of services to all destinations across the globe.

Cyclone Shedding
On-site confidential document and product shredding & recycling service.
Destruction and recycling of computers, hard drives, monitors and office electronic equipment.

Cyclone Archive
Secure document & data storage and records management.
Hard copy document storage and tracking – data storage – fireproof media safe – document scanning and upload of document images.
Cyclone Couriers operate from 8, Upper Stephen Street, Dublin 8.
Cyclone Archive, International and Shredding operate from 19-20 North Park, Finglas, Dublin 11.

www.cyclone.ie   email: sales@cyclone.ie   Tel: 01-475 7246

THE MARRIED WOMAN

Fran O'Brien

Published in 2005

MARRIAGE IS FOR EVER …

In their busy lives, Kate and Dermot rush along on parallel lines, seldom coming together to exchange a word or a kiss. To rekindle the love they once knew, Kate struggles to lose weight, has a make-over, buys new clothes, and arranges a romantic trip to Spain with Dermot.

For the third time he cancels and she goes alone.

In Andalucia she meets the artist Jack Linley. He takes her with him into a new world of emotion and for the first time in years she feels like a desirable beautiful woman.

WILL LIFE EVER BE THE SAME AGAIN?

www.franobrien.net

THE LIBERATED WOMAN

Fran O'Brien

Published in 2007

AT LAST - KATE HAS MADE IT!

She has ditched her obnoxious husband Dermot and is reunited with her lover Jack.

Her interior design business goes international and TV appearances bring instant success.

But Dermot hasn't gone away and his problems encroach.

Her brother Pat and family come home from Boston and move in on a supposedly temporary basis.

Her manipulative stepmother Irene is getting married again and she is dragged into the extravaganza.

When a secret from the past is revealed Kate has to review her choices …

Available from McGuinness Books

www.franobrien.net

ODDS ON LOVE

Fran O'Brien

Published in 2008

Bel and Tom seem to be the perfect couple with successful careers, a beautiful home and all the trappings. But underneath the façade cracks appear and damage the basis of their marriage and the deep love they have shared since that first night they met.

Her longing to have a baby creates problems for Tom, who can't deal with the possibility that her failure to conceive may be his fault. His masculinity is questioned and in attempting to deal with his insecurities he is swept up into something far more insidious and dangerous than he could ever have imagined.

Then against all the odds Bel is thrilled to find out she is pregnant. But she is unable to tell Tom the wonderful news as he doesn't come home that night and disappears mysteriously out of her life leaving her to deal with the fall out.

Available from McGuinness Books

www.franobrien.net